The Giniràlla Conspiracy

Vijitha Yapa Publications
Unity Plaza, 2 Galle Road, Colombo 4, Sri Lanka
Tel. (94 11) 2596960 Fax (94 11) 2584801
e-mail: vijiyapa@gmail.com
www.srilankanbooks.com
www.vijithayapa.com

ISBN 955-1266-02-1

Characters, institutions and organizations in this publication are fictitious. Any resemblance to real persons, institutions, and organizations is purely coincidental.

First Edition August 2005
First Reprint December 2005

Printed by Tharanjee Prints, Maharagama

The Giniralla Conspiracy

Five Journals of Sujatha Mallika

by

Nihal de Silva

Vijitha Yapa Publications
Sri Lanka

Also by Nihal de Silva

The Road From Elephant Pass
The Far Spent Day

Dedication

To the poor of Lanka,
marginalized and suffering,
on whose behalf so many have done ... so little,
in fifty-seven years of independence

Acknowledgements

My sincere thanks go to
Professor Yasmine Gooneratne who kindly consented to edit my manuscript, and then contributed so much more.

And to
Carl Fernando, my old friend who knows all about faraway places and wild creatures, and has an unerring eye for my inaccuracies.

Editor's Note

My cousin Tilak had directed him to me. The old man had thinning grey hair, a belly that drooped over his belt buckle and the red veined eyes of a drinker.

I didn't like him.

The fellow said he was a retired policeman who had worked in the archives section at headquarters. He carried a small parcel wrapped in brown paper and tied with string. It contained some journals that had, he claimed, been picked up during a police raid on a terrorist camp. The subsequent investigation into the affair had stopped abruptly following orders from above. The books, he said, were not needed anymore.

He was probably lying.

The package contained four ordinary monitor's exercise books and a few loose papers. They appeared to be diaries belonging to a young woman and chronicled her life as an undergraduate and later as a journalist. During this period she claims to have stumbled on a conspiracy to overthrow the government.

The old fellow wanted five thousand rupees for the books and went away in a huff when I offered him just one thousand. He must have felt a thirst coming on, for he came back later and accepted my offer.

I started on the journals that evening … and stayed up all night. I read and reread the books over the next few days. Sadly the journals were incomplete, the fourth book coming to an end just before the conspiracy unfolds.

I mentioned the missing diary, and my frustration, to a journalist I knew. He, probably short of ideas for his 'Art Snippets' column, ran a paragraph on the subject in a newspaper the following Wednesday.

A few weeks later a small parcel, addressed to me care of the newspaper, arrived by post. To my surprise and delight it turned out to be the missing fifth journal. No sender's name or address,

There are two intertwined stories in the journals. One is the writer's own tragic history, the other is what she refers to as the Ginirälla Conspiracy. The latter is a plot I find so terrifying that I can hardly believe it. I have tried to verify some of the events described in the journals but have met only aggressive denial from the authorities. Even the killings referred to in the journals are officially ascribed to other causes.

So the questions remain: Are the journals the creation of a traumatized and over-imaginative mind? Or was the nation, especially the city of Colombo, saved from a firestorm by the courage of a young village girl and the sacrifice of the enigmatic man who loved her?

I don't know the answers to these questions. I have just deleted the dates and changed all the names. One cannot, these days, be too careful.

Nihal de Silva
2005

JOURNAL I

Let a hundred flowers blossom
and a hundred schools of thought contend

Mao Tse-Tung

1

Being called a bitch helps to steady my mind.

Someone far more savage than those who stand before me now had after all, called me 'bitch'. I had been beaten senseless at that time, a bitch assaulted almost to death! If I could have survived that, I tell myself, surely I can survive anything.

My first day at Jaypura University!

I had been warned that the rag would be severe and had tried to prepare myself for it. There is no way to avoid being ragged; it is something to be endured and then forgotten; one more torturous obstacle to overcome on the way to my goal.

I had convinced myself that, having faced so many tragedies and setbacks in the past, I could survive one more test. How was I to know it would be like this? At this moment I only want to run away but lack the courage to do even that.

I had prayed for mental strength to meet this challenge. I had hoped too that my native place and my parents' poverty would endear me to the seniors. I am from the South and I had heard that this would count as a point in my favour. I am poor too; even these 'champions of the downtrodden' would not believe how poor I am.

But no one seems to care.

The physical proximity of the seniors terrifies me. I had not expected so much anger and aggression from them. They seem to really hate us and I can't understand why. We are just like them, only one year younger. Where is the crime in that? They seem intent on bruising our bodies just as they crush our spirits. I hate it when they press so close to me as I stand on the bench. I can smell their stale breath and feel the spray of spittle on my hands as they jostle each other just inches away from me. It makes me feel ill.

I can't bear it.

'My name is … ' a treacherous tongue chooses this most terrifying moment to rebel against me. Panic stricken, my mind begins to scream:

Say it, say anything! Just don't get noted or you'll be singled out later.

I am standing on a bench before a crowd of seniors, all of them shouting obscenities. The tables and chairs in the canteen have been pushed aside to make room for the introduction ceremony. The freshers are huddled together in a corner behind me, afraid to speak to each other, all waiting fearfully for their turn. I feel perspiration bead my forehead as I strain to speak. My hands, clasped tightly before me as if in prayer, begin to shake.

I feel my vocal chords straining with effort but the words will not come.

'Nama kiyapang, bälli,' a bearded fellow holding a foot rule yells above the general hubbub. *'Umbata katak nädda?'*

State your name, bitch. Don't you have a mouth?

'My name is Sujatha Mallika. I'm from a village called Angunuwewa. My father is a farm labourer and my mother is a housewife. I am an only child.'

The lies flow easily, one after the other, like rainwater

pouring off a cädjan roof.

The questions and jeers rain in from all around.

'So after one look at you, your father gave up having any more children?'

'Why did you come here? Why didn't you go to Dubai as a domestic servant?'

'Why don't you work in the city as a prostitute?'

How can I answer these questions? I feel my eyes beginning to smart and bite my lip to control myself.

The bearded senior raises his hand and the noise subsides. He asks:

'In which courses have you enrolled?'

'Arts. Department of Sociology and Mass Communications.'

'What school did you attend?'

'Maha Vidyalaya, Tanamalwila.'

'Are your parents sending money to support you?' the bearded fellow demands.

'No. They have no money to send. I hope to get a Mahapola Scholarship.'

That, at least, is true.

'What will you do if you don't get Mahapola or a bursary?' a heavily built girl asks from the rear.

'I will have to give up and go home,' I say bravely, knowing that I have scored a point. I sense that they have lost interest in me … for the moment.

'Umba bähäpang. Eelanga satha geneng,' the beard yells.

Get down, you. Bring in the next creature.

One by one trembling newcomers are made to climb on the bench and introduce themselves. Those who are better dressed than the others, or have studied in a school in Colombo, are herded to one side. The others are sent to my corner.

The safe corner for the 'have-nots'!

A boy with a severe limp is next. As he comes up to the bench one of the seniors calls out:

'Moo nondiyek ney? Madamakata dānna thibunā.'

Isn't this fellow a cripple? He should have been put in a home.

The boy tries to climb on the bench but is unable to do so. When he places his crippled leg on the bench, it doesn't have the strength to lift him up. When he tries to lift his good leg, the weaker right leg buckles under his weight and he has to grab the bench to stop from falling.

'Nägapang, bälligey puthā. Nätthang umbey anith andath kadanavā.'

Climb up, you son of a bitch. Or we'll break your other leg.

The boy finally sits on the bench, folds his left leg under his body and tries to push himself up with the strength of his arms. The seniors jostle each other to get a better view of the spectacle, laughing and jeering as they watch.

'Okā minihekkda, panuwekda? Balapanko badagāna häti.'

Is this creature a man or a worm? Look how he crawls.

The bench wobbles dangerously as the boy straightens himself; he is upright at last. I see that his face is covered with perspiration and his spectacles have misted up. Despite all this he seems calm and unafraid, ignoring the taunts of the seniors crowding around the bench.

'Ado nondiya, kiyapang umbay thorathuru,' the bearded fellow calls out.

Cripple, tell us about yourself.

'My name is Mithra Dias. I studied at Royal College

in Colombo. My father works in a bank. I have been admitted to the Faculty of Management Studies & Commerce.'

The perfect victim!

Mithra Dias is neatly dressed, he has been to a good school in Colombo and his father is a bank official.

In addition to all these negatives, he has a serious physical disability.

I am relieved that the seniors have found a victim to amuse themselves with. It means that, for a little while at least, they will leave me alone. Just the same I can't help feeling a twinge of pity for the wretched fellow on the bench.

I have seen the effect weakness seems to have on bullies. When Pincha's white cow gave birth to a calf that couldn't walk properly, the village dogs sensed its weakness immediately. Although there were many other calves, a pack of dogs harried the disabled one, day after day. In the end, despite all the efforts of its brave mother to drive them off, the dogs tore the little animal to pieces.

I can't bear to watch another spectacle like that. I look down and try to shut my ears.

It had been drilled into my mind at an early age that my only chance of escape from poverty is through education. The long hours of study by the light of a bottle lamp, the endless weary miles on foot along a forest road for tuition classes, and the pleas to other children for textbooks they no longer needed had finally won for me good results at the A level examinations. Looking back it seems as if those were the easy tasks. It was the prospect of being ragged, of being physically in thrall to unknown men and women that had terrified me. I had wanted to give up university, and very nearly did. My friends had thought I was mad. After all, they said, while it will be unpleasant, thousands of other students have endured ragging and survived.

They didn't understand that it is different for me.

It was Father Basil who convinced me that I had to go through with it. He reminded me again and again of the life plan I had prepared with so much care. He told me that only I could turn it into reality and now it was up to me to follow through. Father Basil knew of my problem, for he was the only one in whom I had confided. He understood but would not make allowances for my terror. He finally convinced me, after many weeks of counselling, that I had, in some deep hidden recess, the courage to face up to the challenge. So here I am.

Now I am not sure that I have made the right decision.

The crippled boy is still being interrogated. The bearded leader has his foot on the bench. He jerks his foot from time to time, making the bench wobble. The poor fellow has to flap his arms desperately to save himself from crashing to the ground.

The seniors think this is very funny.

'Is your father also a cripple? Is this a family disease?' one fellow asks amidst general laughter.

'No,' the boy answers calmly, 'I had polio when I was a child.'

A group of seniors tell those of us standing in the 'have-not' corner to follow them. The 'have' group, standing in the other corner, are told to stay back for further questioning … and insult.

They make us stand in formation, as we did at school assembly. Nalini, a girl I had met at the registration desk that morning, is next to me. She is a Buddhist but has studied at a Christian convent in Galle. She has lied to the seniors about her school and has got away with it for the moment.

A dark-skinned girl with protruding teeth gives us our instructions.

As from now, all seniors are to be addressed as *jesta uththamayo* ... august seniors. There is to be a very strict dress code, but when the dark girl goes on to describe it, I want to cry. As a form of harassment they want all the girls to dress ... exactly as I am dressed already.

Everyone is to wear a *gamey gowma,* the village gown, a loose single-piece dress made of printed cotton material that comes down to the ankles. Rubber slippers are the only permitted footwear, no shoes or sandals. Jewellery is not permitted and hair is to be worn in two plaits, held in place by ordinary rubber bands.

I squirm with shame as some of the others look at me and smile knowingly. My white frock with little pink flowers nearly brushes the ground and I am proud of my new Bata slippers. As for jewellery, I have never owned any.

The boys are also given their instructions. Shirts to be worn outside the trousers and no belts are allowed. Rubber slippers, of course, and hair cropped short.

*

The midday meal is served in the main canteen.

I am feeling ill after standing to attention in the sun, listening to the 'august seniors' lecture us on how we are to conduct ourselves during the rag. I am thirsty, hungry and terrified that I will faint!

We quench our thirst at the tap meant for washing our fingers. We are then instructed to pick up a plate each and form a queue. We move slowly past a crew of kitchen staff serving rice and curries directly from cauldrons placed on a counter.

Some lecturers have come into the canteen and happen to stand close to us. I want to kneel on the floor and worship them because their appearance compels the seniors to move off. It is as if a foul odour has been blown away by a sudden breeze.

I see the crippled boy Mithra in the queue. He seems distressed and his clothes, crisp and white when I had seen him earlier, are now stained and crumpled.

The seniors manage to pass a message to us from the far side of the canteen. No fresher is to eat beef or fish, only vegetables and rice.

Some of the others, including Nalini who is seated next to me, are incensed. How can they survive on cabbage curry and mallung? They grumble to each other knowing the seniors can't overhear them. I don't mind, though, for we never ate beef at home, and fish was a rare luxury served only to my uncle.

The lecturers leave after they finish their meal, and the seniors surround us once again. But the afternoon, although extremely strenuous, is easier on the mind. Some of us are taken to the courtyard and trained in performing a perahära.

All temples of any size and significance conduct a perahära, especially when religious relics are to be carried from one place of worship to another. These processions include drummers, dancers, acrobats, stilt walkers and elephants. The boys are given the tougher parts; the stouter ones are made to lumber along as elephants.

I am selected as a dancer and, after the first awkward minutes, play my part with just enough competence to avoid being singled out.

Another group of seniors descend on the courtyard. There is a lot of shouting; threats are hurled at the group conducting the rag. The raggers respond with counter threats and, for a while, it looks as though they will assault each other.

One of the elephants just behind me mutters:

'Ung kelagaththoth apita hondai.'

Good for us if they hammer each other.

The raggers remaining in the courtyard are clearly outnumbered because the bearded leader has taken the other group of freshers elsewhere. They mutter threats at the newcomers and walk off towards the canteen.

The new group of seniors tell us to remain where we are. One of them brings a stool; another man climbs on it and prepares to address us. He is dressed in neatly pressed clothes and shiny brown shoes, very different from the sandals and rubber slippers worn by the raggers.

He addresses us in Sinhala.

'My name is Harith Jayakody. I belong to the Independent Student Federation. We are opposed to the ragging of freshers. The raggers belong to the Socialist Students Union. The SSU undertake the rag to frighten you and to force you to join them. They are aligned to the JSP and are powerful today because the JSP has many members of Parliament.

'We are smaller in numbers but we will protect you whenever we can. Don't be afraid of them. Stay together and survive the rag; then come and join our union.'

The boy jumps down from his stool and comes towards us. He stops to talk to one or two freshers. He is so tall that I can see him over the heads of the other boys as he moves closer.

'He's handsome, isn't he?' Nalini whispers. 'I feel like joining his union right now.'

'Be quiet, he will hear you,' I whisper back, for he is quite near to us now. 'We must be careful till the rag is over.'

Suddenly he is towering over us. It frightens me.

'What is your name?'

'Sujatha Mallika.'

'Department?'

'Mass communications.'

'I will try to protect you,' he says confidently. 'Join our union when this is over.'

I don't answer.

How can I answer when he is standing so close to me?

He stares at me for a moment, waiting for some response; he then frowns and moves on.

'He's interested in you,' Nalini breathes. 'Why didn't you answer him? I think he was upset.'

'I don't want anybody to be interested in me,' I say harshly. 'I just want to be left alone.'

One boy in the village had been 'interested' in me; we had been in the same class in school at Tanamalvila. He thought I was proud and aloof when I didn't respond to his advances. How could I have told him that even the thought of his interest filled me with loathing?

My aunt had been deeply suspicious of the career path I had selected. She wanted to marry me off and took great pains to find a suitable partner, an older man teaching in a government school. She was hurt and confused when I told her that I would kill myself rather than agree to such an arrangement.

She meant well but she should have known better.

A boy yells:

'Let's get out before the other devils come back.'

He uses the term *perethayo* – unclean spirits, which in my opinion is just right.

We collect our files and run, the girls towards the halls of residence within the campus, the boys to theirs outside.

Nalini and I have been assigned to Alwis Hall, located at the rear of the campus, behind the Science Faculty. The three-storied building with a steel gate across its dingy entrance still seems luxurious when compared with my aunt's house. But she keeps her clay-lined floor spotless and the tiny house always smells clean and fresh; of wild flowers and garden produce, of paddy drying on a mat, of smoke from a cooking fire. What would I not give to be back with her for just one hour?

I had noticed a strange smell in the hall when we entered it that morning to leave our bags, a smell of mustiness and also of latrines. I had found it suffocating and wondered how I could possibly put up with it. It is better now that someone has opened all the windows and aired the rooms but still ...

The freshers have been assigned a long dormitory on the first floor. Steel bunk beds are arranged in rows, ten on either side of the room. Tiny lockers have been placed in the space between each set of beds. Common toilets and showers to serve the forty freshers can be accessed through a door at the far end of the dormitory. Nalini tells me that senior girls, four to a room, are housed on the second floor. The hall canteen, providing us with breakfast and dinner, is on the ground floor.

The matron, Mrs. Prelis, is an unsmiling woman whose thick-lensed spectacles seem to flash as she moves her head from side to side. She informs us of the house rules. No men are allowed in the hall, meals will not be kept for those who are late and the hall gates will be locked at 7.30 p.m. each evening.

I look at Nalini and catch her eye. From her amused glance, the first for that terrible day, I know we share the same thought. This place is a wonderful refuge: why not spend the next three months inside the hall? We could leave only when the rag is over!

Nalini is afraid of heights so I volunteer to take the upper bunk. We are both desperate to use the toilet but when I get there I am puzzled by the porcelain seat and cistern.

How does one use these things?

Nalini notices my confusion and endears herself to me by not shaming me in public. Without a word she pulls the seat down and then works the handle of the flush. Having done this she calmly goes into the next cubicle and leaves me.

Without seniors around to harass her, Nalini turns out to be a chatty character with a nice, if slightly wicked, sense of humour.

The hall dining room is on the ground floor to the left of the main entrance with the kitchen at the rear. The food, bread with dhal and fish curry, would have been adequate if the curries had any taste. I wonder if the caterer does this deliberately to make the students eat less, for surely it would not have cost very much to add a little salt and seasoning? When times were hard at home we had eaten red rice, grated coconut and a single green chilli. But that simple meal had tasted better.

Much better!

'The matron couldn't have got fat eating this rubbish,' Nalini grumbles. 'Look at her, she looks like a *bathala gediya.*'

A sweet potato.

From that moment the matron is christened Bathalaya.

She walks round the room talking to the freshers: when she reaches our table she looks morosely at us.

'Where are you from?' she asks a chubby girl seated next to me.

'Panadura, madam,' the girl answers. 'I'm Amali.'

Nalini kicks me under the table.

'Ask her if she eats our food,' she whispers.

'Be quiet.'

'At least ask her if she eats *bathala.*'

'Will you shut up?' I say anxiously, looking down at my plate. 'You'll get me in trouble.'

The hall gates have been locked and the senior girls keep to themselves on the other side of the dining room. For the first time since we entered the campus that morning we are able to put aside our fears and relax a little.

*

Someone screams.

I wake up confused and disoriented. I have no idea where I am. Female voices wail and call out from all sides of the dormitory but I can't make out what they are saying.

The lights are switched on. I see some girls run out

of the room and they are laughing. There is water all over the floor and dripping off the beds.

Those wretched seniors have thrown bucketfuls of water over us.

Nalini sits on the edge of her bed. She has covered her face with her hands but from her heaving shoulders I know she is crying. I jump down and nearly fall when my feet slide from beneath me. Nalini is soaked, her cotton nightdress clings wetly to her body. I sit down beside her and jump up again when I realize that her bed is dripping with water.

I tell Nalini she can sleep with me in the upper bunk. I hate it. I hate having someone so physically close to me but I have no choice, for she has nowhere to go. I turn away and squeeze myself against the railings at the edge of the narrow bunk. I can hear her sobbing from time to time.

I have learned a new word today – bucketing. Why did these seniors inflict such misery on innocents like us? How can they possibly consider bucketing good fun? Hadn't they been freshers themselves? What transforms them into devils after just one year?

Nalini settles down after a while and, from her breathing, I know she is asleep. I toss and turn but sleep doesn't come.

I have never slept on a mattress before. This is quite a thin one, and is spread on a board. Just the same it seems to envelop me in its softness. I feel as if I might sink into it and be suffocated. In my home as a child, and later in my aunt's house, I had always slept on a mat spread on the tamped clay floor.

I long for the familiar surroundings of Angunuwewa, especially at night. The sound of wind lifting the woven cädjan of the roof, of night birds calling by the wäwa, the rare trumpeting of an elephant on the far side of the water. I miss my cousins, Loku and Punchi, who always sleep huddled together on the mat next to me. My aunt Seela spreads her mat on the far side and we keep the little ones comfortingly between us. Her husband always sleeps in the tiny open veranda of the hut.

I had felt safe there.

I must have fallen asleep eventually but then I dream of her.

I can't see her face and she doesn't speak to me but I know it is she. She spreads her arms as if to embrace me.

If you loved me, why did you go away and leave me in hell?

2

There are nearly seventy students in my class. Nalini is reading for a degree in Sociology and Anthropology while I have selected Sociology and Mass Communication. We leave the hall together soon after breakfast and manage to reach the faculty without running into the seniors.

We have two lectures today, each of them two hours long.

'Why only two lectures?' Nalini grumbles. 'We struggle so much to get here and now they won't even teach us.'

'The seniors will catch us when we go for lunch,' I tell her, knowing very well why she is unhappy.

'*Jesta uththamayo!*' she says with a grin. 'I'll give them 'august senior' once this rag is over.'

She has recovered her good humour. By the time we have spread her mattress to dry in the sun, she is making plans to foil the inevitable attack that will take place tonight.

I don't make friends easily, preferring to keep everyone at a safe distance. But with the seniors surrounding us like wolves, I need at least one person I can rely on. Fate must have brought Nalini and me together in the queue at the registration desk.

She is a happy person, full of mischief and fun to be with. I sense that she wants to be my friend … at least for now. After the rag, who knows? She might find me too dull.

They are waiting for us outside the canteen.

'Umbala eeyey pänala giyaney? Ada balamu beraganivida kiyala.'

You ran away yesterday, didn't you? Let's see if they will rescue you today!

The raggers are out in force. Some of the seniors carry sticks and bed poles to use as weapons. Nalini catches my eye with a resigned shrug. There will be no rescue today.

They split us up, twenty to each group. Nalini and I are separated but I find the crippled boy Mithra in my group. We are taken to a corner of the quadrangle and made to stand in three rows.

We are each given a rag name. Our given names are not to be used till the rag comes to an end.

Mine is 'Milkmaid'. Mithra is predictably named 'Nondiya', meaning cripple, while another boy, a bulky chap with round, staring eyes, is called 'Avathāre', meaning apparition.

They ask those who can speak English to raise their hands. Mithra raises his hand without hesitation and, after that, two others follow.

I am not going to raise my hand. Father Basil had convinced me that my life plan could not be achieved without a good knowledge of English. For six years he had taught me, raising me from complete ignorance till I was able to read and understand most common books in the language. I soon began to appreciate the richness of it. I am still not confident enough to converse fluently. I suppose I can if I have to, but I have no wish to advertise the fact.

Although I am writing this diary in English, I do so only to practise my skill. No word of English is spoken on campus outside the lecture theatres.

I am not going to tell the seniors the truth, for if I do

it will mark me out for special treatment.

I am right. They make Mithra and the other two move to the side of the group and kneel. I see Mithra's face twist in pain as he lowers himself on to the uneven ground. His jaw clenches as he struggles to balance his weight on his one good knee.

They start questioning us individually but, from what I overhear, their questions are strange and meaningless, calling for equally meaningless answers. I wonder about it for a while, knowing it to be some test, but find no answer till a girl standing next to me says:

'Gihin ennadada?'

Literally this means 'shall I go and return?' but is a common term in Sinhala meaning, 'may I take leave of you?'

But I say *'Gihin ennan'.*

I understand at last.

Rural southerners speak a slightly different dialect.

For 'is it true?' we ask *'äththei?'* instead of *'äththada?'*

For 'shall I do it?' we ask *'karranei?'* instead of *'karranada?'*

The seniors have not believed the accounts we gave of ourselves. They are trying to segregate us by dialect.

The questions take forever.

I am hungry and my throat is parched. We have been standing in the sun for nearly an hour when they finish with the last of our group, a girl they had named 'Kanduli'. Mithra's face is drawn in pain and he puts his hands on the ground from time to time to take the weight off his bad knee. One of the seniors would spot it and yell at him to straighten up.

I expect them to release us so we could have some food, but it is not to be. The seniors divide us into two groups. There who fail the dialect test are put with Mithra and the other two English speakers, and ordered to stand in the sun. The rest of us are allowed to stand in the shade of a tree.

The bearded leader comes up and there is a discussion with the other seniors. He turns and addresses us.

'My name is Kumudu Prasanna. I am one of the elected leaders of the SSU. Many of you will wonder why we conduct this rag, why we subject you to this punishment. I want to explain the reasons so that you will understand the importance of it, the need for it. One day you will realize that this is not about you and me, it is about nothing less than saving our motherland from the rot and corruption that are destroying it.

'I know that you believe you should be left alone to do your studies and collect your degrees. You think that you will then find good jobs and earn big salaries, that all your problems will be solved.

'But you are wrong!

'None of you will get jobs. You will have to go back like beaten dogs to your villages and explain to your parents that all their suffering was in vain. Is that what you want to do?

'Do you know why you will never get a job? Because a corrupt system reserves all the jobs for people from the cities, for the children of people who are already rich! There is nothing there for you. Nothing!

'All the money your parents spend, all the effort you put into your studies and all your suffering will be utterly useless unless we are able to change this rotten system.

'That is why the rag is so important for it has three objects.

'The first is to make everyone equal. Some of you are accustomed to privilege. The rag will teach you that those privileges only earn you suffering.

'The second object is to teach all of you discipline. You know nothing yet about the corrupt system that works to help the rich and oppress the poor. You must learn to follow wise leaders who will show you the correct path.

'Finally we want to teach you the truth. We are starting on a great struggle to cut out the cancer of corruption from our society. When you realize the great wrongs that have been done to your forefathers, and to you, you will rise up with us to put this right. Don't think we are alone. Students from all over the country, thousands and thousands of them, are being prepared for this great task.

'Listen carefully to your leaders and join hands with us. Our moment is coming and it will be soon.' Kumudu drops his voice to a whisper and continues. 'A word of advice to all of you, don't even dream of opposing our cause … for the punishment given to traitors will be terrible.'

Kumudu speaks with great intensity. He gestures with his clenched fist from time to time and stares intently at each of us in turn, as if daring us to contradict him.

Kumudu stalks off to address the next group of freshers. Although it is now too late for lunch, I hope they will allow us to rest and have a cup of tea.

Again it is not to be. Perahära practice is resumed and I am given a stick and an old paint can to use as a drum.

'Hoi Nondiya, umba adha aliyek weyang,' one senior yells.

Hey cripple, you will be an elephant today.

The elephants are to lead the procession. The unfortunates selected to play elephants have to crawl on all fours over the stony ground and then, when the perahära comes to a halt every ten yards, raise one hand like the elephant's trunk and pretend to trumpet.

I see that the crippled boy is already suffering, having knelt, and then stood, in the sun for so long. Crawling with his bad leg will be hard enough but to lift one arm, while keeping his balance, will be impossible.

But they force him to do it, laughing when he falls on his face. They keep us at it, going round and round the quadrangle till I fear I will faint from weakness and exhaustion.

I hear a thud behind me. Turning, I see a girl dancer sprawled on the ground. I drop the tin can and rush to help her. When we turn her over we see that she is unconscious.

It is the timid girl the seniors had named Kanduli. She has a cut on her lip and her face is bruised. A boy runs off to fetch some water. I expect the seniors to object but find that they have quietly moved away and left us alone.

We rush to a garden tap to wash our faces and drink water. Then, before the wretched seniors can return and get hold of us again, we help Kanduli to her feet and hurry to the hostel.

Once we are safely in the dormitory, all the girls are furious … and brave.

'Those sadists … '

'We should complain to the Dean.'

'He's useless. We should go to the police … '

'Did you see what they did to that Nondiya? His hands were bleeding.'

'How can we survive without food? I'm dying of hunger.'

I am too tired and depressed to speak. I crawl into the upper bunk and fall on my face. This rag won't end in a few days; it will go on for months and months. It will go on till the seniors get bored with it.

When will that be?

Is it true, what that union leader Kumudu told us? Are there no jobs for poor people like us? Are the jobs all reserved for wealthy urban folk?

If that is true then my careful life plan is a mirage; all the hard work I did will be wasted, all my fine hopes will be dashed.

But Father Basil had been confident and he had made me believe. Surely he would not have lied?

*

We jostle each other to serve ourselves at dinnertime. The meal of lumpy white tubes of pittu with coconut milk and dry fish curry is surprisingly palatable. Maybe it is just our famished condition but there is very little talk as we try to fill ourselves as quickly as possible.

The senior girls glower at us from the other side of the dining room. They leave us alone except for an occasional lump of soggy pittu that comes flying across the hall. Bathalaya, the matron, pretends not to notice what is going on.

'Those wretches are going to duck us again tonight,' Nalini says, scowling angrily. 'I feel like hiding behind the door with a broom and whacking the first one who enters the dorm.'

'What if it is Bathalaya who comes in?' another girl asks. 'You'll get the sack for hitting matron.'

We all laugh and that draws some angry looks from

the seniors. They are certainly planning something unpleasant for us tonight.

'Do we actually have a broom?' I ask quietly.

Nalini looks at me in some surprise.

'Yes. I saw one in the dorm,' she says with a puzzled frown. 'Why do you ask?'

'The dorm door opens outwards,' I say hesitantly. 'I thought, you know, if we put the broom across the frame and tie the door handle to it, they won't be able to get in.'

'Where'll we get rope at this time?' another girl asks.

'There's a clothes line in the balcony.'

Nalini's face breaks into a gleeful grin.

'Meyki sadda näthuwa innawā,' she says, *'häbai eyā podi ekek nevai.'*

This one waits quietly but she's not a small one.

The broom is too long to fit on the frame but it sits neatly across the wall. The girls wrap the clothesline round the handle of the door and then securely on the broom. There are giggles all round when we finally go to bed, secure in the knowledge that the seniors will not be able to harass us till morning.

I dream I have walked to the far side of the wäwa again, deep into the forest. It is well after sunset but there is enough light for me to see my way.

Just as it had been the first time!

I hear an elephant trumpet in the distance. I see other animals, leopard and bear, as I stumble through the forest. I am not afraid. I yearn for one of them to attack and devour me for I want my life to end.

To my dismay they all run away.

I wake up with sorrow welling up inside me like water from a spring.

3

The seniors make us balance files on our heads when we move from class to class. They also make us reverse the slippers on our feet.

On the other hand, the lectures are becoming interesting. Apart from notes, we are given plenty of reference reading to do and these books are in English. It is evident that we will not be able to prepare the tutorials without many hours in the library. There are groans from the students.

Even Nalini, sitting next to me, makes a face.

I had not wanted to go to school. I was terrified that the other children would find out about me. I told my aunt that all I wanted was to stay in her home and look after the little ones. I explained my fears to Father Basil, not daring to raise my eyes further than the end of his untidy grey beard. He had listened patiently, nodding his head from time to time. I could tell from the way his beard moved back and forth.

He understood, but never agreed.

In the end I gave in, not because I lost my fear, but because he kept at me till I said yes. He gave my aunt money for my school uniforms and for my books. I had missed many months of schoolwork during my trouble and found it difficult to catch up. Again it was Father Basil who helped me with my work every evening.

Once I settled down in school, he started talking to

me about the future. He told me that I could build a new life for myself if I was prepared to work hard. He gave me the hope that someday, somehow, there could be a better life for me.

That was when he told me I had to learn English. In a village where no one knew a single word of this new language, it had seemed so absurd. I told him so, but he wouldn't listen.

He was a clever, clever man, Father Basil.

I have to keep it secret, at least till the rag is over. Proficiency in English will, more than anything else, mark me down for harassment.

They are waiting for us at the canteen.

They allow us to serve ourselves, just vegetables and rice again, but they will not allow us to eat. They separate us into two lots as before. Those of us who come from remote villages are referred to contemptuously as dirty, 'kunu' freshers. Those who come from the cities or appear to be wealthy are now called 'alayo', whatever that means. They keep us waiting and wondering till the bearded Kumudu Prasanna comes in, followed by his close supporters.

He stands on a table to harangue us:

'Kunu freshers, today we will teach you how to be united. How to live like brothers and sisters,' he says, turning his head to stare at each of us in turn. 'You might not like what you have to do, but one day you will thank us for it.'

As Kumudu is speaking, seniors come into the canteen with sheaves of banana leaves. They spread out, tossing a single cut piece into the centre of each table. Another group of seniors come up, one to each table, and stand by looking expectantly at Kumudu. I notice that the boy at our table is a thin fellow in a very ragged pair of brown trousers and a shirt with long sleeves rolled to his elbows.

When Kumudu raises his hand, the boy takes Nalini's plate and turns it over on the banana leaf.

Nalini is outraged:

'Aney.'

The senior turns on her furiously.

'What did you say, bitch?'

Terrified, Nalini just shakes her head. Brown trousers stares at her for a while and then speaks to the rest of us.

'Turn your plates over on the banana leaf,' he orders.

This can't be true. The banana leaf has been brought as it was cut from the tree. It is unwashed and covered with a layer of dust.

'Turn your plates over,' the fellow yells angrily. 'Anyone who doesn't do as I say will get no food and will spend the afternoon under the table.'

Slowly and reluctantly we tip our plates over, trying to keep each plateful separate from the next person's, for there are six of us at the table. It isn't any use because the senior takes a short stick from his belt and mixes all the food together, as though he is blending cow dung with clay to apply on the floor of a house.

Kumudu is still standing on his table at the other end of the canteen.

'Now that the food has been mixed together,' he says, 'we want all of you to eat from the same banana leaf. We are all one family, so you must show your solidarity by eating from one dish. We want you to learn this lesson. You must also learn to trust your leadership when we say this is for your own good and future development.

'As you know, alayo have been given special lessons

in discipline. So far they have obeyed the leaders so, … as a reward, we will be serving a special mallung only for them.

'Part of your training is to appreciate the food you have been given. Many people in our country are starving. There must be no waste. Every one of you must finish all the food, every grain, on the banana leaf.'

I know that Nalini is looking at me but I keep my eyes lowered. Even speaking to each other will only attract the attention of one of the seniors. But when I try to separate a small portion of rice to one end of the leaf, brown trousers notices and uses his stick to mix it up again.

Two seniors come out of the kitchen carrying an aluminium pan; another comes with a long spoon. He starts serving a portion of the green vegetable on to the middle of the banana leaf on each table. But they only serve the 'alayo'. I watch them go past our table and serve the next one where Mithra is seated.

They tell us to start eating. The rice is full of grit from the unwashed banana leaf but we dare not stop. I try to take my food from the top of the pile but that only delays the inevitable.

A girl sitting at the next table screams:

'Mällumata Kärapottho dāla.'

They've put cockroaches in the mallung.

There are shouts of horror from all over the room. The seniors crowd round tables assigned to the 'alayos'. They are all laughing and shouting.

'Kārpalla kärapothu mällung. Umbala duppatunta denney owa nedha? Däng kāpalla!'

Eat the cockroach mallung. Isn't this what you give

the poor? Now you eat it!

The thought of crushed cockroaches mixed in the food makes me ill. I can feel my stomach churning dangerously. Although they have not served us that mallung, I know I will throw up if I eat another morsel.

And I feel ashamed.

I should feel sorry for the alayo but all I feel is relief that it is they who are being subjected to this treatment, and not us.

Despite the shouting and threats, the alayo at the next table refuse to eat. A fair girl seated next to Mithra, and facing us, is clearly unable to cope with the horror. Her eyes are wide, the whites showing all round; her hands are gripping the edge of the table and the tendons of her neck are standing out, taut with tension.

A senior reaches over her shoulder, mixes some rice and mällung with his fingers and tries to force the handful into her mouth.

She throws up on his hand and on the table, vomit spewing across the banana leaf like dung bursting out of a sick cow. The senior, a short fellow with a scraggly beard, howls in disgust and wipes his hand on her hair. Tears pour down the girl's face; her eyes have a look of madness. I have seen eyes like that before, when Kusuma's daughter was possessed by a demon. The girl puts her head down and rests it on the edge of the table.

More seniors gather round the table. One fellow takes a stick and mixes the food with the girl's vomit.

'Dhäng bathata hodith thiyanawā,' he yells gleefully. *'Kāpalla!'*

Now there is gravy for the rice. Eat!

The alayo sit still with their eyes lowered. They don't obey the seniors but they don't defy them either. They wait.

Some of the seniors laugh.

The senior with vomit on his hand must think they are laughing at him because he gets very agitated. He screams at the alayo to obey him but still no one moves, stunned into stillness by the horror of it.

'Umba, Nondiya,' he shouts, *'kāpang.'*

Cripple, you eat it.

When Mithra ignores the order the senior catches him by the scruff of his neck and forces his head onto the table. With his free hand the senior pulls the banana leaf closer and then … pushes Mithra's face into the foul mixture.

Jesta uththamayo are not august seniors, they are animals!

All the other seniors gather round that table to watch; some of them are cheering. Even the fellow assigned to our table has gone over. Nalini touches my arm. We look at the others and, without a single word being spoken, leave the table and sneak out of the canteen.

No one notices us leave.

*

I am worried about money.

I had told the seniors the truth; my aunt has no money to send me. It is not the whole truth though, for Father Basil had given me one thousand rupees when I left the village. But that is all I have till they release the Mahapola funds.

I have been selected for the scholarship but we do not know when the money will come. I have already paid four hundred and fifty rupees as hostel fees and I will have to pay separately for each meal, even when the seniors prevent us eating it.

What will I do when the money is finished?

*

Nalini and I have no lectures this afternoon. We manage to reach our hostel without running into any other seniors.

Nalini is furious.

'How can we go on like this? These are not human beings; these are devils! What is the Vice-Chancellor doing? Why can't he take some action? If they don't stop, I'm going home. I can't take this any more.'

I try to calm her down:

'We have survived for three days now. Think about how we did that. By not getting noted, by not challenging them, by doing whatever they told us to do. We can survive another three days, then another. This rag will be over one day.'

Nalini looks at me strangely.

'There's something about you I don't understand,' she says at last. 'You are so quiet yet …'

'Nali, I struggled so hard to come here, I am not going to allow these devils to chase me away.'

'But how can we stand it?' Nalini asks despairingly. 'You saw what they did today to that girl and then to that Mithra fellow. Cockroaches in the food and then the vomit! What if it had been us?'

'But it wasn't us,' I tell her. 'We survived today and now we're safe here.'

'You are a hard one, Suji. Don't you feel sorry for them?'

'I feel sorry for them,' I say. 'I do, really. But mostly I'm glad they didn't do it to us.'

'What will you do if it us next time?' Nalini asks me. 'Will you eat food with cockroaches in it?'

'I'll try. I will surely vomit but I'll try,' I tell her. 'That's what they want. Obedience. I'll obey them.'

'How can you even … even say that?' Nalini asks wonderingly. 'They are torturing us like this so they can laugh a little. Why are they doing it?'

'Most people like to inflict suffering on others,' I say harshly. 'No point in asking why! Victims like us can only learn to endure it and … survive.'

'But how can you endure torture?'

'I've endured worse.'

I know I've made a mistake because Nalini looks at me expectantly, waiting for me to go on. I ignore her gaze, collect my towel and go for a shower.

I hate the bathing arrangements at the hostel.

The water comes out of a pipe. Nalini tells me that there should have been a 'shower rose' at the end of the pipe, to scatter the water over you. These 'shower roses' have been lost or broken years ago, so now a stream of water thuds on to your head from the open pipe. You are told to finish quickly in order to save water, and because others are waiting to take your place.

And the water has a strange smell, an unpleasant odour of chemicals.

How different it is in the village, for a bath in the wäwa is the most joyous activity of the day.

The midday meal has to be prepared first. Rice to boil and then two vegetables, lotus roots from the wäwa or something taken from the garden and a small piece of dry-fish for my uncle. The rest of us never ask for, and are never given, fish or meat.

When the meal is cooked and put aside my aunt will announce the magic words we have been waiting for since morning.

'Wäwata yamu!'

Let's go to the wäwa.

The little ones and I would follow her to the old bund where kumbuk trees grow in a long row. Only women and small children come to our spot; the men of the village go further away.

The little ones bathe in the shallows but I wade out till the water comes to my waist. The older women all wear a *diya reddha* for bathing. This is a long strip of cotton fabric that is wrapped round the body to cover it from breast to knee. I was sometimes given a used sarong belonging to my uncle that I had to launder afterwards by pounding on a rock.

We bathe and bathe till our skin is wrinkled and pale. When I am finished I sit in the shallows and play with the little ones. My aunt is very patient and sits in the shade, chatting with the other women till we tire of it.

Why does water in the city smell so strange?

4

On the way to our morning lecture we meet the crippled boy, Mithra, coming out of the Management Science Faculty.

Nali, ever the forward one, speaks to him while I hang back feeling awkward.

'You must be Mithra. I am Nalini and my shy friend is Sujatha,' she says as she drags me forward.

I'm not really shy. A little, maybe! It's just that I don't feel comfortable near strange men.

But Mithra doesn't have a threatening face and his eyes, behind the spectacles, have an expression that surprises me. After the incident in the canteen the previous day, I thought he would be crushed; I expected to see fear. Instead his eyes have a touch of … gentle amusement.

How is this possible? How can you be amused when you are a cripple and everyone is picking on you?

'Hullo. Yes I am Mithra. I saw you both at the next table yesterday,' he says with a small smile. 'I wonder what treat they're preparng for our lunch today.'

'Something awful, I'm sure,' Nalini says, suddenly depressed.

'My guess is they'll give us earthworms,' Mithra calls over his shoulder as he limps away. 'Worms are very nourishing.'

*

I am late for lunch and at the tail-end of the queue. Nalini has run off to the bookstall promising to be back in a minute. I had waited for twenty minutes and then decided to go alone.

There are some seniors about the place, keeping an eye on us, but not as many as yesterday.

'Aren't you Nalini's shy friend?'

I turn to find Mithra standing immediately behind me.

'I'm not shy,' I am forced to say. 'Nalini just says these things.'

'What is your course?'

'Mass Communication.'

'Ahh, so you want to be a journalist, do you?' he asks casually.

I am so surprised that I smile. I almost never smile and certainly haven't done since I entered this hell. The smile just slips out without my realizing it.

I see Kumudu, the union leader, bearing down on us. His face is thunderous. I realise immediately that I have made a bad mistake.

Oh no! How could I have been so foolish?

Freshers are not allowed to speak with each other. I had not only chatted with one of the hated 'alayo', but had gone so far as to smile. The seniors will take it as a sign that I am treating the rag with contempt.

To my surprise Kumudu ignores me and turns on Mithra.

'May nondiya kellanwa sōdanawa methana,' he shouts furiously. *'Moota pādamak ugannanna oney.'*

This cripple is trying to get round the girls here. We must teach him a lesson.

The seniors crowd round and drag Mithra out of the

canteen. I don't want to watch but can't tear my eyes away from the scene just outside the window.

They force him to roll his trousers up to his knees. When his crippled leg is exposed, they begin to shout and jeer.

'Oka kakulakkda, sathekkge waligayakkda?'

Is that a leg or an animal's tail?

'Oyi wandurekkge kakulakkda?'

Is that a monkey's leg?

'May korāta kello elawanna denney kohomada?

How can we allow this cripple to chase girls?

They make him kneel on a pile of rock stones some contractor has left in the garden. Mithra crawls on to the uneven pile but is unable to balance on his weak knee. He keeps falling over.

They won't allow him to use his hands for support.

I sit at a table with some girls from the Arts Faculty. They are free to chat because the seniors are busy torturing Mithra in the garden.

Thanks to me!

You fool. Why did you talk to me? Didn't you see that an evil spirit possesses me? Didn't you know that I only bring sorrow and suffering to those who come near me? Now you are paying the price for your foolishness.

I am hungry and the seniors are leaving us alone for the first time … but I cannot eat. I desperately want to be alone; I always do when I am stressed. I slip out of the canteen and return to the hostel.

When Nali joins me later she tells me what had happened after I left.

The raggers had kept Mithra kneeling on the rocks till he had fainted and fallen down. He had cut his face when he fell but that had not been serious. He had more painful injuries on his knees and had not been able to walk.

Luckily some seniors from the other union, the ISF, had come by later and taken him to the Health Centre for treatment.

*

When we return to the dormitory after dinner we find that the broom, and the cord we had used to secure the door, are missing. All the girls join in the search but finally realise that we have been very foolish. While we were enjoying a surprisingly quiet dinner, the seniors have taken away our device for securing the door.

They must have prepared a special treat for us tonight.

The girls search the dormitory for some suitable bar, but without success. They gather in a circle, unwilling to get to bed, for everyone is certain that something very unpleasant has been planned. There is no shortage of ideas.

'Let's stay up all night, then we can be ready for them.'

'We can fill some basins of water. Bucket them when they come.'

'Let's go and complain to the warden. She'll have to take action.'

I say softly: 'Let's pull up a bed.'

The others go on, ignoring me.

'I can't stand this. If they don't let us sleep at night then I'm going home.'

'I had a good job. I don't know why I gave it up to

come here.'

'If I tell my father what's going on he'll come and set fire to this university.'

Nali says:

'Shut up, all of you! What did you say, Suji?'

I feel awkward when their eyes turn on me.

'These metal bunk beds are very heavy,' I say hesitantly. 'If we pull the nearest one across the door, we can tie the handle to the frame.'

'And what will we use to tie it with?' Nali asks softly. 'They've taken the rope.'

'Let's tear one of those curtains into strips,' I say, pointing at the drapes that hang from the windows. 'If we twist it well, and tie the ends, it will be strong enough.'

They are all quiet for a moment. Nali says:

'Mey kella meeyek wagey inney, häbai mukatiyekgey moley.'

This girl waits like a mouse but has the brain of a mongoose.

Although I feel secure behind the barricaded door, I don't fall asleep for a long time. I can't get the image of poor Mithra out of my mind. All he had done was make a casual remark but I had made the mistake of turning around.

And smiling!

I cannot remember when I last smiled, for what is there in my life to smile about? Oh why had I allowed my teeth to show at that one inopportune moment?

Now poor crippled Mithra has to pay the price for my folly.

I dream of Yasawathi.

I know it is she although a devil mask covers her face. It makes her head huge, like an elephant's. Two fangs protrude from the upper jaw and curve back from the corner of her mouth. There is blood dripping from the fangs, crimson gobbets that stain her cheeks. Angry devil-eyes glisten madly as she comes towards me.

She is carrying a heavy stick.

I turn to run. I can't see where I am going; my eyes are filled with tears and I dare not stop to wipe them away. I can hear her voice close behind me as I run, chanting over and over:

'Bälli. Bälli. Bälli.'

Bitch. Bitch. Bitch.

I know she is going to kill me. I know she wants me dead.

I trip over a root of a tree and fall down. I feel a searing pain as my elbow hits the ground but I roll over and get to my knees. I join my hands together and beg her not to hit me.

'Mama väradi keruwey nähä.'

I didn't do anything wrong.

But the devil mask doesn't change, for Yasawathi isn't listening. She never listens.

She raises the stick to strike me.

*

The Mahapola funds have come at last. It isn't a day too soon as my money is nearly finished. Nali and I join the others rushing down to the bank soon after the morning lecture. I go to the canteen for lunch, relieved of at least one of my many worries.

The 'boga set' is there in force today.

Kumudu and the SSU refer to the Independent Students Federation (ISF) by this name because they are thought to flaunt their wealth. The ISF refer to the SSU as 'Jeppo' because they are aligned to the Janapriya Samajawadhi Peramuna (JSP), the leading leftist political party.

Harith Jayakody is there, moving between the tables and talking to the freshers. Nali and I fill our plates and move quietly to one of the vacant tables near the door of the canteen.

Some seniors from the 'boga set' come over and speak to us kindly, asking how we are coping with the rag, telling us not to be afraid. Nali answers their questions and they soon move away to speak with some others.

Harith comes over to our table. He speaks directly to me.

'You are Sujatha, aren't you?' he asks, smiling easily. 'Which is your hostel?'

'Alwis Hall,' I answer shortly, wishing he would go away.

'Where are you from?' he persists. 'What school did you attend?'

'My village is called Angunuwewa.' My eyes are on my plate. I am trying hard not to look at him. 'My school was Tanamalwila Maha Vidyalaya.'

'You know, you don't have to be afraid of me,' leaning over, he says softly. 'I will not harm you.'

I have to look at him then.

'I am not afraid of you,' I say angrily. 'I just wanted to …'

Kumudu is standing at the entrance with some of his members. He is staring in my direction and his bearded face seems to bristle with anger. Harith glances around casually and, seeing Kumudu standing there, strolls off.

More and more SSU members came in; Harith and his friends drift away through a door at the far end of the canteen.

We are told to report to the upper playground for further training in 'political awareness'.

The SSU have arranged a platform and a public address system. We are told to gather round; Nali and I stand at the back in the shade of a giant mara tree. Kumudu is the trainer.

'How many of you know that there are over forty thousand unemployed graduates in the country?' he asks. 'Raise your hands.'

A few brave hands go up.

'It is quite true. Believe it,' Kumudu goes on. 'Why do you think they are unemployed? Is it because they are fools? Because they are unable to hold down a job?'

He looks at the faces of those in front, not really expecting an answer.

'No, of course not! These graduates are as good as any of the others; better even. They can do the job … but they are NEVER selected. To understand the reason for this, you must go back in history, to colonial times.

'When the British occupied our land they gave jobs to the minorities. There were also some Sinhalese families who supported the invader. These traitors were rewarded with vast tracts of land and with prominent jobs.

'The favoured ones learned English so they could lick the invader's boot. Once their positions were secure, their children were educated in the English medium in the best schools in the cities. They spoke this foreign language in their homes in preference to their mother tongue. Meanwhile the children of patriots could only educate themselves in Sinhala in poor rural schools.

'Everyone expected the system to change after independence. Everyone expected change after the Sinhala Only act. But did it? Many of you may, in your ignorance, think that it has. There are forty thousand graduates out there who learned the truth when it was too late. They came to university full of hope; confident that they would find a good job as soon as they graduated. Now they know that all the sacrifices their parents made, all their own efforts, were in vain.

'So why is it they can't get jobs? Because rural folk can't speak English like the city folk … just that! They tell us to study English for six months and then compete with those who have spoken the language since childhood. How can we?

'They never give the jobs to us; those jobs are reserved for the children of the privileged.'

Kumudu is now grasping the microphone with both hands. His bearded face is covered in perspiration; his eyes widen as he turns his face from side to side to glare at the freshers standing in a semicircle before him. His voice has risen and now thunders at us across the playground.

'Do you fools understand what I'm telling you? You think you know everything but you know … nothing! Do you realize that your hopes and plans for the future are all illusions? Can you see that unless we can change this rotten, corrupt system we are all doomed?

'Those in power will do anything to keep things as they are. They want to keep all the benefits for themselves and they want to keep us in eternal poverty. They control the government and the armed forces. And they have the wealth.

'We have nothing but our numbers. If we are divided

they will surely crush us.' Kumudu pauses for a long moment and seems to gather himself. His voice rises to a scream.

'But if we are united, if we are fearless, we will triumph. If you trust us, your leaders, we can and will change this unjust system. Nothing and no one can stop us.'

He pauses again and his voice drops to a whisper, harsh and threatening:

'We have chosen you to join us in this noble struggle. A cause that will help you, as it will help all poor young people who want to better their lives. Those who refuse to join us automatically support our enemies, for the rich rely on the apathy of the poor. So remember! Those traitors who refuse to join us will be crushed without mercy.'

The meeting is over.

The freshers begin moving away in small groups. Nali and I follow them, hoping our instructions are over for the day.

A tall boy with long hair parted in the middle comes to the microphone and says harshly:

'Indapalla!'

Wait.

'Api athara vesiyek innawā. Eki mehe ävith thiyenney minihekwa hoyanna. Api ekita honda pādamak ugannana oney.'

We have a prostitute in our midst. She has come here with one intention: to get hold of a man. We must teach her a good lesson.

I don't like this at all. I stand still, unable to breathe.

'Sujatha Mallika, meheta vareng.'

Sujatha Mallika, come forward.

I pray for the earth to open and swallow me. Many freshers are laughing. Someone nudges me from behind; the crowd moves apart to make room for me. I walk forward like a clockwork toy with no control over my hands and feet.

This can't be happening. What did I ever do to deserve this?

I am standing before the platform. Through brimming eyes I see Kumudu and the other leaders standing there. The boy with the microphone speaks again.

'Sujatha Mallika, this is not the place to look for a husband. We shall teach you a lesson today to make sure you remember that.'

I stand there trembling, speechless at the injustice of it.

What awful punishment have they planned?

Two senior girls come forward and stand before me. One of them has a closed saucepan in her hand. They are both grinning in anticipation.

One of them walks round, twisting my arms behind me, holding them tight. The other girl uncovers the pan. I see that the pan is filled with cold cooking oil, acrid and black from repeated use.

They pour it slowly on my head making sure it dribbles through my hair and then onto my face and body. I can't open my eyes. My mouth and nose are clogged. I know I will die now. I wish I would die now.

I hear them laughing as they go away.

My eyelids are gummed shut, eyeballs on fire.

Don't let me go blind. Oh please, don't let me lose my sight.

Nali saves me.

I learn later that she had stood there in public and removed her underskirt. I feel her hand on my shoulder, soft material wiping my face.

Nali cleans my nose and mouth and I am able, at last, to breathe freely. She holds me tight till I stop shaking and then, with the help of some others, guides me to the hostel. They have to carry me part of the way.

The stink of rancid oil is being gradually replaced by the sharp fragrance of Lifebuoy soap. I manage to open my eyes.

The sunlight streaming through the window is like fire, searing my brain. The pain recedes after a minute but every object in the shower room is blurred.

I scream in terror then, sure that my sight is lost. I am a beggar already, but to be blind as well? Then with water cascading on my face from the outside, and my tears welling up inside, the film of oil gradually slips away and my sight returns. I sit on the floor under the shower and cry.

Tears of relief!

I go to the mirror fitted at the end of the shower stall. My hair is plastered to my skull and across my face. My eyes are inflamed; blood vessels spreading like tiny red worms.

I stare at my face, filled with despair. I know very well what has brought this about.

Will it never end?

As I am about to turn away I see something on the plastic shelf under the mirror, a rusty half of a razor blade. My hand goes out under its own volition and picks it up.

I can solve this now. One quick slash across this hated face and the problem will be gone forever.

I lift my hand with the razor between my thumb and forefinger. I stare at the mirror again, strangely pleased to see that my hand is steady.

Do it!

Nali is standing behind me, looking puzzled.

'What are you doing, Suji? What have you got in your hand?' she asks worriedly. She takes the blade and puts it back on the shelf.

'You've been here for hours. Wipe yourself or you'll catch cold.'

*

I dream of her again!

Although her features are covered by hair that the wind has blown across her face, I know it is she from the jagged front tooth. He had done that when he came home one night, drunk as always. The heavy pot of rice had caught her full in the face, cutting her lip and breaking that upper front tooth.

She is calling out, trying to tell me something. I can see the lips moving but can't hear her. The wind is carrying her words away.

I see her features now. There is a look of infinite sadness on her face when she realises that her words do not reach me. She turns and walks slowly away.

5

There is a letter for me on the common room table.

I pick it up hurriedly, knowing it is from Father Basil. Only my Aunt Seela and he will want to write to me, and Seela can't write very well. I run to the dormitory, glad that I have decided to give up lunch for some peace in the deserted hostel.

I don't open the letter till I am safely ensconced in the upper bunk.

Samagi Sevana,
Angunuwewa
12th October

My dear Sujatha,

I hope you are well and not being treated too badly. Your little cousins Loku and Punchi ask about you every time they pass me on the road. They miss their clever big sister very much.

I know you must be very lonely there. I also know that much of the rag is degrading and utterly inhuman. It must be especially hard for you to understand why senior students wish to be so cruel to innocent newcomers. Many of the seniors, I am told, have their own psychological and material problems and tend to take out these frustrations on the freshers.

Dear Sujatha, that is the way it is and you must accept it. You have faced the terrible difficulties of your life with so much courage that I know you can face this challenge as well. Remember that while they can subject you to physical torment, they cannot touch your mind – unless you consent to it. You must be mentally strong. I know you can be.

Remember also the plan we prepared together, so many years ago. Keep it in the forefront of your mind at all times. You have achieved so much of what you set out to do and you are now so near your goal. Don't let anyone or anything keep you from achieving your dream.

I have spoken of you to a former student of mine in Colombo. I am happy to tell you that she has willingly agreed to send you, by money order, five hundred rupees every month. I hope this, together with the Mahapola payment, will be enough for you to manage with.

Please write when you are able to find the time. I pray for you daily.

Fr. Basil Fernando S.J.

I read the letter again and again. It lifts me out of my despair, a little higher with each reading. I feel as if new blood is being slowly injected into my veins, giving me new strength. I am thankful now that Nali had walked into the shower room when I had that razor blade in my hand.

When I first met him, I had been very frightened of Father Basil.

Well, I had been frightened of everyone. He sensed it and never came close to me. He would sit on the front step of Aunt Seela's hut, looking out at the garden, and talk. He talked and talked although I, lying on a mat just inside the door, never replied or asked a question.

At the beginning I closed my ears to him, too overwhelmed by the horrors that filled my mind and the unremitting ache of my injuries. But he kept coming back every day and gradually, as my body healed, I began to listen.

He had a deep voice, Father Basil, melodious and strange to my ears. He spoke of things I had never heard of, about planets and stars, about the habits of birds, about the wonders of the sea that I had never seen, of the strange creatures that lived in it. He talked about the ancient heritage of our people, of the modern city of Colombo, of strange and wonderful lands across the sea.

He would come close to noon, when my aunt was preparing the midday meal. After a time I even began to look forward to his visits. When I was able to walk about I'd watch out for him coming up the footpath that led to our home. I would then run inside and sit near the door with my back to the wall. Father Basil continued to sit on the step facing the garden. He never asked me to come outside.

He started bringing books of children's stories. He would read a section in English, of which I understood not a word, and explain it to me in Sinhala. He always stopped at a point when something dramatic was about to happen and that would drive me wild.

But I never spoke a word.

One day I was seated near the front steps watching a pair of Kondayas building a nest, so engrossed I didn't realize that Father Basil had arrived and was preparing to sit in his usual place a few feet away. I wanted to run. I really did, but I was afraid to stand up. Father Basil didn't look at me; he just opened his book and began to read.

I was able to look closely at him when he bent over the book. He was old, older than I'd expected from hearing his voice that was rich and strong. I saw untidy grey hair above an equally untidy grey and black beard. Thick reading glasses perched on a nose like an eagle's beak. Tall, thin, stooped.

I sat outside after that. Not too near, and still without speaking, but outside just the same. That was when he started pointing out the birds in our garden. He could recognize and name a bird with one casual glance and there were many that came there, different ones every day. He would name them in Sinhala and in English and, after a time, the names would stick in my memory. Tailor Birds, Drongos, Babblers, Bulbuls and my favourites, the lovely Sunbirds.

One day while Father Basil was busy reading a story I spotted a bird I had never seen before, small with black upper parts but a breast of such fiery red, I thought it would burst into flames. I waited impatiently for him to look up and identify the bird but his eyes were on the book, reading slowly. Desperately anxious that the bird would fly away I blurted out my first words to him:

'Balanna. Ara mokāda?'

Look. What is that?

'*Gini kurulla,*' he told me casually before returning to his book. 'Scarlet Minivet.'

The next day he gave me a small notebook and a pencil with instructions to record the birds I saw in the garden and those I saw near the wäwa when we went to bathe. It was very difficult for me at the beginning but I learnt with time. Size when compared to common birds, general shape, colour and where I had seen it.

Father Basil would then bring his bird book when he came to visit, a fat volume by someone called Henry. It was written in English but had coloured pictures of most birds. Father Basil would listen to my descriptions attentively while tugging at his beard, eyes behind those thick lenses filled with interest. He would then make humming noises as he thumbed through the book.

'Ahh,' he would say finally as he showed me a picture. 'Isn't this the one?'

He would then turn to the text and tell me something of that bird's habits, what it ate, how it found food and when it nested. Sometimes he would tell me that the bird I picked in the book could not have been there at that time. I would get very angry then, arguing vehemently with him. I think he sometimes did it just to tease me, to draw me out.

One day he gave me the book, making me promise to look after it carefully. I couldn't believe it. No one had ever given me, nor had I ever owned, anything of value before.

I was happy in those days. Happy till my aunt told me that I had to go to school.

'You have already missed a lot,' she told me. 'Father Basil has spoken to the principal and he has agreed to take you in. You have to walk to the main road and the bus will take you to Tanamalvila.'

The prospect had terrified me.

What if they find out about me? School children always find things out. What will they say to me? How can I face them?

'No. I don't want to go to any school,' I told my aunt

desperately. 'I just want to stay at home and look after the little ones.'

'You are only thirteen,' my aunt had replied. 'You can't give up now. Father Basil insists it is time for you to go back to school.'

I cried and cried, pleading with my aunt but she was adamant.

On the night before the first day of school I ran away to the forest, hoping wild animals would kill and eat me.

*

A hubbub of excited voices wakes me.

I roll over and see several girls running into the dormitory. Nali comes hurrying in; she is breathing rapidly and looks upset.

'They are fighting,' she gasps. 'They are hitting each other with iron rods and chairs. It's … it's awful.'

'What are you talking about? What's happening?'

'Where were you? Didn't you come to the canteen for lunch?'

'No. I didn't feel like eating.'

She looks at me for a moment.

'We served ourselves but they wouldn't let us eat. We had to remain standing while Kumudu and a girl called Renuka made speeches about the importance of discipline; that we had to trust the leadership and rubbish like that.

'Then they told us to let the plates remain on the table, remain standing and only use our left hand to feed ourselves.'

'Nali, you're a lefthander,' I point out. 'You would have been all right.'

Nali allows herself a quick grin.

'Yes. I'm the only one who was able to eat anything,' she said. 'But before even I was able to finish... the ISF fellows charged into the canteen from all sides.'

That would have been the right wing student body, Harith Jayakody's group.

What do I care if the unions fight each other?

I think that, on the whole, it is good for us. I turn back to Nali who has got her breath back and is probably thinking the same thing.

'So what happened next?'

'The ISF came well prepared. They must have brought outsiders also because there were people with them that we had never seen on campus. They had clubs and chains in their hands. The Jeppo had no weapons so they grabbed the chairs and started fighting. They were hitting each other and running between the tables. Anyone who fell down got whacked.

'It was horrible.

'We left everything and tried to escape but the doors were blocked. We ran near the serving counter to get out that way but the staff had closed the kitchen door. We were stuck there, forced to watch.'

Nali's eyes grow bigger as she recreates the scene in her mind. We are seated on her bed now; the other girls have gathered in small groups, discussing the violence in shocked whispers.

'I think they had targeted the Jeppo leaders. Two men cornered Kumudu and beat him with clubs. I wasn't one bit sorry when I saw him fall down. Very good for him!

'Then the Police came in two big trucks. Everyone started to run away, they even jumped through the windows. Some of our boys broke down the kitchen door and we escaped through that.'

We have a quiet evening in the hostel. Even the senior girls appear to have been shaken by the violence. They talk quietly to themselves and don't bother with us.

Nali is again her chatty, inquisitive self.

'Are your eyes all right now?' she asks. 'They looked awful when they were covered in oil.'

'Mm. Yes. Still hurts a bit when I go outside.'

'They were very mean to you yesterday, weren't they?' she goes on. 'I mean … everyone knew it wasn't your fault that Harith talked to you.'

'Yes,' I say sharply, not wanting to take this further.

'So why do you think they did it?' she persists, giving me a sly look. 'They must have a reason, surely.'

'How would I know?'

'I saw that Kumudu rascal speaking with the girls who did the job. I'm sure he was instructing them.'

'Mmm.'

'You're not surprised, are you?'

'No, I suppose not.'

'The rotter was jealous, wasn't he?' she asks. 'He didn't like Harith speaking to you.'

'I suppose so,' I say wearily, wishing she'd get off the subject.

'Aren't you even a bit bucked that he is interested in you?'

'He's a sadistic monster. Even thinking of him makes me ill,' I say furiously. 'Anyway I don't want anyone to be interested in me.'

'But …' Nali begins, but I cut her off.

'Stop talking about it! Please stop.'

I read the letter again before I go to bed. It is like a

long *'thangus'*; a fishing line leading back to my home, keeping me connected. I fold it carefully and place it under my pillow.

No dreams.

*

Lectures go on as usual the next day; a few of us visit the library afterwards. Some senior students poring over books give us unfriendly looks but don't accost us. We go nervously to the canteen for lunch.

To our intense relief there are no activists from either union to be seen. The freshers hold their plates out joyfully for a serving of the insipid fish curry. For me, as a vegetarian, the meal is no different, but being able to have it without harassment elevates it to a feast.

We keep looking nervously at the door, expecting the Jeppo to come charging in, but nothing happens. The room gradually becomes noisier as we gain confidence and start talking freely.

Mithra limps over to our table. I haven't seen him since the day they made him kneel on the rocks. He still has a dressing across his right eyebrow and a wide smile on his face.

'Nalini, Sujatha, how are you keeping?'

'Never mind us,' Nali replies. 'How are you? Your knees must be badly cut.'

'Ahh, nothing that a bit of sticking plaster won't cure,' he says airily; the eyes behind the lenses seem to sparkle. 'And you Sujatha? Are you all right now?'

'Yes. Yes I'm all right,' I say quickly, wishing he would go away. If the Jeppo come back suddenly and catch him speaking with me again they'll really make him suffer.

'Your eyes are still a bit red,' he says easily. 'You should get some drops for them.'

'No. I'm all right,' I answer. 'Really.'

'Well don't let them frighten you,' he goes on quietly. 'There is a limit to what they can do … and you can take that.'

I look at him with some surprise. We had, all of us, been sorry for him, not only for his disability but seeing him as a perennial victim. The girls had wondered how long it would take them to break his spirit; make him give up and go home. And here he is, advising me about courage!

'That scoundrel Kumudu seems to have it in for you,' Nali says. 'Why does he go out of his way to torment you?'

'He was also at Royal,' Mithra answers quietly, 'two years ahead of me.'

'What? That rascal was a Royalist?'

'Mm.'

'I don't understand,' Nali goes on with a puzzled frown. 'Then why does he … '

'He was a grade five scholarship student transferred to Royal from some remote village school,' Mithra explains. 'I think he was one of those who were unable to cope with the … change.'

'What do you mean?'

'His classmates mocked him, you know, called him names like 'gamaya' and 'godaya', Mithra says. 'It never stopped … even in the senior years. He was never … accepted. I think Kumudu took it very hard.'

'So he wants his revenge on all Royalists?'

'I think he wants his revenge on the world.'

Mithra nods pleasantly and limps away; his whole body sways with each stride as he bends to support his wasted knee.

The raggers have been quiet for nearly two weeks. Occasionally a few of them would corner some of the freshers and give them a difficult time but these incidents only took place on a small scale. Nali has heard that many of the leaders, including that awful Kumudu, are still recovering from their injuries and have not returned to the campus. To my intense relief, I manage to escape the attentions of the remaining seniors.

A cancelled lecture gives us a free afternoon and Nali suggests that we go to Nugegoda to see the shops. I have been spending most of my free time in the hostel partly to stay out of trouble and partly because I did not mind, sometimes even enjoyed, being alone. I dither for a while but the temptation is too great. We avoid the main gate and sneak out through a small exit that leads to a lane on the northern boundary of the campus. We are soon on High Level Road waiting impatiently for a bus.

Nugegoda astonishes me. I have never seen anything like it.

It is teeming with people, all of them in a great hurry. It reminds me of a large ants' nest I had once seen in our garden where the ants scurried about from dawn till dusk carrying out a hundred tasks, all of them knowing exactly what needed to be done.

At Nugegoda, one can't stand still on the pavement for fear one would be carried away … or knocked down. Where do all these people live?

I have never seen so many shops, each one filled to the roof with an endless variety of wonderful things. Clothes especially, with plastic figures of tall women in the shop windows, all dressed like queens. Shoes, leather slippers and an entire shop of ladies' handbags; toys that would drive my little cousin Punchi delirious; even me! Then there are TVs with screens so huge they would cover one wall of our home, radios, iceboxes and so many other shiny things I couldn't name. Whatever do they wash in a washing machine?

The pavement stalls are also full of things to buy, more colourful than the shops and even cheaper. The men keep calling out that they have special bargains for us. Nali does not hesitate to pick things up and ask for prices, as if she is a serious customer. I worry that the men will get angry when we don't buy anything but they don't seem to mind at all. I pluck up courage to pick up some items, colourful sleeveless blouses and scandalously short skirts that come almost to my knees. I couldn't afford to buy anything but somehow, just looking at these exotic clothes is thrilling enough for the moment. Some day perhaps I will have enough money to buy what I want!

We come to a stall with piles and piles of brassières. I am anxious to take a closer look for they are in black, white and a lovely shade of beige, like the colour of pale skin. They are padded too and trimmed with lace; very, very different from the ones my aunt had stitched for me from plain cotton fabric.

Nali catches my eye and I know she too is yearning to have a closer look. To our dismay we find that the stallholder is a man, an unshaven ruffian who holds a selection of brassières in his hand and is waving them shamelessly under the noses of the women walking past.

He notices our interest from the other side of the stall and calls out loudly:

'Onäma size ekata thiyanawā. Pol gedi, grapefruit, dodan!'

We have all sizes. Coconuts, grapefruit or oranges!

I drop my eyes hurriedly, scandalized by the man's description but he calls out, raising his voice even more.

'Enna nangilā. Oi gollangey jamanarang walatath fit

eka thiyanawā.'

Come little sisters. We have a fit for your little mandarins as well!

I feel my cheeks burning as some bystanders join in the laughter. Nali grabs my hand and we run away, ducking and dodging through the throng.

Nali leads me to a snack bar. I want a bun and a cup of tea but she insists that I try a strange square pack of chocolate flavoured milk. It comes with a hollow tube that Nali says is a straw. I hesitate because it looks expensive but Nali settles the argument by paying the girl at the counter.

We sit on stools near the plate glass window and watch the people hurry by.

'That fellow is mistaken,' Nali says with a giggle. 'Yours are not little mandarins. More like oranges. Small, but still oranges.'

'Stop it, Nali,' I protest in embarrassment. 'How can you talk about things like that?'

'Why? What's wrong in talking? There's nothing to be shy about.'

'Nothing wrong but I feel … uncomfortable,' I say, looking down. 'So let's not, okay?'

'Oh, all right,' Nali responds with a laugh, 'but you really are a *gamey kella,* aren't you?'

Village girl.

'I suppose so,' I murmur softly. 'I can't help what I am.'

'I didn't mean it in a bad way, Suji,' Nali says hurriedly. 'I like you just as you are. Don't worry about it.'

The buses are packed with office workers, some of them hanging desperately to the edge of the footboard.

Traffic leaving the city seems permanently jammed and deafeningly loud. We have to wait a long time to board a bus bound for Maharagama. We are crushed between passengers carrying briefcases and shopping bags, all clinging to the backs of seats and the overhead railing, as the bus sways from side to side.

I feel suffocated. The physical proximity of so many unknown men and the overpowering smell of sweat combine to make me feel ill. I grit my teeth and hold on, strengthened by Nali's cheerful presence close by.

We get off at the Wijerama junction and walk furtively towards the campus. We creep down the narrow lane but are dismayed to find the small gate leading from it locked with a chain and a heavy padlock.

We have no choice but to sneak in through the main gate. We walk through briskly, keeping our heads down; I can hear the thud of my heartbeat.

We almost make it too, but at the last moment someone yells:

'Eyii. Umbalā freshers neyda? Kohedha giyey?'

Hey. Aren't you freshers? Where have you been?

We run.

We hear them close behind, three or four boys, shouting awful threats as they chase after us. Nali tries to run towards our hostel but I grab her arm and pull her towards the maze of buildings behind the Sociology Department. I run till my heart feels ready to burst and then, when we can go no further, we hide in a darkened corridor, ducking below the half wall that runs along it.

Once safely in hiding, we give way to a fit of giggles. It is the first time we have defied, and then outwitted, the raggers.

'I was going to run to the hostel,' Nali says when she

gets her breath back. 'But they would have found out who we were then, wouldn't they?'

'Mmm.'

'You are a odd one, aren't you?'

Nali is looking at me.

'Why on earth do you say that?' I ask, surprised at the question. 'What's wrong with me?'

'Nothing wrong, no,' Nali seems puzzled. 'You seem to … know what to do … '

'Come on,' I interrupt her hurriedly. 'Let's get to the hostel or we'll miss dinner.'

6

The Jeppo are back. We are leaving the lecture theatre on the first floor when we hear slogans being shouted near the main gate. From the safe vantage of an upstairs window we see the leaders of the SSU being escorted into the campus by a large crowd of supporters.

Kumudu, a part of his head shaved and covered with a dressing, is in the lead. The supporters are making a deafening racket, mostly denouncing the ISF. We watch as the procession goes towards the union office where a small stage has been erected. Kumudu and a few others mount the stage and address the crowd.

The rag starts again and, after the respite we had enjoyed, is even harder to bear. We are forced once again to wear our slippers on the wrong feet and carry files on our heads whenever we walk about. Mealtimes become a period of torture.

They select a number of freshers and begin training them for a musical program. By a rare stroke of luck, Nali and I are not picked for that.

*

The *Bōttuwa* group came in today.

Of those selected to enter Jaypura University each year, some students decline the offer and follow courses of study elsewhere. Those who are next in the various merit lists are then given a chance to fill these vacancies. They come to the campus some weeks later and are referred to as the *Bōttuwa* group, those who have arrived like 'boat-people'.

There are thirtytwo such newcomers and the Jeppo fall upon them like jackals. They might have become bored with us because, while the rag remains in force, there is a slackening of interest in harassing us. The new ones get a double dose of it and suffer greatly.

The blow falls about a week later.

Lunch is a quiet affair that day. For us! The seniors have herded the *Bōttuwas* to one corner of the canteen and are tormenting them mercilessly. A few seniors have their eyes on us but only to make sure we do not serve ourselves from the forbidden dishes.

Mithra limps towards me as I am leaving the room. I see him coming and sense that he is about to do something foolish.

Don't speak to me, you fool, they will murder you!

'Sujatha, there is a new boy here called Palitha. Says he is from a village called Medamulana,' Mithra says rapidly. 'He told them you were from his village, some problem about your parents. The Jeppo are saying you lied to them …'

There is a roar of anger behind us.

'Nondiya, umbata kathakaranna kivvey kaudha? Mey särey nang umba hama gahanawā.'

Who permitted you to speak, cripple? This time you will be skinned.

The other seniors come charging out, attracted by the commotion. Mithra is dragged away to the compound. The rest of us are herded together and forced to watch.

They have him roll his trousers to his knees, exposing his wasted left leg.

They begin to taunt him:

'Balāpalla ugey nondi kakula.'

Look at his crippled leg.

'Balu nättak wagey.'

It's like a dog's tail.

They force him to kneel on the gravel road. I can see that he's in great pain. I want to run forward and appeal to his tormentors, to beg them to leave the poor fellow alone. He had only been trying to help me.

But I know it is useless. They will never listen to me.

One of the leaders, an unshaven fellow with long hair calls out:

'Ugey baduwath ohoma ämbarilāda dhanney nähä.'

Don't know if his equipment is also twisted like that.

There is a roar of laughter from the seniors. I hear another fellow say:

'Ugey kalisama galawalā balamu.'

Let's take his trousers off and look.

They crowd round Mithra and pull him to his feet. Mithra fights back, struggling violently for a time, but they are too many. Two men twist his hands behind him, holding him as he writhes about; another starts to undo his belt.

Someone shouts above the din:

'Vee Cee enavā. Duwapalla.'

The VC is coming. Run.

The seniors release Mithra, who collapses on the ground. They melt away in small groups leaving us alone. I see the Vice Chancellor walk into the quadrangle with one of the Deans. They don't look at us but walk past, engrossed in conversation.

We run to Mithra and help him to his feet. He is panting and his face is dripping with perspiration. His belt is undone and he has trouble standing without help; he still manages a crooked grin.

'Lucky escape, wasn't it?' he gasps as some of the boys help him to limp away.

The dormitory is quiet at last with the lights off and the bed tied securely across the door. I have to think.

Mithra has paid a heavy price for warning me but what am I to do now? I can't remember any Palitha from Medamulana. Who is this fellow? How on earth could he remember me after seven years? What has he told them about me?

The Jeppo will want to know why I had lied. If I tell them that I had concealed the truth because it is painful, will they accept that?

Of course not! They'd want to know all the details. I must prepare a dull story to make them lose interest.

I wish I knew what that student has told them.

I don't sleep well.

I dream of Yasawathi again.

She isn't angry when I go to her house. Her face changes only when I tell her about my condition; that is when she turns into a devil. Her eyes turn to fire; her hair seems to rise up above her head as though caught in the wind. Her lips are drawn back and teeth, betel-red, are bared like those of a rabid dog.

She picks up a piece of firewood as she comes towards me. She is screaming so angrily that spittle sprays out of her mouth. She is saying the same words, over and over again!

'Vesa bälli. Vesa bälli. Ättha kiyapang!'

Prostitute bitch. Prostitute bitch. Tell the truth.

She beats me. She beats me without mercy, as if she wants to kill me, as if she is killing a snake. I stay on my knees, crying and screaming but she grasps my two hands in one of hers and lifts me up. She beats me till I am senseless, falling into a pool of my own blood.

She beats me still.

*

They summon me for an enquiry the next day.

Kumudu is seated on the stage with three others, two boys I know to be committee members and a girl they call Padma. Other seniors have arranged themselves in the students' seats in the empty lecture theatre.

I feel like a prisoner being brought to be judged and hanged.

Padma begins:

'Your name is Sujatha Mallika?'

'Yes.'

'You told us that you were from Angunuwewa. You said your father is a labourer and your mother is a housewife.'

'Yes.'

'Do you realize that telling lies to the leadership is a very serious offence and you can be punished severely for that?'

'Yes.'

'So why did you lie to us?'

'I did not lie. I am from Angunuwewa.'

'We have heard that you are from a village called Medamulana.'

'I was born there but I was taken to Angunuwewa when I was twelve years old,' I answer boldly. 'That is my home.'

'But the people you described – they are not your parents, are they?'

'No. My parents are dead.'

Careful. Be very careful now!

Padma whispers something to the others, listens for a moment and turns back.

'How did your father die?'

'He … committed suicide.'

'Why did he kill himself?'

'I don't know.'

'Was it because your mother ran away with another man?'

I feel as if someone has stabbed me in the chest.

Careful. Don't get angry. Don't break down.

'I don't know.'

'How could you not know? You were there, weren't you?'

'I was ill at the time, and very young. They didn't tell me anything.'

'But didn't she go away?'

'Yes,' I whisper. After all these years it is still as if my heart is torn apart. 'Yes, she went away.'

'Whom are you living with now?'

'My mother's sister and her family.'

'You told us you were an only child. Is that the truth?'

'No. I have a younger brother.'

'Where is he now?'

'Living with my father's sister at Medamulana.'

'What is her name?'

'Yasa …' I choke, unable to carry on.

Don't let them sense anything. Just don't.

'Yasawathi Manike.'

'Why didn't you tell us all of this when we asked you?'

'Because ... because it is very painful for me to discuss it.'

Padma confers with her colleagues for a few minutes. She then turns back to me.

'The leaders have decided to overlook your mistake in this instance. Take this as a warning for the future. You must have full confidence in the leadership and always tell the complete truth. Is that clear?

'Yes.'

'Yes what?' Padma's voice is dangerously quiet.

"Yes, Honourable Senior,' I reply humbly.

'You may go now.'

Yes, Honourable Senior! I am safe ... at least for the moment.

*

Kalinga is coming to the campus!

The Socialist Students Union (SSU) strenuously denies affiliation to any national political party. However everyone knows that they are part of the Students United Front (SUF) that, in turn, is a part of the Janapriya Samarjawadi Peramuna (JSP). Which is why Harith and his union call them Jeppo. We do too, only very quietly.

One fresher tells me that Kalinga is the leader of the SUF and controls powerful unions in all the universities. It is rumoured that Kalinga is already a member of the politburo of the JSP.

The SSU become so heavily involved in preparations to receive him that the intensity of the rag diminishes.

'I hope one of their big shots come every week,' Nali says cheerfully. 'Then they'll be too busy to harass us.'

'I wonder what he's like,' another girl says. 'Must be a bearded ruffian like that Kumudu!'

'I hear he's very powerful. He can close down any campus if he wants to,' a boy tells us knowingly. 'My brother at Kelaniya Campus has heard him speak. He was very impressed; says Kalinga will be a national leader one day.'

'What will he talk about?' Nali asks derisively. 'Bringing the revolution? All these fellows are extremists when they are students, then they get jobs and settle down to exploiting the poor; just like every one else.'

'My brother tells me Kalinga is different,' the boy, whose name is Sujith, replies. 'He really believes in him, my brother. He told me that you only need to listen to him once and you'll also be a follower. My brother is thinking of giving up studies and going in for politics full-time.'

'Is your brother mad?' Nali asks and then goes on recklessly. 'Tell him these fellows are tricksters. They will lead everyone to ruin. They don't care about the poor … they only want power. They …'

'Nalini, don't talk like that,' Sujith says urgently. 'It's very dangerous and anyway I hear that Kalinga really is different …'

'I don't believe it.'

'Don't believe me. Just listen to him when he comes, then you'll see.'

'We'll have no choice, I suppose,' Nali observes ruefully. 'They'll force us to listen to the fellow.'

*

He looks like any other student.

Kumudu and his committee members escort Kalinga towards the stage. An excited buzz rises from the gathering as the visitor mounts the steps and turns to face the crowd. He raises his hands to acknowledge the cheer that slowly swells to a roar of welcome. I look at him closely as he stands a few feet away from me.

A little older than the average student perhaps, above average height, slightly stooped and thin to the point of emaciation. His hair is parted neatly at the centre and falls down to his ears, giving him a studious appearance. He is simply dressed in dark trousers and a white shirt with long sleeves unbuttoned at the wrist. Leather sandals.

As freshers we are forced to the front of the audience, directly below the stage. The meeting has been arranged in the upper playground and a really large crowd has turned up to listen to the man. I see Mithra standing close by. He catches my eye and, ignoring my warning frown, pulls a sour face. I look away quickly, terrified that one of the seniors will notice.

Some of the others on stage address us briefly and then Kumudu rises to speak.

'Fellow students, we are very fortunate today for we have an opportunity to listen to one of the great leaders of our time. Today he is the convener of the Students United Front. I can confidently predict that he will soon be a leader at national level.

'I have worked closely with him for many years so I can sincerely tell you; this man can show us the way.

He has studied the injustices inflicted on our people. He knows the sufferings of our educated, unemployed youth. He knows why these sorrows never go away, why we must always be poor so that the corrupt may prosper. He has a plan. He has a solution.

'Listen to him; believe him; follow him. Together we can destroy this evil system of government that keeps us in eternal slavery.'

Kumudu stops and gathers himself.

'I ask all of you to welcome Kalinga Lokuge.'

The applause is long and loud. Kalinga stands grasping the microphone for some time, staring expressionlessly at the crowd. The clapping rises to a crescendo and then ceases abruptly when Kalinga raises his hand.

He allows the silence to stretch, making us quiver in anticipation. Even Nali gets carried away enough to squeeze my hand. When I think he is never going to speak, he does.

He has a slightly hoarse voice, as if there is something obstructing his throat. He speaks slowly, in clear colloquial Sinhala, emphasizing each word as his eyes move over us at the front of the crowd.

'The future of this country must belong to educated, rural youth. It must belong to you. You have been robbed of this birthright … and you don't even know it. In your innocence you believe that you will find a place in the sun if you work hard and graduate from university. That is an illusion.

'There are forty thousand unemployed graduates who have returned to their villages in shame and despair. Do you think they are less clever than you? Less qualified than you will be?'

Kalinga stops as if he is waiting for an answer from

us. Angry eyes drill holes in our heads.

'No, of course not! So why are there no jobs for them? ... The answer is that those with wealth and power, the corrupt people in the cities, want it that way. They want the jobs and the positions for their own kind. There is nothing left for people like you.

'Do you know how these city dwellers got their wealth and their power?'

Kalinga pauses again.

'I will tell you. When the British imperialists conquered our land, Sinhalese patriots were in rebellion. So the invader gave all the jobs to minorities. The minorities would do anything to keep the invader in power, for their jobs depended on it. Then there were Sinhalese traitors. They were rewarded with lands and positions. They were given licenses to make and sell arrack. Both groups prospered while Sinhalese patriots sank into poverty.

'If that was all, we could say that it happened in past times ... let us forget about it and get on with our lives. But that is not the whole story.'

Kalinga raises his head and with it, his voice.

'No. Bribes from the invader and rewards for treason gave these people position and wealth. Then they were able, not only to acquire more wealth, but also to educate their children in the best schools and to send them abroad for higher studies. So, generation after generation, these families moved to the cities and accumulated more and more wealth and political power. The rural patriots were left in misery, ignorance and degradation.

'They now tell us to compete on an equal footing with the privileged class. We are supposed to go to the city, dress in western style and above all speak English like Englishmen. Can you compete with those who have learned these things from infancy?

'More importantly, … *should you*?

'A few of you will be called for interviews, but that is only for show. When the interview is over they will laugh at you; call you the not-pot fellows. Did you know that?

'Once in a way they will allow one person to succeed. They will put that person on a platform and say: "See. You can become one of us if you learn our ways and are loyal to us. Then you can enjoy the fruits of wealth and power."

'That is only for show, like a lottery winner. For every winner there are thousands of losers.'

Kalinga pauses and lets his eyes wander over the faces in the crowd. He has our attention all right.

There is a deathly silence.

'Our leaders tell us that things are changing. They tell us to be patient. That soon we will be able to claim our rightful place in the sun.

'Do you know what they are planning? They want to teach English in rural schools. They will set up libraries with English books. They will teach our children to sing English songs and to perform the ballet. Then they will say: "Ahh, now you are like us. Come to the city, there are jobs for you."

'Do you believe it? Do you think people with wealth and power want to share it you? Rubbish! This is just another sham to keep us quiet for another generation. Even if they are sincere, you must ask yourself this. Why should we, Sinhalese people who are heirs to this land, have to learn western *thuppahi* ways to get a job?'

Another new word! Am I thuppahi then, because I can read English?

Kalinga bows his head over the microphone. He is holding the stand with both hands and his fingers are corded from the intensity of his grip. I feel the tension grow around me as we wait breathlessly for him to continue.

He raises his head and looks at us. I feel his eyes boring into me, as though he has a special message for me alone.

'The corrupt system will never allow real change. It is foolish for us to expect the elite in the cities to voluntarily give up their wealth and power. Why should they, when their prosperity depends on oppressing the poor?'

Kalinga raises his voice. It thunders at us through the speakers.

'No. We will NOT be fooled any longer. We will not wait any more. We will topple this oppressive system and take control of our destiny. We will cleanse the cities of their corruption. Banish, for all time, the evil western culture with its pornography, gambling, prostitution, with its alcohol and drugs.

'Only when we crush the cities, only when we right the historic injustices inflicted on us by the imperialists, will our people … that means you … gain their rightful place.'

Someone starts clapping. Soon the whole crowd takes it up and wave after wave of deafening applause shakes the air. Some of the boys are shouting and whistling. Even my sceptical Nali is clapping. Only Mithra, standing close by, holds his hands firmly gripped behind his back.

The idiot!

'It will not be easy. Don't ever think it will be. The city folk have wealth, they run the government and they control the police and the army. They will not give up everything just because we ask for justice. The oppressors will act with extreme violence to crush any threat to their position.

'So what force will rise up to challenge the system? The old left tried to get the workers in the cities to rise up. They failed because the workers were already corrupted. They had jobs that they wanted to protect. They yearned for the material things that Western culture dangled before them.

'What about the farmers? What about the people from your village, your parents? Do you think they will be able to unite to topple this system? … No, of course not. They have been oppressed for too long. They are sunk in apathy; they think poverty is their proper station.

'Who then can carry out this patriotic duty and save our motherland?'

Kalinga pauses again with his eyes closed. When he opens his eyes and starts speaking, his voice is a hoarse whisper. He points his finger at us dramatically.

'You!

'Only you can save the motherland from the clutches of this city filth. You are educated. You have the numbers and you are united on campuses and schools around the country. All you need is leadership and training.

'We will give you both. We have a vision. Trust us and be patient.'

Kalinga stops abruptly and stalks off the stage. Kumudu and the others rise quickly and follow him.

In a moment he is gone.

7

I get a full bucket of stinking canteen waste on my head … and I'm delighted.

The seniors have, over a period of days, used some discarded tar barrels to collect wastewater from the canteen. The food residues have fermented into a foul, oily mess with yellow froth covering the top.

It stinks.

We are told to line up, two abreast, and take our turn. I am next to a fellow named Previn from the Management Faculty. Nali is just behind me, poking me with her finger to hurry me on.

The senior stirs the barrel with a stick to make sure that my bucket has its proper share of muck from the bottom. I close my eyes and hold my breath. I feel the putrid mess dribble through my hair and then on to my face and body, and I don't care. My heart is singing.

They have done everything they could to break my spirit but I have stood up and taken it. This is the final torture and now the rag is over. Sujatha Mallika has survived.

Nothing will stop me now!

*

Nali has come with me to the bus stand in Pettah.

She knows that, despite my outward calm, I am nervous about the long journey home. We had left the campus after the final paper was handed in but it is dusk when we reach the bus terminus.

Nali is going to Galle and her journey will take about three hours. Her father is coming to the bus station to meet her and she will be safely home for a late dinner. It is different for me. I have to wait for one particular bus that leaves for Tissamaharama via Ratnapura, Balangoda and Wellawaya. My journey will take all night and I will only be able to reach Tanamalwila very early the following morning. From there it is just a few miles to my home.

We find that the next bus to Tissa is due to leave at 8.00 p.m. Although the bus has not come in as yet, passengers have already formed a queue.

I take a place at the end and turn to Nali:

'You'd better go or you'll be late,' I tell her. 'I'll be all right, really.'

'There's a bus to Galle every half hour,' she answers cheerfully. 'I'll just stay a while.'

'But your father is waiting. He'll worry …'

'Ahh, let him wait a bit. That's what fathers are for.'

Nali must have seen a change in my expression

'I'm sorry, nanga,' she says, puzzled by my reaction yet immediately contrite, 'I didn't mean to upset you.'

She sometimes calls me nanga, little sister, although we are nearly the same age.

'It's all right, Nali. I'm not upset at all.'

'Anyway I'll wait till you are on the bus. Otherwise someone might carry you away.'

'Don't be silly.'

I am glad she is staying and she knows it.

The queue builds up behind me and Nali chats with a middle-aged woman a few places further down the queue. After a few minutes Nali calls me over. The sturdily built woman is carrying a blue travelling bag in one hand. A little girl about twelve years of age stands nervously at her side holding on to the hem of her brown cotton sari.

Nali speaks to her.

'Aunty, my cousin Suji is going to Tanamalwila,' she starts with a bright smile. 'Since you are going to Tissa, can you look after her till she gets down?'

'What can happen in a bus?' The woman allows herself a small smile. 'All right! I can keep an eye on her.'

'Maybe she can sit with you?' I feel mildly embarrassed as Nali persists. 'She has never travelled by herself before.'

The woman seems distracted and nods without interest.

Nali turns to me.

'You look after yourself, nanga,' she says solemnly, 'and I'll see you in a month.'

My eyes are stinging when I hug her.

'You too,' is all I can mumble, 'you too.'

I become conscious, for the first time, of the sounds around me. A radio playing Sinhala music in a kiosk, a lottery seller using a battery powered megaphone, vendors calling out to pedestrians, grinding truck engines and jingling bicycle bells.

A bus pulls into the vacant space soon afterwards. A young fellow with a sheaf of folded currency notes wrapped around his middle finger stands near the door issuing tickets and the queue begins to move forward slowly. I count heads quickly and calculate that I will be able to secure a seat.

'Ammey. Ammey.'

Mother. Mother.

I hear someone call out behind me and turn to look.

A boy is trotting towards the woman; he must have run some distance for he is panting heavily.

'Ahh puthey. Mama bayeng hitiyey umbata wäradei kiyalā.'

Ahh son. I was worried you will get it wrong.

'Moratuweng āpu bus eka bada gāgena āwey. Kohomahari āwaney?'

The bus from Moratuwa was crawling along. I came somehow, didn't I?

He might be about eighteen, medium height but well built. He's in school-uniform white, with shirtsleeves rolled high to expose heavily muscled upper arms.

A good-looking face, and clearly aware of it!

The boy pushes himself into the queue ignoring pointed comments from others behind us. I buy my ticket and the family party follows me into the vehicle. I pick a window seat on the right hand side and am pleased when the woman sends the little girl to sit beside me. The woman takes the window seat on the other side and her son sits next to her by the aisle.

I notice that the boy is looking at me with frank interest and turn away quickly. The bus starts off soon afterwards and I look with amazement at the tall buildings of the Fort as the driver moves the bus into the stream of traffic leaving the city centre. The crowds on the pavements have thinned out just a little and hawkers are closing down their stalls for the night.

I look at the little girl seated quietly next to me. I see big eyes set in a small, pale face, stick-like arms emerging from the puffed sleeves of a pink dress.

'What is your name?'

The child looks down for a while and I think she isn't going to answer; then she looks up with a shy smile.

'Shanthi.'

'Is that your mother and brother?'

'Yes. My brother's name is Nishantha,' she says with pride in her voice. 'He is in the A Level class and will go to university next year.'

'And you? What class are you in?'

'Grade seven,' she says, more at ease now, 'I go to school in Tissa. My brother studies at a big school in Moratuwa.'

We chat easily for some time. The driver switches off the interior lights and conversations gradually die down as the passengers settle down to sleep. I turn my attention to the passing scene and find it too full of interest to ignore.

At first the towns are brightly lit and neon signs flash everywhere. The roads too are filled with hurrying pedestrians and flashing headlights. Soon the towns become smaller and less lively; then we are passing through open country with paddy fields and rubber trees seen dimly in the reflected headlights.

The driver pulls into the main depot in Avissawella; a few more passengers board the bus and move to the back. In ten minutes we are on the road again. I am too excited by the prospect of going home, and of seeing my cousins, to think of sleeping.

I wonder if they will like their presents. It had been a struggle to save the money but I had disciplined myself to manage with the Mahapola payment and save most of the five hundred rupees sent by Father Basil's friend.

Nali had come brassière shopping with me. We didn't have the courage to approach the ruffian at the pavement stall but went to a regular shop with a salesgirl serving at the counter. Two daring lace-edged bras for me, and one for my little cousin, Loku! She will be absolutely delighted, of that I'm sure, but I wonder what my aunt will have to say.

Ratnapura.

I had heard of the town and expected to see gem and jewellery shops lining the main street. Perhaps they do, but they are now dark and shuttered for the night. The driver stops at the main depôt and announces that there will be a break of thirty minutes for the passengers to have their dinner.

I follow Shanthi and her mother to a restaurant by the bus depôt but sit at a separate table. Most of the passengers order rice and curry but I, finding that excitement has dulled my appetite, ask for a bun and a banana.

I want to save money anyway.

I chat with Shanthi for a while when we start off again but she seems tired and falls asleep soon afterwards. The sound of the engine changes to a deeper note as the bus begins to climb. I remember from my first journey to Colombo that the road runs along the southern edge of the hill country, through Balangoda and Beragala, before it turns down to the plains again.

The towns are deserted now, the houses closed and dark. I feel like a visitor from another world, looking at the earth people as they sleep. I want to call out that Sujatha Mallika is passing by.

We had enjoyed the two weeks of semester remaining after the rag was over. Nali had been free with her comments about the rag and the seniors who had been responsible. She had earned some angry looks but no real retaliation. I knew she was asking for trouble and finally persuaded her to keep quiet.

Mithra often joined us in the canteen. Everyone still called him 'Nondiya' but he didn't seem to mind. He had been singled out for special punishment during the rag; the seniors had gone out of their way to torture him. He had endured it all with a reserve of strength, never letting them crush him. He is just the same after the rag is over, calm and slightly amused about everything.

Mithra would make fun of me, calling me his *'rathu sahodariya,'* red sister, because I had been so taken with Kalinga's speech and socialist ideas. But he did it so gently that I was never upset.

Harith Jayakody joined us sometimes. He had an air of confidence about him that I found disquieting. I was unhappy at first when Nali encouraged him to sit with us but he turned out to be all right. He is one of the leaders of the independent union, and a senior, so I suppose it is 'one up' to have him sit with us.

The bus is dark now and most of the passengers, including little Shanthi next to me, seem to be asleep. I make sure the knapsack is under my seat and wedge the cloth sling bag, with my money and personal things, safely between my body and the side of the bus. I rest my head on my arm and close my eyes. I must have fallen asleep almost immediately.

I dream that he has caught me again.

How can that be? He is dead. I saw his corpse and had been so relieved. How can he come back to torment me?

I wake up trembling and find it isn't a dream at all. Someone's hand is on my breast. I am too terrified to move, my mind frozen with shock and revulsion. I realize that the little girl is no longer in the seat next to me. A man in white trousers sits there with his arms folded across his chest. Under the cover of his right arm, his left hand is reaching for me.

Nishantha, the big brother!

I find my fear ebbing away, to be replaced by an anger that almost chokes me.

I am no longer twelve years old, you miserable animal.

I make a slight movement, as though I am waking up, and the hand is pulled away instantly. I slowly insert my right hand into my sling bag and feel around, regretting now that I carry so much rubbish in it.

Where is it when I need it so urgently?

My fingers finally make contact. The tiny pair of nail scissors has a wickedly pointed tip! I wrap my fingers round it and draw it out. I sit still and pretend to sleep. After awhile the hand emerges like a rat from a burrow and reaches for me.

As I feel his hand touch my breast I stab at it with my right hand, driving the point towards my chest. I am so angry I want to pierce the back of his hand, to inflict the maximum damage. The point hits something hard, his wrist perhaps, and glances off. It must have hurt him just the same because the hand vanishes in an instant and I hear a sharp intake of breath, a stifled scream.

'Ahhhhh.'

I have no tears for him, only a warm sense of satisfaction.

'Para bälli.'

Filthy bitch.

You'll always say that, won't you, when a woman refuses to lie down for you?

I turn away from him and pretend to sleep again. I

keep the scissors firm and ready in my hand. I hear him muttering threats, awful things he will do to me if he catches me alone.

He gets tired of it after a few minutes and wakes his sister. Little Shanthi stumbles across the aisle and collapses sleepily into the seat beside me. Nishantha, the great seducer of women, returns to the seat by his mother.

To my intense surprise I find that the whole incident has, for some reason, cheered me up. I fall into a dreamless sleep soon afterwards.

*

I am already awake when the conductor calls out that Tanamalwila is just ahead. The sun is still below the trees on my left but the forest is coming alive in preparation for a new day. As I am, now that I have returned to the environment that I know and love!

Tanamalwila had been, for me as a schoolgirl, a town of some importance. Having seen the city, I realize now that it is no more than a junction with a collection of small shops, a school and a post office. I love it just the same.

The woman and the little girl are still asleep when I pick up my knapsack and step into the aisle. Nishantha is awake and his eyes, when he looks at me, are filled with venom. I hope I never run into him again.

I step off the bus and stand by the roadside, watching the heavy vehicle till it turns a corner and disappears. The shops are still closed but there are people moving about, men scratching and spitting, women carrying pots of water and sweeping gardens. I have to travel about two miles along the road to Bodagama and then a mile along a gravel track to get to my village. I am too excited to wait for a bus so I decide to walk.

The houses dwindle away and soon the road runs through scrub jungle. The birds are especially noisy today, as though to welcome me home. I try to take note of some of them for I know that Father Basil will test me.

I have become quite good at identifying birds, good enough to please Father Basil anyway. I can name, with one quick glance, most common birds as they fly across the road. I can also recognize many of their calls and so picture them even when they are hidden in the trees.

I had missed this so much while I was away.

A section of the road is covered with elephant dung, moist and steaming in the morning sunlight. A small herd has crossed the road not long ago, the torn branches and strips of bark showing that they have been feeding as they moved. They must have been at the wäwa, my village tank, during the night and left at dawn to seek shelter in the deep forest.

I come to the track that leads to my home. There had been a name board once but an elephant had knocked the post down and no one had bothered to replace it. There was no point to it. We know where our homes are … and who is the outsider who will want to visit?

I have only walked a short distance when I hear a familiar sound behind me. There are no buses along this track so the villagers depend on two-wheel tractors for transport; and bicycles, of course. A few of the farmers use tractors to take their produce to town and they take villagers along as well, when there is room in the little trailers.

I am pleased to find that the driver is Lahiru Aiya from my village. He pulls up immediately.

'Mey apey Sujatha kella neydhai? Adhaidha äwey?'

Isn't this our Sujatha girl? Did you come today?

'Ow aiya. Towmey indan ävidinna hithunā.'

Yes brother. I felt like walking from the town.

'Naginna. Naginna. Mama geniyannan.'

Climb in. Climb in. I will take you.

Lahiru Aiya wants to know all about Colombo and I want news of the village. Long before the questions are answered to our satisfaction we are at the bund and then the village comes into view.

My mouth goes dry.

There had been eighty-four families when I left, eighty-five if you count 'Holmang Martin' who lives alone in a tiny hut at the far end of the village. Most of the houses are like my aunt's, built by plastering a framework of twigs with clay from the wäwa. The floor is lined with a mixture of clay and cow dung. Layers of woven coconut fronds carefully arranged over a lattice of jungle sticks give the houses a snug, waterproof cover.

People of the city call our homes wattle and daub huts; hovels unfit for decent people to live in. But it is all that poor people can afford. There is plenty of clay in the wäwa, the jungle yields a limitless supply of sticks and the coconut fronds come from our own trees. The house, and the surrounding yard, are swept daily and kept scrupulously clean. The interior is wonderfully cool in the heat of the day, snug and warm at night.

What do I care what foolish city folk say? This is my home and I wouldn't exchange it for a palace.

Sarpin Māma is seated on a bench grating an areca nut. He looks up and allows himself a rare half-smile.

'Duwa! Dändhai äwey?'

Daughter! Did you come just now?

I am surprised and touched; he has never called me daughter before. Not once.

'Ow māmey. Punchi-amma ko?'

Punchi-amma means small mother. Seela is my mother's younger sister.

'Kussiyey äthi.'

In the kitchen.

He returns to his task as if regretting the smile. He is a lean man with arms wiry from years of hard manual labour. I look down fondly at his lined face as if seeing it for the first time.

He hardly ever speaks if a grunt or a single word will do. He works hard from dawn till dusk every day in our own garden and as a labourer in one of the adjoining villages. They had so little for themselves and yet my aunt had taken me, the unwanted orphan, into her home without hesitation. And the silent Sarpin Māma has provided for us year after year with his daily toil; the family has never, that I could recall, gone without a meal.

But once in a way he has a need to get drunk!

When he fails to come home at dusk we all know he is at it again. He would buy a bottle of *kasippu,* a potent local brew produced in the next village, and make his way to a lonely spot by the wäwa. My uncle, who never utters an unnecessary word at home, would drink the fiery liquid straight from the bottle and sing at the top of his voice.

Päl kavi.

After the monsoon, chena cultivators clear areas of jungle and plant crops. They build little watch huts high in a tree and sit through the night to guard their crops against wild animals. They make up songs to keep themselves awake and the animals at a distance, lamentations of loneliness, of poverty and hardship.

The villagers tell my aunt that these are the sad songs Sarpin sings to the wäwa.

My aunt Seela is cleaning a jak fruit, sitting on a little stool. She drops the knife on the floor and stands up, a happy smile spreading across her face.

'Duwa.'

Daughter.

First the uncle, now the aunt!

I drop my bags and kneel on the floor before her. I join my hands together and, bending over, touch her feet with my forehead. She grasps me by the shoulders and helps me to my feet. She cups my face in her hands so I feel the callouses on her fingers against my cheeks. She speaks softly.

'We missed you so much.'

I start crying then, a salty stream of tears pour down my face as though to drain all the fluid from my body.

8

I wait in the garden for my little cousins to come back from school. I see them coming, tiny figures in the distance in once-white uniforms, and hide behind the tamarind tree.

They trudge wearily to the gap in the fence and turn into the garden. Punchi has a stick in her hand and is swinging it at the weeds on the side of the path. I make my voice as deep as I can and growl:

'Whose children are these? I've come to take them away.'

They stand still with just their eyes scanning the garden, like deer alarmed by a snapping twig. Loku takes a few steps towards the tree, her sister following cautiously.

They scream when they see me, shrill excited shrieks that cut through the quiet of the afternoon and hurt my ears. They fling themselves into my arms so clumsily that I lose my balance and fall to the ground, my cries adding to the din. Seela comes running out of the house thinking someone has got hurt but stops when she sees us.

Both girls are jabbering at the same time as we scramble to our feet. I call out to Seela.

'Punchi ammey, wäweta yamudha nānna? Mung denna kalaväddo wagey gandai.'

Auntie, shall we go to the wäwa to bathe? These two stink like polecats.

There are howls of protest but then the girls run inside to put their school bags away and get ready.

The gravel road through the village leads to the wäwa. The wäwa is overgrown with lotus and silted in many places, getting worse every year. It is no longer used for cultivation. The water has receded with the drought but, near the old bund, there are places with waist-deep water in which the villagers bathe.

I walk ahead with the two girls hanging on to me on either side. Loku is fifteen now and pretty. Punchi is only eleven. A noisy, skinny, joyful eleven!

Near the bund we meet three boys walking the other way. I recognize Ranjit who had been in my school, but he doesn't look at me. Instead he speaks to the others just loud enough to be overheard.

'Her head is swollen, now she lives in Colombo,' he sneers. 'She thinks she is too good for people like us.'

I should be angry at the injustice of it but, for some reason, I'm not. Instead of anger I feel a great sadness. Ranjit had been a keen student but his results had not been good enough for selection to university. He is stuck in the village and faces a future without hope.

There is another reason for his anger.

Ranjit had believed he was in love with me. He would loiter about after school hoping to find some time alone with me; he even sent me a letter declaring his devotion. He had been confused, and later infuriated, by the lack of response on my part.

How was I to tell him that his interest petrified me? How could I tell him my silence was due to no fault of his?

I walk a few more steps but then my feet stop of their own accord. I turn and call out boldly:

'Ranjit.'

He stops and turns. I raise my hand and beckon

to him, a gesture I would not have dared to make a few months earlier; life on campus has given me new confidence. Ranjit stands undecided for a moment and then walks slowly towards me.

He stops a few feet away and looks at me sullenly. What can I tell him that will help in any way?

'I haven't changed, Ranjit,' I say gently. 'I am still your friend.'

'You were never my friend,' he answers harshly. 'That priest put ideas into your head … and turned you against me.'

He stares at me angrily for a moment, then spits and turns away.

The most wonderful moment is that first plunge into the wäwa. The water is sun-warm at the surface and mud-chilled below. No stink of pipe-borne chlorine. While Seela washes the school uniforms by pounding them on a rock, the girls and I wade into the water.

Punchi prances around in a pair of knickers. Loku, conscious now of her status as a 'big' girl, has a 'diya reddha', a length of thin material, wrapped modestly round her body. As I have! We wade further and the material billows like a sail, making us shriek with laughter as we try to cover ourselves. Fortunately men folk are not encouraged to linger at our bathing place.

We bathe by getting on our knees and bending over so that our heads sink below the surface, striking the water violently with our hands at the same time. I have never understood why village folk slap the water in that particular way; perhaps it is to frighten crocodiles.

I sit on a rock wiping my hair. Two other family groups have joined us and one of the women speaks briefly to me. My aunt has gone in the water to bathe and the little ones are still splashing each other in the shallows.

I let my eyes wander over the wäwa.

The life of the village revolves around it, but anyone can see that the wäwa is dying. Year after year the monsoon rains have washed silt into it; a man can now wade across most parts of the wäwa. Lotus plants and reeds have so choked the surface that fishermen can no longer cast their nets. Deep gullies are eroding the bund but no repairs have been carried out in many years.

Why should the government in Colombo care about what happens to an obscure village tank?

But it is still a wonderful haven for birds. In a few moments I have spotted jacanas and swamphens skulking about on the lily pads. Further away, some painted stork have immersed their half open beaks in the water. Keeping their heads very still, they are stirring the mud with one foot, hoping some unwary prey will slither straight into the open beak-trap. A fish-eagle is circling the water on motionless wings.

*

We eat, squatting on our heels as we always do, from a tin plate balanced on one hand. My aunt has prepared country rice with 'polos' curry and a 'mallung' of leaves from our garden. As a special treat she gives me a long green chilli.

I had longed for this meal for many long months.

When we have washed our plates and put them away I take out my gifts. Punchi is delighted with the brightly coloured hair clips and bangles I have brought for her;

Aunt Seela beams with pleasure when she sees the folding umbrella. Loku is trying hard to hide her impatience as I keep her waiting till the end.

She opens the little plastic bag, looks inside and blushes in confusion. She squeezes the bag shut and turns to rush away. Her mother says:

'What is it, babā? Let me see.'

Loku gives her the bag reluctantly. She watches Seela with wide eyes, biting her lip in anxiety. Seela opens the bag, peers inside and then touches the brassière with her finger. She has a frown in her eyes as she looks at me.

I use an easy smile to hide my own uncertainty.

'Kamak nähä, punchi ammey. Adha kawuruth ova andinawā.'

It's all right, aunty. Everyone wears these today.

Seela is not convinced. She hesitates for a minute and my heart sinks, but she surprises me by nodding.

'All right,' she says, looking hard at the trembling Loku. 'But you must always tell me before you wear that … thing.'

'Yes, amma,' Loku says obediently. I can see she is bursting with excitement. She runs into the house.

9

The board with the words 'SAMAGI SEVA SEVANA' is new. A group of small boys have been playing cricket in the compound; one little fellow is now threatening the umpire with his 'pol pittha' bat.

A small house with a tiled roof and lime washed walls stands at the back of the compound. Partially covering it in the foreground stands the community centre.

I look at the old building fondly. A half-wall separates the open veranda from the garden and the grey-brown thatch slopes down to almost head height at the entrance.

Father Basil lives in the little house but he spends most of his time at the community centre. The nursery school is at the back of the building. After my A Levels, Father Basil had persuaded me to assist the regular teacher. There had been twelve little ones when I left and I wonder how many there are now. I can hear them chattering away at the back.

I walk into the veranda. I have forgotten how cool the interior is; the shade envelops me as I try to adjust my eyes to the gloom. The reading room is on the left, the long table and wooden benches exactly as they had been when I left. I have spent countless hours here, preparing for the A Levels, for it was the only place in the village with an electric light, thanks to the solar panel Father has fitted.

The office is on the other side. I hear a cough; he is there.

He has been reading and it is the untidy grey-black mass of hair that I see first. He looks over the rim of his spectacles as I stand at the door and a slow smile spreads across his face. He smiles a lot, especially when I'm around.

It warms me.

'Sujatha, my child, I was expecting you,' he says, marking a place in his book and putting it down. 'You look … well. Sit down. Sit down and tell me about your first semester.'

'I survived, Father, just as you said I would.'

'Yes, I knew you would, but I'm proud of you just the same. Tell me about it. Was it very … hard?'

'Yes, Father,' I answer slowly, the ups and downs of the last four months tumbling through my mind. 'Yes, it was very hard at times but it was worse for some others.'

He is so easy to talk to. He just sits there tugging at his beard and nodding his head to show his interest. I tell him about the rag, about the seniors who conducted it and about my friends Nalini and Mithra. I see his brow knit in a frown when I tell him about the cruel treatment to which the crippled Mithra had been subjected.

'What about your … background,' he inquires softly. 'Did they give you any trouble about that?'

'Not at first. They accepted my story. Then a boy named Palitha came with the late entrants. He is from Medamulana. He told the seniors that I came from the same village.'

'And?'

'They held an enquiry; asked me why I had tried to mislead them. I told them that I had not lied. I had not told the whole truth because it was very painful for me.'

'Did you tell them the … whole truth then?"

'No,' I reply with a strained smile, 'only a little bit but

.... just enough so they would believe me.'

Fr. Basil regards me gravely for a minute, than asks very gently.

'The other thing! Did it cause any more trouble for you?'

'Yes,' I answer, feeling a bitter taste at the back of my throat. 'Yes, it did. Many times. I ...'

'Yes?'

'But I'm learning to cope with it, Father.'

He is not convinced but lets it go.

'Good. I'm glad to hear that,' he says as he walks round the desk. 'Come along then, I have something to show you.'

He is proud of his new medicine room.

A small storeroom has been cleaned out and some crude racks fitted to the wall. The shelves are well stocked with bottles of common medical products. Cotton wool, bandages, rolls of sticking plaster and a large bottle of surgical spirits lie on the counter near the door.

A club in Colombo has donated the medicines and Father Basil has arranged for a doctor from Wellawaya to come to the village once a month for a medical clinic.

The children in the nursery stop their lesson and run to meet me. They surround me, clinging to my dress, tugging to attract my attention. Their yells of 'Suji akka, Suji akka,' drown the teacher's attempts to restore order.

I find, to my surprise, that I remember their names. Champa and Sunil. Kumari, Rehka and Manel. I sit on the floor to chat with them. The teacher gives up and goes to talk with Father.

No one knew why Father Basil had selected our

village. He was already established here when, after my trouble, Seela brought me to her home. There was no community centre then and Father Basil worked in his home at the back of the compound.

My aunt told me there had been no Christians in the village when he first came; and I know there are no Christians in the village today. If he had come seeking converts to his faith, he has been a complete failure.

But he has helped almost every family in the village at one time or another. I know how he helped me regain my sanity.

He has, he told me, very little money of his own. What he did have was an endless array of friends in far off places, friends who would do his bidding without asking questions.

There is Miss Decima, a lady I have never seen, who sends me five hundred rupees every month because Father Basil has asked her to. He writes letters asking for medicines, for clothes and dry rations during periods of drought, for a tricycle for Lalith who lost his legs in a motor accident. Letters seeking funds to build the community centre.

No one, it seems, says 'NO' to Father Basil!

As I say goodbye and turn to go he calls me back.

'Wait,' he says, and his eyes behind the glasses are amused although his face seems stern. 'I have a task for you.'

'Yes, Father?'

'I have arranged for a group of older children to come here in the evenings. I want you to teach them English.'

'But Father,' I protest. 'I don't know how to teach....'

'You remember how I taught you? Same thing.'

'But I am on vacation ...'

'They need your help, duwa,' he reminds me gently. 'You will enjoy it.'

What could I say?

'Yes, Father.'

No one says 'NO' to Father Basil.

*

I slip easily into the routine of life at home. Saturday mornings are for gathering firewood from the forest. Normally Aunt Seela would go, taking the girls along to help. Now that I am home she passes the responsibility to me.

I love the job.

We wind lengths of coir rope round our waists and find rags to wrap our hands with when handling thorny scrub. I pick up the kathi from behind the front door and run my finger along the concave edge.

Razor-like.

'Wäwa ainey dhara ahulapalla, ähunadha?' Seela calls out worriedly as we walk away. *'Käleyta ringanna epā.'*

Pick firewood along the shores of the wäwa, do you hear? Don't creep into the forest.

We say yes, knowing very well that the whole village depends on the forest for firewood and all the dead wood in the open has already been collected and used. We will have to go deep into the forest to find enough to last the week.

Green wood is of no use to us. We have to look for trees blown over by storms or killed by lightning. If a herd of elephants have passed by, then there will be plenty of branches torn down and stripped of leaves. But we have to reach the deep forest for that.

We walk to the end of the village and then along

a footpath that runs by the edge of the wäwa. The sun has not had time yet to suck up the dew from the grass on either side; drops of moisture hanging on the blades scatter sunbeams into minute rainbows. Punchi, having by far the most energy, skips as she leads the way.

She is singing under her breath.

The water birds are feeding busily along the shore. Pansil-white egrets, openbills and spoonbills are patrolling the shallows. A purple heron stands as still as a statue with its beak poised to strike. Sandpipers, plovers and unrecognisable brown bird-creatures skitter about the foreshore. We disturb some lapwings that dive at us with cries of alarm.

Did-he-do-it. Did-he-do-it.

Punchi wants to stop and look for chicks but a sharp prod from Loku gets her moving again. The footpath disappears after a while and we have to pick our way carefully through the knee-high grass. I see some buffalo shapes at the water's edge further along the shore and decide not to get too close.

We turn into the forest.

It is easy to get lost in a forest, even for those of us who know it well. Without consciously thinking about it, I note that the sun is behind my left shoulder as we step into the scrub jungle. On our return, provided it is before noon, all I have to do is keep the sun before my right shoulder to find the wäwa. By itself that isn't enough for, if there is a sudden storm, the sun will disappear and we will be lost.

As we thread our way deeper into the forest, making detours to avoid patches of dense thorn bush, I snap protruding twigs, allowing the bent end to hang down conspicuously. I am pleased to see the little ones doing the same thing as they walk along. We will have clear markers to follow on our way back, just in case we need it.

We collect twigs and dry branches as we go along. Sometimes I have to use the kathi to cut a dead branch off a tree and into manageable lengths. We hide the small bundles under bushes to collect on our way back.

Punchi spots a palu tree in fruit.

The noise of feeding hornbills attracts her attention and she points it out to us. It stands tall and unmistakable above the surrounding scrub. If the hornbills are quarrelling, the fruit is ripe.

The flesh of the little fruit is surprisingly sweet and Punchi would have rushed forward if I hadn't restrained her. The feast attracts not only birds but also forest animals, especially deer and pig that feed on the fallen fruit.

And bears.

There is no wild animal we fear more than bear. Buffalo can be spotted at a distance and carefully avoided. Herd elephants are rarely aggressive and can be seen, and avoided, if one is alert. Even lone male elephants have wonderfully acute hearing and move away when they sense our clumsy approach.

Not bears.

Bears are fools. Greedy, dangerous fools. When they are feeding on termites they are so happy that they never hear a villager approach till he is very near; then the bear gets very angry and attacks. After surprising a bear, a man called Jemma in the next village has only a red-brown scar where his eye and nose had been.

Next to termites, bears love palu fruit!

I make a cautious approach, warning the girls to be

quiet and keeping them close behind me. The animals hear us just the same and we are able to see spotted deer and a small herd of pig crash away through the scrub.

The rough-barked palu tree stands tall in the centre of the clearing. Fallen palu fruit cover the forest floor immediately under the tree. Deer and pig had been feasting on it when we disturbed them.

No bears.

Small as she is, Punchi can climb like a monkey. She places one foot on Loku's shoulder and the other on mine as we squat facing the tree, then balances her weight against the massive trunk as we stand up. At full stretch Punchi is able to grasp the lowest branch and pull herself up. The small round leaves of the tree form a dense canopy and every stem is festooned with tiny yellow ovals. Punchi pulls off her T-shirt as she sits on a horizontal branch and uses it to collect the fruit.

Loku and I are looking up at Punchi when something moves at the edge of my vision. A branch near the crown of the tree sways from side to side … but there is no wind. I grasp Loku by the shoulder to keep her quiet as I strain my eyes to make out what it is. I haven't heard monkeys calling and anyway they feed in troupes. I see it then, a shaggy black shape grasping the trunk.

A bear has been feeding in the tree and is now climbing down. The animal is not aware of us as otherwise it would have made a sign. But it will find out very soon.

I try to control my panic-stricken mind.

Think!

If Loku and I remain where we are the animal will see us as soon as it reaches the ground. In its surprise, it will almost certainly attack us. If we run away and hide, the bear might not see Punchi; then it will be all right. But what if the bear spots little Punchi in the tree? I can't even think about what might happen.

From the way we are standing Punchi must have realized that something is wrong. She opens her mouth to speak but stops when I put a finger to my lips. I move under her and spread my hands, gesturing urgently with one of them.

Jump. Please baby, don't ask questions, don't hesitate. Just jump. Hurry!

Punchi hesitates, looking at me uncertainly.

A quick glace shows me that the bear is more than halfway down, nearly at the fork of the branch Punchi is perched on. The animal is facing the other way and hasn't seen us.

Yet.

Punchi must have heard something because she turns her head and is confronted with the shaggy black back of the creature behind her. She let out a little squeak of alarm and throws herself off the tree. Her tumbling fall catches me by surprise. A knobbly knee strikes a painful blow on my shoulder as both Loku and I crash to the ground under her weight. Palu fruit rains down from her open T-shirt.

'WROOFF.'

Surprise and alarm are evident in the coughing roar.

And anger!

We scramble to our feet, clawing at the rough grass for support. The bear coughs again, a furious grunt that's louder and even more threatening.

We hold hands to support each other and run. We run till our lungs are bursting but we don't stop. We run till Loku trips on an exposed root and goes sprawling, bringing us down as well.

I can't look back, waiting in terror for the bear's claws to savage us.

The seconds tick by and nothing happens. I stand up shakily and help the girls to their feet. Loku flops down again with a low moan to massage her bruised foot. The forest around us is quiet except for the cicadas.

No bear.

We hug each other spontaneously and the laughter starts then, hysterical with relief. Our clothes are covered with green-brown stains and, looking down at her, I am able to remove bits of grass from Loku's hair. Punchi has painful scratches on her bare belly and knees. But we are alive and that is enough … almost.

I remember that we have lost Punchi's T-shirt and the kathi. Seela will never forgive that. We have to go back.

I do, anyway.

The girls insist on coming with me because they are afraid of being left alone and also because, Punchi says, they didn't want the task of telling their mother that a bear has eaten me.

We would not have been able to find the palu tree easily if not for the hornbills. They have returned to feed and their squabbling and honking can be heard at a distance. When I think we are close enough, I make the two girls climb another tree and approach the clearing with great care.

I hear a grunt and feel a shaft of fear pass through me. I had been brave enough when the girls were with me but now I feel alone and powerless.

Oh please, let it not be the bear.

I force myself to go forward and peer into the clearing. The palu tree now stands still and quiet in the centre; the hornbills have flown away once again.

No sign of a bear.

I pick up a stone and, taking aim at the tree, fling it into the clearing. It hits a branch and crashes to the ground. From behind a tussock of tall grass that has concealed it completely, a huge boar emerges with a loud snort of alarm. It races away and disappears into the forest.

A space of a heartbeat is enough for me to dash in and collect the kathi and Punchi's T-shirt.

We return to the edge of the wäwa with relief. I am glad we don't have to go to the forest again till next Saturday.

*

For the first time in many weeks I dream of them again.

I'm lost in the forest and it is night. The moon is full and bright in the sky but under the trees it is as black as death, black as the shadow of evil.

I hear the angry 'WROOF' of a bear close behind me and start to run. I hear the grunts and snarls getting closer and know it will catch me. I reach an open glade and, as I emerge into the moonlight, I risk a hurried and fearful glance over my shoulder.

The bear is close behind me. Its body is monstrous and bear-like but it does not have a bear's head. The features are human with mad, staring eyes and bared teeth.

Drooling.

From the grey hair floating behind the head I know it is Yasawathi.

When I turn to run, terrified beyond thought, I see her at the far end of the clearing.

She is so beautiful, my mother.

She has spread her arms to receive me and I know that, if I can reach her, she will keep me safe. She will never allow Yasawathi to destroy me.

But as I run towards her, reaching out in desperation, she moves away, just out of reach.

Are you going to abandon me again? Isn't once enough?

There is a look of unbearable sorrow in her face, as though she wants to help me but cannot. Her figure fades away and I am alone with the bear. I run and run till I trip over a stone and go sprawling on the ground. I roll over in terror and find the Yasawathi-animal towering over me.

I know what you mean to do. I know you will rip out my belly and eat it.

I see the awful claws spread out as the forefoot is lifted to strike at my body. I hear my own despairing cry.

Seela has lifted my head and holds it to her breast.

'Andanna epā, duwa. Baya wenna deyak nähä.'

Don't cry daughter. There is nothing to be afraid of.

I feel my body trembling violently; I cannot shake off the terror that floods my mind. Seela strokes my head. I also see that the two little ones have crawled to my mat, hugging me in turn.

Punchi says:

'Baya wenna epā, akki. Mama innawā.'

Don't be afraid, big sister. I am here.

My fear drains away as I realise that I have a family now and I am safe with them around me.

10

I tell Father Basil about Kalinga.

'There is a lot of truth in his words, Father,' I say. 'People with wealth control the government and the system. They want to suppress the lower classes; they want to keep us poor forever.'

'What have they been teaching you, child?' Father Basil's eyes are twinkling. They always do when I start an argument with him. 'You are not from a lower class. You might be, of course … but only if you think you are.'

'No Father,' I answer quietly, 'only you treat me as if I am a princess. Every one else knows the truth. I am not ashamed of that.'

'I don't treat you at all like a princess,' he replies sternly. 'I treat you like a wonderful young lady with a bright future. Others will see that too, if you will give them a chance.'

'Let's not talk about me then,' I say in some confusion. 'What about the thousands of poor rural students who come into the university? What are their chances of getting jobs when they finish their degrees? Do you think they will be given a fair chance to compete with urban folk from the upper class?'

'You have learned the skills needed to compete. They can also learn, if they want to.'

'They don't have someone like you to teach them,' I point out. 'They make so many sacrifices to come to university. They have so many hopes and dreams. When they can't find jobs they are so ashamed that they can't even go back to their villages. So many students kill themselves in despair.'

'Being poor is only a handicap, duwa. It is like a race, with the poor starting further behind. But they can win, if they run fast enough.'

'For just one or two, that may be so,' I answer, 'but for the vast majority, there is no chance. You know very well, Father, that the urban rich keep the jobs and positions for their own kind.'

'You must accept the world as it is, duwa. If you work hard, I know you can overcome all these obstacles and become successful.'

'Yes, Father. Thanks to you, I know I can do that,' I feel as if I am speaking to myself as well, 'but what about them? What about those thousands of young people who are doomed? Don't I need to care about what happens to them?'

Father Basil looks at me seriously for a moment. He nods and says.

'You are right, of course. You must be concerned about the others, not just about yourself. You must do what you can to help the less fortunate. But it is only when you have won yourself a place in society through your intelligence and hard work that you will have the power to help others. Then you will be able to work actively, to help the less fortunate ...'

'Gradual change might take decades. That won't help those who are suffering today.'

'There is no other way,' he says again. 'You must accept the reality of this world.'

'There is a way, Father. Kalinga has a plan to overturn the whole corrupt system. Then the poor will take their rightful place.'

'What you are talking about is revolution,' Father Basil reminds me gently. 'You cannot achieve justice by way of injustice. That is immoral.'

'What is the morality of keeping people in poverty, generation after generation? When we see the suffering around us, don't we have a moral duty to put things right? Where is the injustice in that?'

'The end does NOT justify the means,' he answers quietly. 'I have explained that to you many times. Revolutions cause immense suffering to innocent people. Victory is achieved only by the letting of much blood. The good you seek does not justify the means your friend Kalinga might want to use.'

'Father, I think ... I really think that, if there are serious reasons to justify the end, if the end is truly worthy, then the means are also justified,' I say hesitantly. 'Otherwise change will never come.'

I wonder if he will fly into a rage for I have never rejected his guidance before. He surprises me with an understanding smile.

He looks into my eyes and says very gently.

'My child, I will not try to change your mind at this moment. You will one day learn the truth from a life experience of your own. I pray that it will not be a painful one for you.'

JOURNAL II

They are not long,
the days of wine and roses.

Ernest Dowson

11

I have decided to join the Socialist Students Union.

Nali is horrified when I tell her.

'Are you out of your mind, nanga?' she moans, holding me by the arm as if to restrain me physically. 'They are a bunch of misfits who can't find a place in society; they want to tear everything down.'

'It is true that some of them are anti-social Nali, but there is a core of truth in what they stand for,' I answer. 'Someone has to help the poor and … no one else seems to be doing anything.'

'You think these stupids are sincerely interested in the poor?' Nali shoots back derisively. 'They are after power and position … for themselves. Surely you can see that?'

'You listened to Kalinga. He is sincere, I'm sure he is,' I say. 'He has a real plan. I want to be part of that.'

'That man is dangerous,' Nali responds seriously. 'You are not to get mixed up with him. Do you hear?'

'He's only dangerous to the rich, Nali baba,' I answer lightly. 'What have I to lose?'

When I walk into the union office to register my name, Kumudu stares at me with an expression I'm unable to read. He doesn't say anything till I fill in the form and pay the small subscription.

He signals to me to join him in the tiny cubicle that serves as his office. I have not spoken to him since the cooking oil incident during the rag and I ignored him on the one occasion on which he tried to speak to me afterwards.

I stand in front of the cluttered table and feel as if I have walked into the cage of a dangerous beast.

Father Basil told me never to show fear; it only makes your opponent more vicious, and the attack more severe.

I can hear the thud of my heartbeat but keep my face still and my hands folded across my chest.

'I am glad you have decided to join our union,' he says, looking into my eyes with great intensity. 'You will not regret your decision.'

I nod but I don't answer. I avoid his eyes and look at his hands, now clasped together and resting on the table. Big hands with thick, calloused fingers; hands of a man who is used to manual labour … or strangling children.

'Good,' he goes on. 'You will be attending sessions, for information about our work and for training in your tasks. I will see you there.'

I nod again and turn to leave.

'Sujatha.'

I turn at the door and see that he is standing. 'Yes?'

'I regret … what happened during the rag,' he says slowly.

I am forced to look at the face, dominated as it is by those devil-eyes and heavy black beard. His expression repels me.

I turn without speaking and slip out of the door.

I have been looking forward to meeting my friends.

It will be such a relief to sit and talk about the holidays, about our plans for the term, about anything we feel like, without the wretched seniors trying to bully us. Just the same, the bubble of pure joy that seems to explode in my head when I see them seated together catches me by surprise.

Mithra sees me first and his mocking grin spreads from one ear to the other.

'Menna enawā apey gamey kella.'

Here comes our village girl.

Nali jumps up to greet me.

'See? The village gown has not been shortened by even one inch. Her hem is still dragging on the ground,' Mithra goes on. 'When is this girl going to smarten up?'

'Oh shut up, Mithra,' Nali says, still joining in the laughter.

'Seriously. Just look at her.' Mithra can't be stopped when he's teasing me. 'No lipstick, no powder and those awful pigtails hanging behind her head! Just like two *gärandiyas.'*

Gärandiyas are rat snakes.

I raise my fist to whack him and he covers his head with his hands.

Nali says:

'My nanga doesn't need lipstick and powder, you *pottaya*. Just look at her.'

Pottaya is a blind man.

'I've joined the SSU,' I blurt out to cover my confusion and change the subject. 'I just signed the forms.'

I am looking at Mithra when I say it and see his expression change in an instant. The laughter leaves his eyes and they go very still. There is something there that I can't make out. A moment later he is at it again, making fun of me.

'She is now going to destroy the rich and save the poor,' he mocks. 'When she stands for parliament, the village gown will be her symbol.'

'Oh, nanga, I told you not to do it,' Nali wails. 'Now those fools will fill your head with their socialist rubbish and you will not want to join us.'

'I'll never do that, Nali,' I assure her warmly. 'But when I come to power I might lock this Mithra up for worrying me so much.'

'Who has been worrying you?'

I turn and find Harith standing behind my chair. Nali swears that he is the best-looking man on campus.

He looks at me with a kindly smile.

'So our Sujatha has joined the Jeppas?' he asks easily. 'What a shame, I was hoping she would join us.'

'That's the thing, Harith,' Nali responds. 'I told her and told her but would she listen? No. She's just smiles and does what she wants! I'm wild with her.'

'What about you Mithra?' Harith asks. 'We need people like you in the ISF. Nalini is with us. Will you also join?'

Mithra looks amused; most things seem to amuse him.

'No, Hari,' he says easily. 'I won't join any union. Thanks anyway.'

'But why? You'll be safer with us if things get ugly. We can protect our members.'

'Oh, I wasn't thinking of safety,' Mithra replies with a slow smile. 'I just don't like people telling me what to do. Not even you."

I expect Harith to be offended but he returns Mithra's smile and nods.

'If you change your mind, our door is open,' he says.

*

Father Basil has suggested that I visit, and thank, my sponsor. Miss Decima is the lady who has agreed, at Father Basil's urging, to send me five hundred rupees every month to supplement the Mahapola scholarship.

The difference between life and death!

He has given me the address, an apartment in a place called King's Court. I wrote to Miss Decima and she wrote back suggesting I come on Saturday morning.

As the day approaches I begin to feel nervous. What if she doesn't like me? What if she decides to cancel the sponsorship? How will I manage?

Nali agrees to come with me for moral support.

King's Court turns out to be a tall concrete box with a huge cavern for parking cars at ground level. A grumpy security guard frowns suspiciously at us till we mention Miss Decima's name. He then waves us towards the flashing lights of a metal box set in the wall.

Nali presses a button and the doors slide open. There is no one inside.

'I'm not stepping into that,' I say firmly. 'What happens if we get stuck?'

'Come on, nanga, it's only a lift,' Nali explains patiently. 'People use it every day.'

'How will we breathe when the air finishes?'

'I won't breathe; you can have my share,' Nali says, giggling. 'Will you just get in? That guard fellow is staring at us.'

The door closes before we can make our minds up.

'There, did you see that?' I point nervously. 'It's a trap.'

Nali presses the button and the doors slide open again. She catches me by the hand and drags me inside.

Nali pushes another button and I feel the box moving.

Yasawathi has locked me in a box again and I can't breathe.

I shut my eyes and hold my breath till it comes to a stop; the doors open once again.

Miss Decima is a motherly lady with short hair and thick-lensed spectacles that make her eyes look enormous. If she is surprised to see two girls when she has invited only one, she gives no sign.

'Which of you is Sujatha?' she asks.

Nali steps aside and pushes me forward.

'I'm Sujatha, madam,' I say, looking at her nervously.

Her face lights up with a smile, warm and comforting. I know it is going to be all right.

'Father Basil tells me you are a very bright student,' she says, 'but goodness me, he didn't mention that you're such a lovely child.'

Don't talk about that. Oh please don't talk about that!

I look at the floor.

'Come in. Come in,' she goes on. 'Who is your friend?'

'This is Nalini,' I murmur, glad to change the subject, 'she is my classmate. I didn't know the way so …'

'I'm happy to meet you, Nalini. Please sit over here.'

Miss Decima has prepared an enormous feast and insists that we try everything on the table.

'Father Basil told me that the rag was very severe this year,' Miss Decima says. 'I'm glad you were able to survive it. Do the seniors still give you trouble?'

'No. They leave us alone now,' Nali answers, 'but there is tension between student factions. We have to avoid being caught in the middle.'

'And you? You are good friends, are you?' she asks. 'Do you look after each other?'

'Oh yes, madam,' I answer promptly. 'Nali is my best friend. We … try to help each other whenever we can.'

Miss Decima is easy to talk with, so we chat for a long time. She questions us about our families and later tells us about her own. She has lost her husband many years ago and her two daughters are studying in the United States. I have the impression that she is lonely and glad that we have paid her a visit.

She holds my hand when I turn at her door to say goodbye. She presses something into my palm and folds my fingers over it so I am not able to see what it is. I open my fist while waiting for the lift and find a green note resting there.

A thousand rupees!

I am so excited that I forget to hold my breath in the lift. There must have been enough air because we reach the ground floor safely.

Nali says: 'Let's go shopping.'

'But Mithra …'

'Ah, I'll give him a call,' Nali says. 'We can go there afterwards.'

Mithra has invited us to his home in Havelock Town, wherever that is. We have promised to go there after seeing Miss Decima.

'What do you want to buy?' I ask.

'I don't want anything, nanga. I want to get a proper dress for you.'

'What? I don't need a dress. Anyway I can't afford it.'

'Now you can.'

I look at the green note, now damp in my hand.

'But …'

'No buts. You are coming with me.'

House of Fashions is incredible.

I cannot imagine such a collection of clothes in one place, or so many people buying them. How much money is needed to pay for the armloads of clothes the shoppers are carrying away? I had thought the pavement stalls and the shops at Nugegoda were so wonderful but this is something else. Separate floors for women and men, separate sections for dresses and undergarments. Areas for display of shoes, belts and handbags; and a whole aisle of shockingly transparent night dresses. Do women really wear these things? They might as well walk naked!

Had it been necessary to ask someone for prices I would have run out of the shop; luckily every article is price marked. We are able, when we think no one is watching to take a quick look and assure ourselves that the green note will stretch far enough.

'Look at this, Nanga,' Nali whispers excitedly. 'This will be nice on you. Why don't you try it on?'

'Are you crazy? How can I change here in the open?'

'No silly, you can take it into that cubicle and try it.'

'Are you sure we are allowed to do that? Will they say I'm trying to steal it?'

In the end we both squeeze into the little changing room with an armful of dresses. Once we have the door firmly shut and don't hear any alarms go off we are able to enjoy ourselves.

It's not easy for two of us to try on dresses in a space meant for one; we complain and giggle as one extracts a knee or an elbow from the other's face.

We make a lot of noise.

As we wait outside the shop for Mithra to pick us up I wonder if I have been foolish. Should I have saved the thousand for an emergency? And that dress, silky blue with a hem only a few inches below my knees, will I ever have the courage to wear it in public?

A silver car draws up with a grinning Mithra in the front seat. Nali opens the rear door and we scramble inside to the luxury of leather seats and air conditioning. The driver pulls away just as a frowning policeman comes striding up to the vehicle.

'So what have you girls been buying?' Mithra asks.

'It's Suji, I got her to buy a party dress,' Nali says. 'You should see it.'

'What are you doing, Nalini?' he demands. 'Are you trying to ruin our village girl?'

'I'm not spoiling her, you idiot,' Nali says. 'What's wrong with buying one nice dress?'

'What's wrong? She'll cut her hair next, then she'll start using lipstick and makeup,' Mithra goes on. 'When she goes home to her village, her aunt will chase her away with a broomstick. That's what's wrong.'

'Oh shut up, Mithra,' I say crossly. 'I'm not cutting my hair and anyway, I haven't even decided if I'll wear this dress.'

The car enters a narrow lane and then turns through a gate to stop under a covered porch. I am nervous about meeting Mithra's family, wondering what they will think of us. We conceal our anxiety by helping Mithra to climb out of the car.

She is nice, Mithra's mother.

She makes us comfortable in the sitting room and stops to chat while Mithra goes inside to change. It is a large, airy room with windows opening on to a well-tended lawn. My home would easily fit inside it.

'I'm glad he has made friends with you,' Mithra's mother says. 'He didn't have … in school, you know, many friends.'

We just nod, not knowing what to say. She goes on:

'We were very worried, during the rag. We thought they would pick on him, because of his disability. He never told us anything that happened.'

'They were very wicked to him,' I tell her, 'but he is strong. They tried hard but were never able to … crush him.'

'I'm glad but …'

'Our batch-mates admire him for that,' I go on. 'He has many friends now. Really.'

She appears to be relieved. She leaves the room as Mithra returns, followed by a little girl of twelve or thirteen. He places one hand across her shoulders.

'This is my little sister, Mihiri. We call her Meeya,' he says with a grin. 'Meeya, this is my friend Nalini and the ugly girl over there is Suji.'

'She's not ugly,' Meeya says shyly.

'Of course she's ugly,' Mithra pretends to be puzzled. 'Are you blind?'

'You're the one that's blind,' Meeya answers firmly. 'She's …'

Mrs. Dias walks in with a tray of food, sandwiches and cutlets. The butter cake is still hot from the oven, she warns us.

I have never tasted homemade butter cake before. I decide that, given a choice, I'd eat nothing else for the rest of my life.

The cake must have loosened her tongue because Meeya suddenly asks:

'Which one of you is aiya's girlfriend?'

Taken by surprise we both point to the other and then burst out laughing. Seeing that our antics are upsetting Meeya, I say:

'Your aiya is not interested in us, baba, he thinks we are too ugly. He is interested in a very nice girl called Padma.'

'Truly?'

'Yes,' Nali says with a giggle. 'Only thing is, she's a bit fat.'

Meeya looks at us uncertainly. Before she can say anything another vehicle turns into the drive and stops near the porch. A door slams and we hear footsteps in the corridor outside the sitting room.

'Who the hell are these women?' a gruff voice asks.

A mumbled answer comes from Mrs. Dias.

'Mithra … friends … campus …'

'Bloody riff-raff,' the heavy voice barks. 'Get rid of them. I'm expecting some people from the office.'

'But Clement …'

'Do it.'

Nali and I jump to our feet.

'I'm so sorry,' Mithra tries to smile but his eyes are glazed with mortification. 'You mustn't mind my father. He can be … very abrupt at times.'

'It's all right, Mithra, it's all right,' Nali says awkwardly. The atmosphere has changed. 'We must be going anyway. Thank you for inviting us.'

'Wait,' Mithra calls out as we hurry towards the door, 'I'll tell the driver to drop you at the bus stand.'

'No, Mithra,' I tell him, 'we can walk up to the road.

Please don't worry.'

Anxious as we are to get away, we have to slow down to allow Mithra to accompany us up to the gate.

'Please don't be upset by what my father said. It is not you he is angry with,' Mithra says apologetically, 'it's me.'

'What do you mean?' I ask. 'What have you done?"

'I got polio.'

'What? What are you talking about?'

'He was a great sportsman, my father. He played cricket for Royal and the SSC.' Mithra whispers shakily, his eyes on the ground. 'He wanted his son to follow in his footsteps. Instead … I became a … cripple.'

I want to cry.

I reach out and clasp the hands holding the crutches.

'It's not your fault, baba,' I say impulsively. 'You are brave and kind and … wonderful. Don't let that foolish man upset *you*.'

12

Harith has invited us to a party at his home.

He often joins our circle at the canteen and I must admit he is good company, always ready with a funny observation; most often the objects of his ridicule are SSU members.

'It will be very grand.' Nali's eyes are shining. 'We must go for it.'

'Too grand for a person like me, Nali,' I say ruefully. 'Why do they waste money to celebrate a birthday anyway?'

'It is his twenty first, you silly girl,' Nali tells me. 'That is a very big event. There'll be nice boys there, not these university *yakos.*'

'You can have the nice boys, Nali,' I tell her firmly. 'I'm not going.'

But she doesn't let up. She keeps at me and at me till I finally, against my better judgement, agree to go.

My new blue dress makes me feel that everyone is staring at me. Nali says I look very smart in it but I don't feel comfortable. Is the hemline too daring? Will Harith's friends laugh at me? What will Father Basil say if he hears about it?

Oh why did I agree to this?

No one on campus takes much notice when we slip out of the gate. Sitting in a nearly empty bus going into the city gives me a chance to catch my breath.

'What happens at these parties?' I ask nervously.

'The girls usually sit together. The boys stand around the table with the drinks. When they've had one or two, they pluck up the nerve to chat with the girls.'

'Drinks?' I ask, thoroughly alarmed now. I know only too well what men do when they drink. 'Are you saying the boys will be drunk?'

'Not drunk, nanga,' Nali says, 'just a drink or two to give them courage. Can you believe the poor mutts are too scared to speak with us unless they've had a couple?'

'I'm not sure I like this,' I say worriedly. 'I don't want to talk to any strange boys, especially if they've had drinks.'

'Don't worry nanga,' Nali squeezes my arm. 'I'll be there.'

'Well, don't go away and leave me with them.'

The house is huge.

A man in a white jacket and black trousers greets us at the door. I think he is someone important in the household till Nali whispers that he is one of the stewards from the caterer. We walk carefully over granite floors and under dazzling multiple lights; chandeliers, Nali says they are called.

Sliding glass doors in the sitting room lead to a wide expanse of lawn, bright with garden lights. We wait nervously till Harith spots us.

The boys must have had their confidence boosters because some of them are already chatting with the girls. The girls are dressed very grandly. They seem to have stepped out of magazine covers. Some are in dresses, cut low and daring, others wear tight trousers with tiny tops showing many inches of bare skin at the waist. One has a ring inserted in her navel. They seem to know the boys very well; they call out to each other and there is much laughter. I sit and pray for the evening to finish quickly and, in the meantime, for no one to notice me.

'Machang, who are those two?'

'Friends … campus …' Harith's voice is lost in the chatter.

'Wow! Introduce me at once.'

A moment later Harith saunters over with a boy whom he introduces as Amal or Kamal. Another boy joins them and soon there are four or five young men standing before us, all of them talking at the same time. Someone calls Harith away.

Amal – Kamal asks: 'Would you like to dance?'

'What?' I really am taken aback.

'Dance with me, you know,' he says pointing. 'The band has started playing.'

Some couples are gyrating on an elevated wooden floor at the end of the lawn. A three-man band is playing western music with a heavy beat.

'I … don't dance,' I blurt out in surprise. 'I don't know how to.'

'It's very easy,' Amal – Kamal offers. 'I'll teach you.'

'Yes, yes, we'll all help,' one boy says while the others murmur encouragement.

I begin to squirm with embarrassment.

'Are these fellows worrying you, Sujatha?' A familiar voice at last; I'd recognise that drawl at any time. I look up with relief to find that Mithra had joined our circle.

'No Mithra, just tell them I'm useless at these things,' I say, more confident now. 'There are lots of nice girls sitting over there.'

'Ahh, we've danced with all of them. We want to teach you.'

'Not today.'

They finally leave us and drift away.

Mithra takes us closer to the band to watch the dancers. The couples on the boarded floor are very graceful, each in their own style. It is very glamorous and exciting, like watching TV.

The music changes to something I recognize.

Baila.

The boys in the village sometimes dance to these tunes.

I think Mithra must have made some sign. At the next moment, Nali grabs my hand and hustles me onto the floor. She keeps hold of my hand and starts moving to the beat.

The other dancers see what is happening and gather round us in a circle. They clap their hands to the music and shout words of encouragement.

I stand like a dummy, wanting to die.

I shake my hand free of Nali's grasp and start dancing. I have no choice. At first, I only make the smallest movements with my hands and keep my feet still. Then, as if of their own accord, my feet begin to move to the rhythm.

No one laughs at me, except Mithra who is standing nearby, a broad grin on his face. Harith comes up behind him and says something; then he helps Mithra on to the dance floor. We stand in a small circle, the four of us with Mithra moving just his upper body, and dance.

And dance!

We forget to check the time.

Harith had promised to have a vehicle ready to take us back before the eleven o'clock hostel curfew. It is past that when we leave the party.

We are in trouble.

'What are we going to do?' Nali asks me. She speaks in a whisper, as if she fears the driver will tell the matron.

'I don't think security at the main gate will stop us,' I say.

'Maybe. But that bathalaya matron will lock the hall door at eleven,' Nali continues worriedly. 'We'll have to wake her to get in.'

'Never mind,' I say gaily. 'We had a good time. It was worth it.'

'You little scamp,' she replies, pretending to be angry. 'You made a big fuss at first but you secretly enjoyed it, didn't you?'

'Mm. It was fun when the four of us danced; not when the other boys came close.'

'All that's fine but what do we do now?' Nali asks, starting to worry again. 'We'll be suspended if we are caught.'

When I make no answer she says:

'You have a plan, don't you?'

The security guards are either too sleepy or they are too impressed by Harith's car when it draws up at the gate to ask any questions. We slip through and hurry towards the hostel.

It is eerie.

The drive is dark except for the light from the guardhouse behind us. Our shadows are gigantic as they stretch out ahead.

Nali grips my arm so suddenly I nearly scream.

'Do you think it's midnight now?'

'I don't know,' I whisper. 'What does it matter?'

'That's the time the dead rise up to take the living.'

'Oh shut up, Nali,' I say shakily 'It's scary enough already.'

'But it's true. I read it in a book,' Nali goes on in a hoarse whisper. 'The spirits of the restless dead come looking for virgin girls at this time.'

You idiot Nali, you're the one they'll be after then.

'I'll turn you into one of the restless dead if you don't shut up.'

'It's true.'

'Shut up.'

We climb the shower room drainpipe. I had made a note of that drainpipe during the rag, marking it as an escape route from our dormitory in case the seniors were waiting for us at the main entrance. It is a sturdy metal pipe and the windows in the long shower stall are never locked. It is an easy climb for a village girl used to scrambling up mango and guava trees. Nali struggles a bit but manages it without getting trapped by the spirits of the dead.

*

The SSU insist on an extensive course of 're-education' for new recruits. They divide us into batches of twenty each. Classes take nearly two hours and include lectures followed by very animated discussions.

The teachers are young men and women from outside the campus.

They talk about many things we already know of and also of things we don't know or haven't thought of.

They explain the meaning of something called GDP by which the prosperity of a country is measured. But, they say, if the rich get richer and the poor remain the same, the GDP will still indicate that the country is prospering. Our teachers tell us that all the programs financed by the donor agencies are like that; they only benefit the rich. The poor are expected to wait for generations for the wealth to 'trickle down', like crumbs falling off a table for the dogs beneath to feed on.

They tell us about the great powers that colonised undeveloped countries to secure cheap raw materials and to create markets for their finished products. How the colonialists, and their successors the local upper class, require the poor to remain hungry in order to provide cheap labour for their factories and estates.

They show us how hopeless the prospects are for a graduate seeking employment. How the system uses the English language as a barrier to keep rural students out of the race for good jobs.

I attend the SSU education programs faithfully. What is being taught appears to be clearly logical and self-evident. I wonder why people in authority do not see the truth of these teachings.

I work faithfully for the SSU and believe wholeheartedly in their cause, which is now mine. Yet I find it difficult to make friends with the others in the movement, even the girls in my own re-education group. I spend all my leisure hours with Nali, Mithra and Harith.

I lead a double life.

*

They ask for volunteers for the Ginirälla program. Ginirälla means wave, or tsunami, of fire.

The Ginirälla group is to be an èlite corps trained for special tasks. We are given to understand from the beginning that theirs will be the key role. Volunteers are to be carefully screened and only a fortunate handful will be selected. Once in the special corps, training is to continue during every vacation.

The prospect of not going home for vacations is a knife in my heart but I want, with even greater fervour, to be part of this great struggle. I want to be at the forefront of it, and it is clear to me that joining Ginirälla will give me the opportunity.

I volunteer.

They ask six of us to stay on after the rest of the class disperses, four boys and one other girl. We are given applications to fill out, information about our homes, families and economic condition. The lecturer then interviews us, one at a time.

I find the questions very strange; much of it is about what I would do if faced with an unusual situation. I learn later that it has to do with something called psychological profiling. They make us swear an oath that none of these matters will be discussed outside that room, not even with the others who have volunteered.

It is very exciting.

Two weeks later I am summoned to the union office. Kumudu is seated in his cubicle studying a sheet of paper. He looks up when I enter, eyes like black pits in that hairy face.

'You volunteered to join the Ginirälla project?"

'Yes.'

'It will be very hard. Are you sure you want to do this?'

I feel my heart lurch with elation. Have I been selected?

'Yes. Yes, I want to join.'

He tugs thoughtfully at his beard as he stares at me. I begin to feel uncomfortable. I cannot remember ever having had a normal conversation with him, or ever wanting to.

'You have been selected,' he says slowly, 'but I have decided to cross your name out.'

'What?' I protest, furiously angry. 'You can't do that. I volunteered and have been selected. This is something I want to do.'

He closes his eyes and remains silent for a while. When he opens them again he has a strange expression and his voice seems to have changed as well.

'I am glad that you truly believe in our cause,' he says softly, 'but Giniralla is not for you. There is a lot of useful work you can do for the cause as an ordinary member.'

'I am much stronger than you think.' I am pleading now. 'I want to be involved. Let me join. Please!'

'I don't doubt your strength,' he answers quietly. 'But there's another side of your character … that makes you unsuitable. I'm surprised the profilers missed it.'

'What do you mean?'

'At a critical moment, I suspect that you will refuse to … obey,' he answers thoughtfully. 'You might fail to trust the leadership.'

'How can you say that?' I demand angrily. 'I do trust the leadership. I have carried out all their instructions …'

He studies me gravely for a minute; I feel uncomfortable and drop my eyes to his hands, spread palm down, on the table.

'Let me ask you this. If you find some policy or action by the leadership unacceptable to your conscience, what would you do?'

'I would … protest, I suppose,' I say with some hesitation.

'And if the leadership overrule your protest and insist that you obey, what then?'

'If it is a serious matter, I suppose I'll … leave the movement.'

'Once in Ginirälla,' he says slowly, 'you will not be allowed to leave.'

I notice that his fists are now clenched tight.

'You can't be serious.'

'This is a serious business. I don't think you have any idea how serious it is. It will be … well for you to remember that.'

That brooding look is still in his eyes.

13

In the very first semester of the new academic year the Vice-Chancellor suspends Harith and his committee.

Dr. Gunapala is new to the campus. The previous VC, Dr. Mendis had been a strict disciplinarian; too strict perhaps and also too sympathetic towards Harith's union. He made no secret of his contempt for the SSU.

The SSU campaigned for two years to have him removed. After repeated demonstrations, and parliamentary support from the JSP, the minister was finally persuaded to remove Dr. Mendis.

Dr. Gunapala is a respected academic. He is a popular choice, at least with my union, on account of his unquestionable Marxist sympathies. That faith is justified when a brawl breaks out in the canteen between members of the two unions. The new VC promptly suspends Harith and the other committee members of ISF.

The ordinary members of the ISF are furious. They huddle together in little groups to plan a series of demonstrations demanding justice for their suspended leaders while a small inner core want to do something even more drastic to show their disapproval.

From the whispered conversations that come to a stop when I pass by, I guess that they are planning something extreme. What surprises me is that Mithra, who is not even a member of the union, seems to be thoroughly involved.

I am walking towards the main gate one evening when Nali grips my arm so hard I gasp in pain.

'He ... he's coming back,' she stammers. 'He only left a few minutes ago and now he's coming back.'

'Who?' I ask, trying to free my arm. 'What *are* you talking about?'

Nali is staring at the gate as if in a trance. I recognise the VC's car. Dr. Gunapala has rolled down a shutter and is speaking with one of the security officers.

'I can see the car,' I tell Nali. 'Why is that a problem?'

'It's Mithra,' she wails, grasping my arm again. 'He's there. He's in the VC's office.'

I see the shutter roll up and the car begin to move towards us.

'What's Mithra doing there? What have you idiots planned?'

'He's going ... to urinate on the VC's chair.'

'What? Are you serious?'

'Yes.'

The car is hardly twenty yards away. The VC will park under the porch and walk into his ground floor office.

And Mithra will be caught in the act.

If Nali had run inside the moment she spotted the car, she might have been in time to warn him. It is far too late now.

'Oh why did you send Mithra?' I ask desperately. 'He can't even run.'

'All the others backed out,' she says despairingly, dropping my arm. 'He'll be sacked now.'

I turn my head and look at Nali. From the corner of my eye I can see the car moving towards us, now just yards way. I count to three and step in front of it.

Nali's scream rings in my ear as I suffer a crunching blow on my hip; searing pain at first and then my side goes numb. I feel my body being flung into the air as if in slow motion. I hit the ground and something very solid smashes into the side of my head.

For some hazy moments I hear confused shouts; then Nali's voice and I think she is sobbing. All sounds fade away. I know someone is lifting me up. The pain returns now and I want to scream; no sounds come.

I sense movement of a vehicle.

*

I try to make out whether it is my head or my side that hurts most. I discover that the hip pain is bearable if I don't move my body but my head aches all the time. It throbs, as if a nail is being driven very slowly into my skull.

A nurse sees that I am conscious and calls the matron. A young house officer examines me soon afterwards, shining a little flashlight into each of my eyes and making notes in the bed-head ticket. He prescribes something to put me to sleep.

They only allow two visitors at any one time. Nali and Mithra are standing on either side of my bed.

'You lunatic girl,' Nali says, seemingly torn between anger and concern, 'you could have been killed.'

'Are you sure I'm not dead?' I ask and that draws a wan smile.

'The VC thought you were,' she answers. 'You should have seen him when we carried you to the car.'

'My head aches terribly but the doctor says I'll be all right,' I tell them, knowing they are hiding their anxiety.

'They want to keep me here for a few days. Observation, they say.'

Mithra hasn't said a word; only his eyes are not amused. Not as much as usual, anyway.

'You brainless dolt,' I turn on him furiously. 'Who asked you to volunteer for such a thing?'

'Someone had to do it,' he answers easily, 'and the others backed out at the last minute. Anyway I thought no one would suspect me.'

'It was a disgusting thing to do.'

'Mm.'

'Did you do it?'

'Yes.'

'If I could sit up I'd slap you.'

Mithra only laughs.

'I'll remind you when you are feeling better,' he says.

A nurse comes round to chase the visitors away. Nali squeezes my hand and turns to go. Mithra stays behind for a moment; for once his eyes are serious.

'Suji, you took an awful risk to save me,' he starts quietly. 'I …'

'Shut up, Mithra,' I say sharply to cover my embarrassment. 'You would have done the same for me.

'Oh, I don't know,' he answers with a crooked smile. 'I have only one leg left.'

'Yes, you would,' I tell him firmly, 'and there's another thing.'

'What?'

'If you ever … ever do anything stupid like that again, I'll break your crutches.'

'All right,' he says seriously as he turns to leave.

'Mithra.'

'Yes?'

'Did you actually do it, I mean, on his chair?"

'Sure,' he says with a grin, 'but it wasn't easy.'

'What do you mean?'

'I had to balance on one foot,' he explains seriously. 'No crutches because I needed both hands, you know, to...'

'Oh, shut up. I don't want to hear it.'

'Then it wouldn't come ...'

'What?'

'When you're scared,' he goes on with a laugh, 'it doesn't come in a hurry.'

'Ahhh you horror! Will you go away from here?'

*

The second semester is nearly over when Kalinga comes to our campus again. Most of us are preparing for our end-of-year examinations and could have done without any disruptions. But Kalinga is a very special person, so feverish preparations are now underway. He is to conduct a series of closed meetings, counselling our members in small, manageable groups.

There are about thirty in my group. We are conducted to an empty classroom and a number of senior activists are posted around to keep watch. When everyone is seated and ready Kumudu conducts the visitor into the room.

His head is bowed, long hair falling forward and covering part of his face. The clothes are the same, long sleeved shirt buttoned at the bony wrists and dark trousers. The face, when he turns to look at us, is that of a famine victim, hollow cheeks and thin lips below sunken eyes.

Kumudu introduces him briefly.

Kalinga's voice is unforgettable. Hoarse and strange, as if he hasn't cleared his throat, but the message comes across with raw power.

'You are now with us. This is as it should be, as it must be, for we have the same mother. It is our mother Lanka who is raped and robbed, who is shamed and ground into the gutter. It is our task, our sacred duty to save her.'

Kalinga pauses and lets his eyes run over us.

'Are you with me?'

'Yes,' we murmur.

'ARE YOU WITH ME?'

'YES.'

'We know the enemy. They are the filth that live in the cities. The enemy has power because they have wealth. They have wealth because their ancestors were traitors and thieves. They have wealth because they deal in every kind of corruption. They want you to remain poor so that they can retain their wealth and power.

'There is no force that can clean the filth out of the cities other than you. If you, the poor rural students, unite to sweep away this rotten system, you can bring about an era of justice and prosperity for all.

'You have the numbers. All you need is guidance and leadership.'

Kalinga stops and looks down at the floor before him. The silence drags on till there is restless movement in the seats behind me.

He looks up at last and fixes those intense eyes on us.

'I have a plan; a perfect plan that will sweep away the evil and bring us to power. This plan is only known to a handful of people. It will take us time to put all the elements into place. But each of you has a part to play in that struggle. Your section leaders will tell you how to prepare, what to do. But you need training, some for one task, some for others. Each task is vital to our cause.

'Remember one thing. You must have complete and unshakable faith in your leaders. When the time for action comes there must be no hesitation and no questioning. Only your leaders will see the full picture, you will see only your part of it. You must therefore carry out your tasks whether you like them or not, whether you agree or not. I demand absolute devotion. I demand absolute obedience. It is only then that we will be assured of victory.'

Kalinga's words run through my head, keeping me awake till late that night. It is exciting to be part of a movement that promises to bring justice and hope to the poor. Perhaps the changes will occur in time to help Loku and Punchi and thousands of rural children like them.

I think it strange that Kalinga didn't mention Ginirälla. I suspect that the members selected for this èlite unit have already been sent for special training. I have tried to find out more about the program but had no success whatever. No one is willing to talk about it. I wish again that Kumudu had not blocked my chance to join.

Some tiny concerns creep into my mind. I brush them away but they keep coming back.

Kalinga had said: 'I have a plan to sweep away the evil.'

I, not we! Is this project his and his alone?

I am not comfortable with his demand that we obey our leaders even if we think the action they order is wrong. Sujatha, I tell myself, when a complex and secret project is to be carried out, such discipline is necessary.

I dream of her again!

She is beautiful in a white sari and she is smiling. She

holds out her arms once more to gather me up.

Then a shadow falls across us and I see Yasawathi creeping up behind her; she has something wrapped around her hand.

Something evil.

I scream and scream to my mother to look out, to turn around and face the danger behind her. She doesn't hear me. It is a noose that Yasawathi carries. She slips it round mother's neck and jerks it tight.

I watch in horror as life slowly goes out of my mother's body. Her eyes are on me and it breaks my heart when I realise that the sorrow there is for me, not for her.

14

Harith has arranged a trip to a place called Wilpattu.

We are busy studying for our second year examinations and don't pay much attention. Harith should have been preparing for his finals; instead he spends more time organising the outing.

Wilpattu is a wildlife park in the north west of the country. It is, Harith tells us, an incredibly large forest teeming with animals. It isn't anything special for me but it will be a change to watch animals from the safety of a vehicle rather than on foot.

And I don't wish to let my friends down.

My aunt would faint if she knows I am going on a trip with boys, even though they are only Harith, his younger brother Sidath and Mithra. They are now like brothers to me but my aunt will not think of them like that.

Harith doesn't frighten me anymore; not since we spoke of my problem during the 'paduru gee' festival. This is an annual talent show organised by the cultural society. It is called 'paduru gee' because, during the performance, the audience is expected to sit on mats. We sit on scraps of newspaper.

Harith had been seated next to me.

'Why do you always avoid being alone with me?' he had asked quietly. 'Do you find my company so repulsive?'

I took a deep breath to calm myself. It was only fair

that I answered his question honestly, but so hard.

'Harith, it is not you at all,' I told him as kindly as I could, 'it's me. Something happened long ago that I ... I can't even bear to think about. It's impossible ... impossible ...'

I had bent over and choked up, unable to go on.

'It's all right, Sujatha,' Harith said, thoroughly alarmed. 'Don't talk about it if it upsets you. But you need help with this. I can arrange for you to see a good doctor ...'

'No. No, they will only say I'm mad ...'

'I want to help you,' Harith had said. 'I can help if you will only let me.'

'You can't help me ... no one can.'

'I don't believe that at all. It's all in your mind,' he had answered calmly.

'You can help me by being a friend."

'But ...'

'Please.'

'All right,' he said with a sigh. 'All right, let's be friends then.'

I was comfortable with him after that.

*

There is really nothing to compare with the joy of setting out on a long journey with good friends. The examinations are over and this is the first day of our long vacation.

I should have been on a bus to my village; instead I am seated in the back of Harith's new Prado, watching the dark shapes by the roadside fall away behind me. Harith is driving with his brother Sidath seated by his side. Nali is fast asleep beside me with Mithra at the other end of the rear seat. The vehicle is loaded to the roof and more things are tied to the hood rack above.

I ignore Harith's grumbling and lower the shutter just a little for fresh air to enter. All his arguments about the efficiency of the air conditioning system are of no avail; I'm not convinced that there is enough air for all of us inside the closed vehicle.

Harith had insisted on leaving at five in the morning. We have to get to Kokmotai campsite, wherever that is, in time to have a river bath before lunch. It is impossible for Nali and I to leave the hostel at that time so I had appealed to Miss Decima to put us up for the night.

Miss Decima was delighted to have us but not at all happy about my going on a camping trip with boys. I took Mithra to meet her and that proved to be enough.

Mithra can charm anyone.

I am too excited to sleep. As dawn breaks I see the name boards flashing past, Marawila, Madampe and Chilaw, places I have neither seen nor heard of. The road is broad and straight and the Prado is flying.

Harith turns off the main road to find a breakfast spot. He parks under a solitary tree overlooking a huge lagoon.

He pulls out folding chairs and a small table. Within minutes we are seated comfortably in a circle eating seeni sambol sandwiches and boiled eggs. Just sandwiches for me but I don't mind at all. Sidath pours hot coffee into plastic cups.

I notice lots of birds along the waterline, egrets and ibis, open-bill storks and pelicans. Sidath seems to know something about birds but to the others they are all 'kokās'. They are only interested in big animals, elephants, leopard and bear.

Nali wants to know where the ladies' room is. Harith

laughs and points to a clump of bushes on the other side of the road.

Puttalam is disappointing, a dull town except for the brilliant blue of the lagoon with fishing boats bobbing up and down in the water. We turn right at the junction.

The road is now narrow and uneven. Small villages sit listlessly between stretches of scrub jungle. Many of the houses have huge concrete tanks shaped like cooking pots. Mithra explains that they are for collecting rainwater.

It takes about forty-five minutes to get from the main road to the park entrance. Harith goes to the office to pay the park fees; we get down to stretch our legs.

Nali and Sidath start a battle that is to last for the next three days.

'How old are you?' Nali asks him. 'It can't be much because you haven't even started shaving.'

'I'll be sixteen soon,' Sidath answers with a cocky grin. 'I bet you don't shave either.'

'You cheeky little brat,' Nali responds warmly. 'Remember I'm the oldest girl here. You will call me akki and obey me at all times.'

'Akki? Why should I call you akki?' the boy shoots back. 'Maybe I should call you aunty.'

'I'll aunty you,' Nali growls as she advances on Sidath threateningly. The boy jumps off the bonnet of the vehicle and skips away. Harith returns with a bundle of papers and a tracker, a stocky middle-aged man with a morose face. Harith introduces him.

Sena.

Through the gate and into the park.

I notice at once that this forest is different from the jungles in the south. I had grown up near scrub jungle where groves of trees are interspersed with extensive areas of thorn and shrubs. Wilpattu is a forest of trees.

The sandy track runs through dense forest and opens, from time to time, into grass-covered plains. In the centre of each plain is a natural reservoir of water. The track curves gently round the wetland to re-enter the forest on the far side. The others groan in dismay when each villu turns out to be empty of animals except for buffalo and pigs. I could have told them that the animals would by now have retreated to the forest for shade, and nothing much should be expected in the mid-morning heat.

But I don't.

Kokmotai campsite is at the far end of the park and the drive seems very long but I enjoy it. I suppose it is a combination of being in the jungle and, at the same time, being safely cocooned in a comfortable vehicle.

I know better than to get accustomed to luxury but this one time is not going to harm me.

We reach the campsite at last; a shady clearing on the bank of a rocky stream the tracker calls Moderagam Aru. The boys, with Sena to help them, start to set up camp. The first thing they do is to rig a long grey tarpaulin under a kumbuk tree by the edge of the stream. They bring the provision boxes from the Prado and stack them on a side. Harith assembles a small table and places a gas cooker on it.

He dusts his hands and announces:

'OK girls, get started.'

'What do you mean?' Nali asks suspiciously.

'Start cooking,' Harith seems surprised at the question. 'Don't you want to eat?'

'Is that why you brought us?' Nali demands, clearly outraged. 'To cook for you fellows?'

'Of course,' Harith answers with a laugh. 'Didn't you girls know that?'

Nali is all for staging a strike and I soon realise the reason. She can't cook. I calm her down and get her to help me sort the packages. We persuade Sidath to fetch us a bucket of water for a start.

The boys work hard, even Mithra in spite of his disability. By the time we have rice boiling nicely they have put up two neat tents and call us to inspect the toilet arrangements.

We have been waiting anxiously to see this.

Metal uprights, in a rectangle about four feet by five, make up the frame. A heavy green canvas hangs around it. The entrance, facing away from the camp, has an overlap for added privacy.

Nali is happy. She runs to the camp and comes back with a strip of paper that she pins to the entrance.

LADIES ONLY.

There are cries of outrage but Nali is firm.

'I'm not sharing the toilet with a bunch of messy boys,' she says callously. 'You can use the jungle.'

'We should have told you to put it up yourself,' Sidath grumbles, stretching his hand out. 'See? I even got a callous from digging that pit.'

'Poor baby! We'll let you use our toilet,' Nali says grandly, 'since you are only a little boy.'

'Shut up,' Sidath growls. 'I don't want to share with YOU. The jungle's good enough for me.'

We drive round parts of the park that afternoon. Animals are scarce but we see herds of deer and then a solitary sambhur stag. And a herd of elephants on the far side of a villu, grey-black shapes just big enough for us to be sure they are not buffalo.

Sena shows us the remnants of the holiday bungalows at Kalivillu and Manikepola. The cement floors and parts of the walls remain but that is all. They have fallen into ruin during the period when the park was abandoned. It must have been a wonderful experience to live in those houses; for they overlook open villus that would attract many animals and birds.

It is dark when we get back to camp, eerie too till Sena builds a bonfire using deadwood from the riverbank. Harith hangs two lanterns in the cook tent.

'OK girls,' he says sweetly. 'Dinner.'

I know that the two words Nali uses are improper and I haven't heard a girl use them before. It is amusing to see the shocked expression on Harith's face though. I decide to make a deal.

'We'll cook the dinner,' I tell him, 'only if you'll promise to take us to the other side of the river afterwards, so we can bathe.'

The boys are very helpful, really. When the meal is ready Harith helps us to scramble across a massive pile of rocks to the far side of the river. I have selected a sandy spot with shallow water that is better for bathing than the muddy near bank.

The jungle behind us is dark and forbidding; Nali gets nervous at the last minute.

'Don't leave us here,' she tells Harith. 'You'd better stay on this side.'

'Sure,' Harith laughs. 'I don't mind watching you girls bathing.'

Nali uses the two bad words again and makes me laugh. In the end we force Harith to sit on a rock facing the other way. He keeps threatening to turn around and we threaten to throw water on him.

We make enough noise to drive any wild animal away.

The boys grudgingly admit that our cooking is good. I know that this is due to the combination of real hunger and the feeling of contentment that the jungle brings. They would have found anything palatable.

We wash up and put away all our provisions. No one wants the day to end so we sit listening to the sound of water flowing through the rocks.

And talk.

Nali enjoys needling Sidath.

'You can send the little boy to sleep in our tent,' she tells Harith. 'He can hold my hand if he gets frightened in the night.'

'Who are you calling a little boy?' Sidath cries angrily. 'I'm not frightened of the jungle … even if I was, I wouldn't hold your hand.'

'Why did you hold my hand then, when you brought me a bucket of water?'

'I didn't. I didn't,' Sidath appeals to Harith. 'Tell her not to tell lies, aiya.'

'How do I know what you did?' Harith answers. 'Anyway I think Nali likes you. You can hold her hand if you like. We don't mind.'

'Actually I wanted to be Nali's boyfriend,' Mithra butts in, 'but if you're keen on her I'll step aside.'

'Chee! Are you mad?' Sidath is outraged. 'You're all mad. I'm going to sleep.'

The little tent Harith has set up for us has a ground sheet that zips up neatly to make us feel secure. To my intense relief there are two net-covered openings for fresh air.

The boys have a bigger tent and Sena the tracker is to sleep in the vehicle.

The sounds of the jungle seem louder now that the conversations are over. Two owls keep calling to each other near the river, a peafowl cries like a cat; the loud cry of another animal upsets Nali.

'What is that?' she asks nervously. 'It seems very close.'

'A deer,' I tell her. 'Something must have frightened it.'

'Yes, but what frightened the deer?'

'Ahh it could be anything. Maybe even our fire,' I say reassuringly and then, from pure mischief: 'Or a leopard.'

Nali grabs my hand.

'Oh no,' she says. 'I don't like this at all.'

'Don't worry, babā,' I tell her. 'Leopards don't attack people. The jungle is really very safe. Much safer than the city.'

Nali isn't convinced and falls asleep holding my hand.

*

I see a leopard for the first time in my life.

I have seen footprints of leopard in the forest near my village and I have listened to stories about leopards related by villagers. None of these prepare me for the stunning beauty of the animal we see that day.

We are returning after a long circuit in the park and are close to the camp. The vehicle rounds a bend and standing in the middle of the track, hardly ten yards from us, is a magnificent yellow and black beast.

The leopard turns its head and stares boldly at the vehicle. Then, as I hold my breath, it walks towards us, passing by the driver's seat and the open shutter by which I am sitting. I see the black rosettes in their bed of yellow fur so close that I might, had I the courage, have reached out and touched the splendid beast.

The leopard continues down the track and disappears round a bend.

Dinner is over. We are still talking about our close encounter with the leopard, trying to relive the experience. Nali is concerned that a big leopard was seen so close to the camp. She keeps glancing over her shoulder and the forest beyond the circle of light.

Sena the tracker has joined us. He tells us about a bear he had encountered some weeks earlier.

'What's on the other side of the river?' Mithra asks. 'Is it all forest or are there villages?'

'Only jungle for many miles,' Sena says, waving his arm. 'Like Block III in Yala. Only here no outsiders coming to do buildings.'

Sena insists on speaking in English even when the questions are put to him in Sinhala. Harith smiles tolerantly when Mithra raises an eyebrow.

'Are we allowed to drive the jeep across?' Sidath asks. 'Is there a track?'

'No. Vehicles not allowed. Anyway can't go … no road,' Sena says. 'Have to go on foot.'

'What is there to see?'

'There are ruins there. People say it is Kuveni's palace, all covered in jungle.'

Harith sits up and takes an interest for the first time.

'Really? Kuveni's palace from Prince Vijaya's time?' he asks. There is suppressed excitement in his voice. 'Can you take us there?'

'Yes. I know the way ... but is against the rules,' Sena says. 'If warden find out, I will be suspended.'

'We will look after your trouble.' Harith solves every problem by looking after someone's trouble. 'Anyway no one will find out.'

'It is long way. Have to start early and carry our lunch,' Sena warns us. 'Can return by evening.'

15

Nali dithers for a while but finally thinks she will be safer with us than with Mithra who is staying back in the camp.

Sena leads the way, slashing at the dense undergrowth with his kathi. We walk in single file with Sidath following Sena and Harith behind me. The vegetation thins out after fifty yards and we are able to walk more easily. We still make detours to avoid heavy thickets of thorn bush.

Nali and I have risen early to prepare both breakfast and lunch. Our food and water is stuffed into the two haversacks we found in camp. Harith and Sidath, who have the porters' jobs, ask if I have filled them with rocks.

Sena seems less confident now about the route than he had been the previous night. He stops from time to time to climb a tree and look for landmarks. Once the sun comes over the trees I realise that we are travelling towards the northwest.

By force of habit, I break twigs and branches of bushes, snapping them and allowing the broken ends to hang down.

It is much further than we had expected. We stop to rest under a tree by the edge of a small clearing. Though we are thirsty, Sena warns us to use the water sparingly as we will not find natural water again till we get back to the stream.

'Let's turn back,' Nali says. 'It's dangerous to walk so

far from camp.'

'What do you say, Suji?' Harith turns to me. 'Do you also want to give up and go back?'

'I told you not to bring these girls along, aiya,' Sidath cuts in, 'they cry for their mothers at the slightest hardship.'

'Oh shut up, you big baby,' Nali responds warmly. 'We'll go on then. Let's see who cries for mummy first.'

There is no turning back after that. The boys pick up the bags and trudge after Sena; Nali makes a face as we stand up wearily to follow them.

It is nearly noon, and the sun is blazing down fiercely when we finally reach the site. They don't look like ruins at first, more like piles of boulders covered by scrub and jungle vines.

But when we look closely we can make out the massive stone blocks and columns underneath. They are ruins all right, but who can tell if it is Kuveni's palace?

We find a tiny clearing and collapse wearily on the ground. We decide to have our meal first and then explore the ruins. We'll have to be quick for we need to get back to camp before dark.

An elephant must have uprooted the small tree by the edge of the clearing for the branches have been stripped of all leaves. I see Sena trying to roll the trunk over with his foot to make more room for us. I am opening one of the haversacks when Sena screams.

His face is contorted with fear as he staggers towards us. I make out the words he keeps repeating and feel my skin crawl.

'Sarpayā gähuwā. Sarpayā gähuwā.

Snake bite.

Sena falls and struggles to raise himself. We run to help him. Everyone is speaking at once.

'What happened?'

'Where is the snake?'

'Where did it bite you?'

Sena is groaning in pain. He stretches out his right foot and I see the bite mark; two punctures on the instep by the ankle. The skin around the bite is already swelling up.

Sena's eyes are panic stricken. He grabs Harith's hand.

'Aney māva beraganna. Doshthara langata geniyanna.'

Please save me. Take me to a doctor.

Harith looks round helplessly. Nali and Sidath are in shock, unable to take in the extent of the disaster. I try desperately to control my own fears.

Think!

I know that I am the only one with any knowledge of the jungle. I have to come up with some plan.

'Harith, make him lie down on the ground,' I say quietly. 'If he moves about, the poison will spread faster.'

Harith looks at me in surprise. I stare back knowing that if he starts arguing with me we'll surely be in trouble.

Sena is sitting with his sarong tucked up, holding his injured foot with both hands. Harith pushes him gently to the ground and tells him to lie still.

'Aney sir, weydanāwa ivasanna bähä,' Sena groans.

Sir, I can't bear the pain.

Harith looks at me.

'Sidath, I need your shoes,' I tell the boy.

'What?' Sidath is still in shock; staring at the tracker's swollen foot in disbelief.

'Sidath, remove your shoes and give them to Suji,' Harith says gently, helping the boy to sit down.

Harith gives me the shoes and watches with a puzzled frown when I remove my tennis shoes and pull Sidath's heavy canvas boots on. They are far too big for my feet but will do for the moment.

I walk towards the fallen tree; Harith comes after me.

'What are you trying to do Suji?' he asks anxiously. 'We are in enough trouble already.'

'We must try to identify the snake. The doctors need to know what … antivenin to use.'

'Are you mad? The snake will bite you as well.'

'We won't go near the trunk … where Sena was,' I tell him. 'Let's twist the branches and see if the trunk rolls over. I just need to see the snake … if it's still there.'

It is scary because the grass is knee high and the snake might be anywhere. I tell Harith to stamp his feet as he walks and we reach the upper end of the fallen tree without mishap. Harith grasps one branch and heaves. I add my strength to his and then we feel the tree begin to roll over. I let go and run towards the spot where Sena was bitten.

There it is. I feel a shudder pass through me as I stare at it.

Triangular head with a white V on the snout; a fat brown body with dark markings.

Tith polonga.

I signal to Harith to let go and step back hurriedly. I struggle to control myself.

'Did you see it?' Harith asks. 'What is it?'

'Russell's viper. We call it tith polonga in the village.'

'Is it bad?'

'The worst.'

'What are we to do?'

Oh, why must you ask me? I am not meant to be a leader.

'Let's sit down and drink some water,' I say slowly, trying to calm my racing mind, trying to form some plan.

'Shouldn't we cut the bite mark,' Sidath asks, 'and … suck the poison out?'

'No. That might make it worse. We have to get him to hospital,' I tell them, 'otherwise he will die.'

'Will he be able to walk?' Nali asks, looking at Sena's prone figure.

'No. We'll have to carry him,' I say. 'If he tries to move about the poison will spread faster.'

'Carry him?' Sidath asks, his voice cracking under the strain. 'How can we carry him such a distance?'

'We'll have to make a stretcher,' I answer, searching desperately for solutions that no one else seems to have. 'We'll have to use his sarong to make one.'

'How do you know all this, Suji?' Nali asks in a tone of wonder. 'You have all the answers.'

I suddenly feel overwhelmed by the responsibility.

'Oh, what are you saying?' A bund bursts inside me and I feel tears pour down my face. 'I don't know anything! It's … it's only from a b …book Father Basil gave me to read to … improve my English. I'm trying to remember. I can't …'

I cover my face with my hands and bend over. I feel my body shuddering. I know I cannot cope with this; I just want to escape.

Nali puts her arm round me and the others gather round.

'It's all right nanga,' Nali says quietly. 'None of us knows anything either. Just tell us what you think is best.'

Harith uses Sena's kathi to cut three sticks, each about six feet in length. He eases the sarong off the injured man finding that he is wearing a pair of faded red shorts underneath. He puts away the cigarettes and matches that fall from Sena's waist.

We fold the sarong in two lengthwise and insert the sticks, two on one side and one on the other. We then realise that the sarong is too short to provide support for the damaged leg. Harith takes off his T-shirt and inserts the handles through the body of it and out through the sleeves. It might just do.

When we prepare to lift Sena onto the stretcher, I am dismayed to see that his condition has worsened. One eye is partially closed and he is groaning pitifully. The swelling has now extended halfway up his calf.

We transfer him gently on to the stretcher. He cries out in agony when we lift the injured foot. Harith speaks to him, asking if he wants some water.

No answer.

Harith looks up in dismay; the thought strikes us at the same time. We had assumed that, even as we carried him, Sena would guide us back to camp. That is not to be.

'How are we to find our way?' Harith asks worriedly. 'I know we walked towards the northwest this morning, but how can we find southeast when the sun is overhead?'

There is no sound except for Sena's groans as we grapple with this new crisis.

'I think … I can find the way,' I say shyly. 'I can try.'

I feel embarrassed when the others stare at me.

'How will you do that?' Harith asks.

'As children in my village, we were sent to the jungle to collect firewood. To find our way back, you know, we break twigs from bushes as we pass along. It's a … habit.'

Harith has a look of wonder on his face.

'And you did that when we were coming out this morning?'

'I … I think so,' I say hesitantly, 'most of the time anyway. I wasn't doing it consciously.'

I carry the kathi and lead the way. Nali follows close behind me with Harith and Sidath carrying the stretcher. I soon realise that, although both boys are strong and fit, carrying the stretcher is awkward. They have to keep it steady too, for Sena cries out whenever there is a jerk or bump.

The main delay is because of me. I have to progress from marker to marker with care, sometimes having to cast around to find the next one. This means the boys have to stand and wait till I give the signal, then repeat the same procedure till I find the next one. It is tedious and tiring.

And very slow.

We struggle on for over an hour when Harith calls for a break. The boys are bathed in perspiration and Sidath looks ready to collapse. We sit down in the shade of a tree to drink some water and rest.

The swelling has spread further up the leg. Sena is mumbling and groaning, turning his head from side to side. Harith pours a few drops of water in his mouth but it dribbles out again.

Sidath holds his hands out. I see that the rough wood

has rubbed raw red patches on his palms. Harith makes him pull off his shirt and uses the kathi to nick the seams so he can tear it. They wrap the strips of cloth round their hands like bandages.

Harith looks at me gravely.

'We won't get to camp before dark, will we?'

'No.'

'Do you mean we'll have to spend the night in the forest?' Nali is horrified. 'We'll be eaten up by animals. Can't we keep going?'

'No Nali, I won't be able to find the way after dark,' I explain carefully. 'The safest thing is to sit out the night and continue in the morning.'

'We are all hungry,' Sidath says. 'Why don't we have our lunch now?'

'That's all the food we have,' Harith answers. 'Why not keep going as long as we can? We won't have any more food till we get to camp.'

The trek is a nightmare in the blazing afternoon heat. Stop and look around for the next marker, signal to the others to come up. Forward to find the next marker, signal again.

Endlessly.

Sidath is drooping with fatigue; even Harith is nearing the limit of his endurance. Sidath trips and stumbles, letting his end of the stretcher crash to the ground. Sena, feeling the impact even in his semiconscious state, screams in pain.

We find a shady spot for the stretcher and gather round the stricken man. The foot has swelled up like a pumpkin; the purple skin around the fang marks is splitting open and oozing blood.

I notice that he is drooling from the left side of his

mouth. We use a moistened rag to squeeze a thimbleful of water between his lips.

We are too tired to eat but Harith says we must, for we will need energy to keep going. We open two of the parcels I had made that morning and share them, leaving the remainder for the night. Half an hour later we start off again.

The walks gradually become shorter and the rest stops longer as we skirt the edge of exhaustion. My mouth seems to be filled with dust and grit and my throat is so parched that it is painful to speak. We only have a single bottle of water left and have resolved to keep it for the night.

Harith and Sidath plod on doggedly but I can see that they can't keep going much longer. The sun is touching the treetops on our right when Harith calls out:

'Let's stop here; I've had … enough.'

He sinks to his knees and lays the stretcher on the ground. He stays in that position with his head down. I can see his chest rise and fall as he tries to recover his breath. Sidath has just thrown himself down on the ground; his eyes are closed. Nali sits listlessly, her face lined in fatigue.

I look around and find a shade tree with very little grass at its base. I use the kathi to clear the ground of small shrubs and animal droppings and call the others over.

Harith groans when I tell him they have to shift the stretcher again. I notice that the rags covering his hands are stained with dried blood. Nali and I help them to shift Sena to the site. We have to get organised before dark.

We gather round the stretcher.

What I see terrifies me.

There is more blood seeping from the area round the wound. The skin is cracking open to reveal naked flesh underneath and all the open areas are oozing. Sena's eyes are closed and I suspect that the left side of his face is paralysed. There is blood mixed with the spittle dripping from the corner of his mouth.

The man is dying.

Harith looks at me; the question is in his eyes.

Oh why are you looking at me? I only read a book about snakes and even that was years ago. What can I know about treating a dying man?

I fight to conceal the despair in my mind.

'All we can do is to keep him quiet and hope that he survives till morning. We can leave at dawn and try to reach the camp; then we can take him to the gate in the Prado.'

Harith thinks about it and nods his head.

'I suppose you are right,' he says. 'There is nothing more we can do.'

'We can light a fire,' I say. 'It will help to keep him warm. Keep animals away as well.'

'Hmm.'

'We need firewood.'

Harith sighs and gets wearily to his feet.

'Be careful,' I tell him, 'there's no one to carry *you*.'

That brings a small smile to his face. He picks up the kathi and walks away. I give Sena a little more water and moisten a rag to wipe his face with. We each swallow a small mouthful of water. We have just over half a bottle left.

Will it be enough for the night?

I make a small pile of dry leaves and grass and set it

alight using Sena's matches. I feed the tiny flame with dry twigs and branches and soon have a healthy fire going.

The brief twilight fades away and the forest grows dark.

We have finished the remaining food and have each had another mouthful of water. I check on Sena again. Even in the uncertain light I can see that the flow of blood-coloured fluid from his mouth has increased. I turn his head to the left to prevent it dripping down his neck. The boys move the stretcher closer to the fire.

Sena has stopped groaning. Is that a good sign or a bad one?

I study the others in the flickering light of the fire. The boys are bare-bodied, streaked and stained with perspiration and grime. Sidath is drooping with exhaustion and soon stretches himself on the ground. Nali, normally the talkative one, keeps glancing nervously over her shoulder. She finally decides to sit with her back to the tree and makes me come over and sit by her side.

The jungle noises begin. Rustles and squeaks in the shrubbery around us, grunts from a passing herd of pig and then, in the distance, a shrill trumpet of an elephant.

Nali grasps my hand.

'Wild animals are calling everywhere,' she says nervously. 'I'm sure we'll be killed and eaten before morning.'

'Elephants don't eat people,' I comfort her gently. 'Anyway if some animal comes, it will pick Harith because he'll make the biggest meal.'

'No,' Harith responds, 'it will pick one of you because your flesh is softer; easier to digest.'

'Oh shut up, both of you,' Nali says crossly. 'It's eerie enough without your nonsense.'

'Don't worry baba,' I tell Nali, squeezing her hand, 'no animal will bother us, especially while the fire is going.'

She calls me baba, baby, when I am stressed by situations in the city. We're in the jungle now and I must take care of her.

That night seems endless.

Mosquitoes torment us all through those dreary hours, driving us to the edge of insanity with their incessant buzzing. I get to my feet from time to time to tend the fire and check on Sena. I'm unable to see his chest rising and wonder fearfully if he is dead.

It gets cold towards morning. The fire has died down and the fuel wood is finished. I snuggle against Nali for warmth and try to sleep.

I must have dosed off because it is a birdcall that wakes me, a sweet, musical whistle. I call out and the others rouse themselves with groans of dismay. We look, and feel, like survivors from some natural disaster.

I crawl to Sena's stretcher; his hands are cold to the touch. I look up at Harith and he hurries over when he sees the distress on my face. The foot has ballooned out. The skin around the bite-mark has disappeared, leaving a huge, suppurating wound. There's more blood dripping from his mouth and the sarong below his groin is also stained with blood.

Harith takes hold of Sena's wrist and feels for his pulse. After several attempts he looks up.

'It's very faint but I can feel it beating,' he says. 'We'd better get started.'

We share the last of the water, half of a mouthful each, and leave. The boys still have the bloodstained wrappings on their hands but the skin underneath must be raw and painful. I see Harith's jaws clench as he lifts his end of the stretcher. Sidath, on the other hand, has recovered some of his good humour after a night's rest.

It's nice to be sixteen.

I lead the way and the pattern is the same. Walk forward; find a broken twig, signal to the others. Repeat.

And repeat.

Nali hears it first, a faint murmur in the air. I listen for a moment and my heart leaps. Surely that is the sound of water flowing over rocks. I tell the others to wait and run forward. The vegetation gets so dense I have to push my way through.

At the next moment I am standing on the bank and my heart is about to burst. There is another vehicle at the campsite and three or four people are standing there looking in our direction.

And Mithra.

I open my mouth to call them but the words don't come. The men see me and come splashing across the water.

I sit on the bank and start crying.

They look at our stretcher with open-mouthed amazement. The warden checks Sena's pulse and then orders his men to carry the stretcher to his vehicle. He instructs one of the trackers to remain with us till we leave; he also makes it very clear that he wants us out of the campsite by noon. Sooner if possible!

I know the warden is itching to pounce on someone but Sena is in a coma and we have probably saved the man's life.

'Sir,' I say diffidently as he climbs into his vehicle.

'Yes?' he snaps.

'The snake … it was a Russell's viper.'

'What? Are you sure?'

'Yes. Yes, I'm sure.'

'I'll tell the doctor,' he says grudgingly. 'You … did a good job, all of you, to bring him back. Thank you.'

We lie in the water. I feel like a sponge, soaking up moisture through my skin. The weariness slowly leaks away.

Mithra is sitting on a rock, listening to Nali relate details of our adventure.

'How did you inform the warden?' Harith asks suddenly. 'He didn't come here by accident, did he?'

'I knew something had gone wrong,' Mithra says, 'so at dawn I … er … drove your Prado down the track Harith, till I saw another vehicle. This other party, they took me to the gate to find the warden.'

'Rubbish, you can't drive!'

'I … know the theory of it,' Mithra says with an easy smile, 'it wasn't too difficult.'

'But how did you use the clutch with … you know…'

'With one leg? That's easy, I just drove in first gear,' Mithra is grinning happily now. 'Every time I touched the brake, the stupid engine stalled. I then had to move the gear to neutral, start the engine and put it in first gear again. No problem.'

'Oh no, this bugger has ruined my vehicle,' Harith groans. 'What am I to tell my father?'

Fortunately the Prado has not suffered any ill effects and starts off smoothly when we leave after lunch. The boys have recovered their high spirits and chatter away merrily.

The reaction just makes me drowsy; I sleep through most of the journey back to Colombo.

JOURNAL III

A belief in a supernatural source of evil is not necessary;
men alone are capable of every wickedness.

Joseph Conrad

News item
20th August

PEOPLES FRONT JSP COALITION SWEEPS TO POWER

The Peoples Front, with its coalition partner JSP, scored a resounding win at the general election held on Wednesday. The coalition has already garnered 115 seats giving it an absolute majority in the 225-seat chamber. 5 results are still to be declared.

The National Alliance government suffered humiliating losses even in its strongholds in the western and central provinces. 7 government ministers have lost their seats.

Reliable sources within the Peoples Front have reported that the JSP is demanding several key ministries as the price of its support. The President, as leader of the PF and the coalition, is expected to announce his cabinet in the next few days.

News item
14th September

MEGA DEVELOPMENT PROJECT IN CINNAMON GARDENS

Construction work on the massive Maya City development project was launched at a lavish ceremony last morning. The multi billion-rupee project will comprise a large shopping mall, cinema complex, amusement park and hotel.

Chairman Lee Kwok Swee promised that the project would be completed in two and a half years. Presidential advisor Suraj Pinto, widely believed to be the man responsible for bringing the investor to Sri Lanka, announced that this was the first of several major projects the new government had planned.

News item
23rd September

FORESTRY PROJECT APPROVED AFTER CABINET TUSSLE

Cabinet approved businessman Somasiri Jayakody's Goldwood project yesterday. The promoters propose to replant degraded forest with valuable timber that will be progressively harvested by the company when the trees are mature. An extent of one thousand acres of scrub jungle in the Monaragala district has been allocated for the project. The designated land lies to the north of the Yala National Park.

A reliable source reports that Mahaweli Minister, Kalinga Lokuge, vehemently opposed the project. JSP Minister Lokuge objected on the grounds that the activity would have a negative impact on block three of the Yala National Park.

We stand for organized terror ...
Terrorism is an absolute necessity in time of revolution.

Felix Dzerzhinsky

16

We won!

I had worked very hard, spending the long vacation campaigning from house to house in the area assigned to my team. I had not wanted to work in my own village, for I knew it would upset Father Basil. Kumudu had placed me with a group working in Tangalle and this had suited me very well.

Kumudu summons a meeting of our members on the very first day of the semester. All the freshers are herded together to one side of the platform; as a final year senior I have a prominent place in front of it. It is hard to describe the euphoria I feel at the moment when Kumudu stands up to speak.

'My brothers and sisters, a new era has dawned on our motherland. Can you not sense it in the air? Can you not feel it in your heart? I can truthfully say that you, each and every one, helped to achieve this great victory.

'Those who are seniors today will agree that it was the discipline we taught you during the rag that gave you the strength and unity for this task. Freshers, you must keep this in mind when you face the rag. Join us when the rag is over so that we can continue this great mission.

'The seniors have met our brother and leader Kalinga Lokuge. All of you will now know that he has been appointed Minister for Mahaweli and Wildlife.'

Kumudu pauses as the applause and whistles echo round the playground.

Why shouldn't we shout for joy? Our own leader is now in a position of power.

When the applause dies down Kumudu surveys the crowd before him; he seems to gather himself.

'Brothers and sisters, this is not the end of our struggle, it is the beginning. It is the first, small step of our journey. Our leader has set a goal for us; that goal will bring prosperity and justice to our people.

'Believe in the goal and trust our leader.'

Kumudu goes on:

'I am happy to inform you that I have been selected to continue Kalinga's work as national convenor of the SUF. It will be my duty to gather all poor students of our land under our banner. The students will give our leader the power to destroy this corrupt system in a wave of fire.

'I will be leaving the campus once a new leader is selected for the union here.'

Nali is seated with me in the canteen waiting for the others.

'You are a sneaky girl, Suji,' she complains grumpily. 'Did you really spend the entire vacation working for those rascals?'

'Oh yes,' I say happily, 'and we won. It was all due to my hard work.'

'I feel like giving you a good smack,' she growls. 'Why didn't you tell me?'

'You would have told me not to go,' I say simply, earning an angry glare. Nali opens her mouth to say something nasty, and then shuts it again when Mithra limps over to join us.

'Oho, so our village girl is going to be in power, is

she?' he asks with his usual grin. 'We'll have to treat her with respect now.'

'I'll give her respect! Just look at the wretch!' Nali demands bitterly. 'She acts like an innocent baby but she's quietly working to bring those maniacs to power.'

We are still arguing when Harith joins us.

He should not have been on campus at all for his final examination had been held at the end of the last semester. Being totally unprepared for it due to his union activities, he had submitted a medical certificate and earned himself another year on campus.

We know that the union on which he had lavished all his devotion is under severe threat. The Independent Student Union has survived, despite its smaller numbers, due to support from the rightist National Alliance government. Now, with the JSP as a coalition partner in the new government, the SSU will make every effort to crush it completely.

I am happy for the SSU, of course, but concerned about Harith.

'Have you come to pay your respects to our new boss?' Mithra asks, pointing at me.

'Oh, be quiet Mithra,' I say, 'otherwise I'll have you ragged again.'

'What about our union?' Nali asks Harith. 'They will come after us now, won't they?'

Harith's grin fades away as he looks at Nali.

'Yes. Yes, they'll attack our members,' he says seriously. 'A man called me on my mobile ... gave me a week to disband the union.'

'And if you don't?'

'The caller warned that ... I would be killed.'

'My God! Do you think he was serious?' Nali gasps.

'I don't know.'

'Are you going to do it then?' Mithra asks, no longer amused. 'Will you disband the union?'

'My father believes that you should never give in when someone puts pressure on you. It only encourages them to push some more,' Harith says with quiet determination. 'No, I'm not going to disband the union.'

*

I manage to catch Kumudu alone in the union office. He looks surprised, for I have always avoided conversation with him.

'Yes, Sujatha?' he asks with a slight frown. 'What brings you here?'

'I have been a loyal member of the union for over two years now. I worked hard during the election,' I start boldly enough but then lose confidence. 'I have now come to … ask a favour.'

'Our members are expected to work because they believe in our cause,' he answers sternly. 'They are not entitled to seek favours in return.'

'I must ask you just the same. It … it is very important to me.'

'What is it? What do you want so badly?'

'It is about Harith Jayakody,' I say hesitantly. 'They have threatened to kill him if he doesn't disband the ISF.'

'So? Just tell the bastard to close it down,' he snarls dismissively, 'and then he'll have no problem.'

'He won't disband the union.'

'He has to pay the price then.'

'He can't close it without losing face,' I say desperately. 'His members are already leaving … the union will not be a threat to us. Can't you leave him alone?'

I realise that my words have made him very angry.

'What is that bastard to you?' Kumudu demands, eyes boring into mine. 'Is he your boyfriend? Is that why you are so concerned?'

'No. I swear he is just a friend,' I say desperately, wondering if I have placed Harith in even greater danger. 'I am asking because he is my friend.'

'You were allowed to keep your … precious friends all this time only because I … I overruled the others and permitted it,' he answers coldly, 'but this is too much. He has to fall in with our demands or … face the consequences.'

I don't realise that I'm crying till I feel the wetness on my cheeks.

'Oh please, please … he is a good, kind person,' I say between sobs. 'Please don't allow anything to happen to him. Please … I beg you.'

Kumudu looks at me with some surprise. I stand before him with the tears pouring down my face, unable to carry on. He looks down at his hands spread out on the table before him.

'All right,' he says with a sigh. 'I can't promise anything but I'll ask the central committee to reconsider their decision.'

I am unable to speak, even to thank him; tears still course down my face, tears of relief now. I turn to leave.

'Sujatha,' he calls after me.

I stop by the door.

'You'd better wipe your face before you leave. People will think I have assaulted you.'

There is, for the first time, a touch of amusement in his tone.

17

Mithra tells me that Palitha, the boy from my parents' village of Medamulana, wants to speak to me. I know that Palitha is following a management course with Mithra. I had previously avoided contact with him for fear that any conversation will inevitably lead to the subject of my family and why I went away.

I could not bear that.

I notice Palitha in the canteen that afternoon. He is sitting alone with an empty cup of tea on the table before him. He looks at me with a strange, lost expression in his eyes.

Is he appealing for help? What can he want from me?

He looks down hurriedly when some others walk into the canteen behind me.

I see Harith and Mithra having their lunch and join them. They are discussing Somasiri Jayakody's forestry project.

'Is your father really going ahead with that project?' Mithra asks. 'It must require a massive investment.'

'I think he's crazy but yes, he's going ahead,' Harith says with a rueful grin. 'Of course he's got this Malaysian group putting up a good part of the money.'

'Has the land been released to him?' Nali asks.

'Oh yes, he's got the land and work has started already. My father is very keen on the project; he spends a lot of time at the site,' Harith says.

'How long will it take to clear the scrub and plant the whole extent?' Mithra asks. 'A thousand acres is a very large undertaking, isn't it?'

'The plan is to finish it in two years, I believe,' Harith has a small worry-frown on his face, 'but there seem to be some local problems. Our work crews have been assaulted and even my father is being threatened. Someone wants him to abandon the project.'

'Is he going to?' Nali asks.

'No,' Harith responds with a grin. 'Jayakody folk don't give in to threats.'

We all laugh.

'Where is this land?' I ask.

'It is south of Monaragala, bordering block three of the Yala Park. That stupid Kalinga objects to the project, saying it will interfere with wildlife in the park. Actually it won't affect the animals at all because we'll allow the area to go back to forest once replanting is done. The man's mad.'

I am walking towards the hostel that evening when I hear someone call my name.

'Sujatha.'

I turn to find Palitha standing there, partly concealed behind a tree.

'Sujatha, I … I need your help,' he stammers. 'Please, can you…'

His condition shocks me, for his forehead is beaded with perspiration; his eyes have a desperate, hunted look.

'What's the matter?' I ask, ashamed that my selfish concerns had kept me from speaking to him earlier.

'Talk to them. Please speak to them … ask them to release me,' he whispers hoarsely. 'I hear that the leaders will listen to you … please.'

'You want to leave the union?' I ask, puzzled. 'Why shouldn't you?'

'Yes … No.' His fear has made him incoherent. 'Assure them … I will never tell anyone, I … I promise. Just let me …'

Palitha looks past me; his expression changes abruptly. He turns and walks away without another word.

Three girls are walking towards the hostel. One of them, Padma, is a committee member of the SSU. She had failed her finals and has returned to campus for a second attempt. She leaves the others and walks up to me.

'What did that renegade want?' she demands roughly. 'What is he doing here?'

'He asked me to do him a favour,' I answer easily. I will not allow myself to be bullied. 'Before he could tell me what it was, he saw you … and ran away. What has he done? Why is he frightened?'

'It's none of your business,' Padma says sharply. 'Don't get involved with him if you want to stay out of trouble.'

*

Nali and I are leaving the faculty building for lunch when we hear a commotion near the gate. There is a fight in progress, with two groups shouting and striking at each other in a furious brawl.

I want to run to the first floor so we can watch the mêlèe from a safe distance but Nali can never resist a bit of excitement. She drags me to the rear of the guardroom where some other students have also taken shelter.

Students are pushing and grappling with each other.

We can actually hear gasps of pain as fists thud into ribs.

'Oh no,' Nali cries out in horror, 'Harith is in the thick of it. I'm sure I saw him.'

One boy falls to the ground, another reels away from the mob holding his head.

The VC comes striding up, followed by the marshals. There is a warning shout; one lot break off and run down the road. The others stand there in a daze, gingerly touching their cuts and bruises.

The VC pounces on them furiously.

'What's going on here?' he roars. 'You fellows are here to study, not to play politics. I feel like sacking the lot of you.'

'Sir, we were just leaving for lunch when we were attacked by SSU members,' Harith speaks up boldly. 'There was no provocation. We were only defending ourselves.'

'Rubbish, it takes two sides to have a fight,' the VC snaps dismissively. 'You're Jayakody aren't you? I suspended you once before. This time I'll have to sack you.'

'But sir …,' Harith begins.

The marshals have been helping the fallen boys to their feet.

One marshal calls out:

'Sir, ekkenekuta pihiyen änalā. Ley hämathänama!'

Sir, one of them has been stabbed. There is blood everywhere.

Once the fighting stops we edge forward till there is a circle of interested onlookers surrounding the VC. The wounded boy had been lying on his face. There is a gasp of dismay when the marshal turns him over, for his shirtfront is soaked in blood.

The marshal cradles the boy's head and I see his face for the first time; the features are unmistakable.

Palitha.

The VC reacts well although he is clearly dismayed by the violence. He hurriedly sends one of the marshals to fetch his car. He turns to Harith.

'Who is this boy? Is he a member of your union?'

'No sir,' Harith says with a puzzled frown. 'I think he belongs to the SSU.'

'Then one of you hooligans stabbed him.'

'No sir, no! We don't carry knives,' Harith protests. 'He … this boy came towards me … then the other SSU fellows attacked us.'

'Rubbish!' the VC thunders. 'Why should they attack one of their own members? It has to be one of you … you're just a bunch of thugs. I'm handing you over to the police.'

One of the lecturers is told to call the police; the marshals are instructed to keep a close watch on Harith and the others till the police arrive. We look on silently as Palitha is lifted to the rear seat of a vehicle and driven away.

Nali is hanging on my arm; I feel her fingers digging painfully into my skin.

'Oh no. Surely they can't think Harith would do a thing like that?' she moans. 'Harith would never carry a knife. How can the VC suspect him?'

'Maybe it was one of the others,' I say for want of a better answer.

'No, no! I know them all … they will never stab anyone,' Nali says and then continues in a puzzled tone, 'but who else could it be? It … has to be one of them. One of the SSU thugs.'

'What do you mean?'

'What if one of them had a knife and … maybe Palitha got cut by accident.'

I feel confused and more than a little frightened.

I have to agree with Nali; the knife must belong to one of the attackers … or to Palitha himself. They had pounced on Harith and his friends without any provocation.

When he met me yesterday, Palitha had been terrified about something. He ran away the moment he saw Padma, a leader of his union. Why should he now join other SSU members to attack Harith?

It didn't make sense.

Harith had said that Palitha had come towards him; the others had attacked them immediately afterwards. What if Palitha had been trying to find refuge with Harith? What if he had tried to exchange some information for protection in Harith's union?

Then the intended victim must have been Palitha all along. They wanted to silence him … and blame the attack on Harith's union.

*

Nali has been in tears since the police took Harith away.

We call his home soon after the incident. Nali speaks to Harith's mother and spends the next ten minutes trying to calm her hysterical reaction. We know there is no purpose in hanging around the police station so I ask Nali to come with me to the hospital.

'Why do you want to visit that loser?' Nali asks callously. 'He's one of them.'

'You're forgetting that poor boy is from my village,' I say, 'and he's a union member.'

'Ahh rubbish,' Nali responds grumpily. 'You're up to something. I can tell from that crafty look on your face.'

'Palitha will know who stabbed him,' I tell her. 'He might trust me enough to tell me the truth.'

Nali isn't convinced at all but she agrees to accompany me.

They don't let us in. The girl at the information counter tells us brusquely that the patient is in intensive care and no visitors are allowed.

We are at lunch the next day when Harith walks in. We jump up excitedly, both speaking at the same time.

'What happened?'

'When were you released?'

'Is everything all right?'

'Did they harass you?'

Harith is, as always, smiling easily but black smudges under his eyes signal the strain he is under. He sinks wearily into a chair.

'The cops searched us and didn't find any knife or bloodstains. Just the same they locked us in a cell for the night,' Harith tells us. 'The wretched VC prejudiced them so much, I was afraid the cops would try to plant some evidence on us.'

'Didn't your father come?' Nali asks.

'It's a good thing you informed them, Nala. My father arrived with a lawyer and created a huge fuss. After that they let us out of the cell even though they kept us at the station till this morning.'

'Is it safe for you to be here?' Nali asks anxiously. 'I mean … those devils might attack you again.'

'My father insisted on sending two of his security

men with me,' Harith answers with an embarrassed laugh. 'They are standing outside even now.'

There is a new girl at the hospital information desk today but she is just as unhelpful. Palitha is still in intensive care, no visitors. When I turn to leave I find a grey haired woman looking intently at me.

I study the worn features for a moment, taking in the lined face and tearful eyes. Who can she be?

'Mey apey Sujatha kella neydhai?' she asks. *'Balanna magey puthata karapu dey.'*

Isn't this our Sujatha girl? See what they have done to my son.

Palitha's mother!

I don't remember the face but I do feel sorry for her as she stands there helplessly, twisting the free end of her sari. I take her by the arm and lead her to a canteen outside the main gate.

We sit at a fly-infested table and order two cups of tea.

'Nända, what is Palitha's condition?' I ask. 'Were you able to see him?'

'No, duwa. He is … unconscious … in some special room. They say … no visitors … allowed. I … don't know what to do …'

Tears are streaming down her cheeks. She makes no attempt to wipe them off. I search my mind for something to say, anything to ease her pain.

'Nända, was Palitha afraid of anyone?' I ask. 'Was he in any trouble?'

She looks stunned.

'Yes, yes! I think something had happened.' she says eagerly. 'He was away for most of the vacation and came home only for the final week. But he had changed, wouldn't talk to anyone, didn't go out.'

'Did he tell you what the trouble was?'

'No. He didn't speak very much but he seemed worried.'

'Do you know where he had been during the vacation?'

Please say yes. If you say he stayed with some relative it will be such a relief.

'No. I don't know. He said it is some kind of training.'

'Had he gone for this training before?'

'Yes. Almost every vacation he went,' she says, 'and was very happy when he came home afterwards. Only this time he was different … afraid.'

*

The Dean announces that Palitha died last night. He had never regained consciousness.

Harith tells us that that the police have questioned 'that bearded thug' Kumudu but have released him for lack of evidence. No one, it seems, is able to identify the boys who attacked Harith's group that day.

Palitha's death makes me realise that there is something going on that is far more serious than I had first imagined. I also realise that I have, by either good or bad luck, stumbled on information unknown to anyone else.

I had volunteered for Giniralla but Kumudu had prevented me from joining. It is obvious to me now that

Palitha had joined the program.

He had attended training courses during all the vacation periods. What kind of training had it been that had taken nearly three years?

Something had happened during the last vacation that had made Palitha want to leave the program. Palitha had wanted me to assure the leadership that he would never tell anyone. What had he seen or heard that had frightened him so much?

Kumudu told me that no one would be allowed to leave Ginirälla!

I try to put my thoughts in order.

I still believe in Kalinga and his cause. I am convinced that Kalinga, Kumudu and the other leaders are totally sincere in their promise to bring a new life to our rural poor. I am convinced that they have a good plan and it will not be long before that comes to fruition. My trust in them is unshaken.

Ginirälla is clearly an important part of Kalinga's plan. In trying to leave the project, Palitha must have become a danger to it.

So they have had to execute him for the sake of their just cause. That cause is so worthy; the needs of the poor are so urgent, that even killing is justified.

Can I accept that?

I'm not sure.

I know I have to keep my doubts well concealed. At all costs I must not to be seen as a threat. I decide to carry on with my studies and my union tasks as if nothing has changed.

But my uneasiness will not go away.

I buy a thick exercise book that afternoon and begin writing an account of all that has happened since I came to Jaypura.

About my work with the union, about what I have heard and seen.

About Ginirälla!

18

We are just two weeks into the final semester when I get Father Basil's letter. I slip away to read it in the privacy of my bunk.

Samagi Seva Sevana
Angunuwewa.

20th October

My dear Sujatha,

I am sorry I was away during your vacation for I had been looking forward to meeting you. Obedience, as you know, is an important requirement in the Jesuit order; so when my superiors assigned me to another project, I had no choice but to comply.

You are now close to your goal. You were full of doubt when we first discussed the plan, so unsure of your own capabilities. But I never doubted your ability; I knew that you would succeed. What you have achieved so far has been ENTIRELY due to your courage and perseverance. I am absolutely sure that you will see it through to the end.

Your final examinations will, I believe, be held in about two months. You must put aside all other interests and activities and concentrate on your preparation. A good result will greatly help your future career.

I have been in touch with Ms. Decima who seems to have become very fond of you. You will be happy to hear that she has offered to pay your fees for the diploma course in journalism at the Open University. You will need to find part time employment while you follow this course. It will be ideal if you are able to persuade a newspaper to take you on as a freelance journalist. But there will be time enough to think about that when the examinations are over.

Your family is well and your cousin Loku has now agreed to help in the nursery school. She is keen on her studies too. I hope she, and the mischievous little Punchi, will follow in the footsteps of their clever elder sister.

I pray for you every day,
Sincerely

Fr. Basil Fernando S.J.

P. S.

I have heard rumours that young people, even students, from our village are being taken to the forest for 'leadership' training. I did not take notice till, one night last week, some young men came to see me. They told me that the work I am doing does not help the poor in the long term, it only dulls their pain for the moment. They wanted me to give up my work and leave the village.

These are all boys I have known since they were toddlers, but they seem strangers now, and so angry. Hinnihamy's son Ranjit, who was in your class, appears to be their leader. I blame myself. If I had spent more time with these young people, if I had found a way to give them hope for the future, perhaps they might not have fallen for this revolutionary nonsense. I must still try to reach them; maybe it is not too late.

Do not worry about this, Sujatha, for this is the kind of situation that we Jesuits are trained to handle. Concentrate on your studies and look to the future, not to the past.

19

News item
12th November

SOMASIRI JAYAKODY SLAIN AT GOLDWOOD PROJECT SITE

Entrepreneur Somasiri Jayakody and his son Sidath (18) were gunned down by unknown assailants while inspecting their project site last afternoon.

The controversial Goldwood project seeks to replant degraded scrub jungle with valuable timber. The government has allocated a thousand acres in the Monaragala district for the enterprise despite objections by their JSP coalition partners.

Goldwood staff report that Jayakody had received numerous threats but had been determined to press ahead with the scheme. Nearly one third of the allotted land has already been replanted.

Jayakody was being driven along a rough track within the project area when gunmen had opened fire with automatic weapons. The driver had been killed instantly while Jayakody and his son appear to have sustained only minor injuries in the initial assault.

The survivors had been taken out of the vehicle, made to kneel by the side of the track and then shot in the back of the head. Police have ruled out robbery as a motive and believe that this is a professional assassination. A special police team from Colombo is conducting investigations.

*

I feel I am being torn in two. The JSP was vehemently opposed to the forestry project from the beginning, so in all probability they are responsible for this killing. I cannot believe that they are mindless thugs so there must, somewhere, be a good and proper reason. Somehow the Goldwood scheme must stand in the way of their grand design, that final plan.

But the person killed is not a distant figure. This is Harith's father … and Sidath, a boy of eighteen.

How can I live with this? How can I justify my support of the JSP, and their promise to liberate the downtrodden, when the price of liberation seems to keep rising all the time?

We try to keep busy; it stops conscious thought.

Harith's mother breaks down when she hears the news and has to be sedated. She is now confined to an upstairs bedroom under the care of an old servant. Harith appears to be outwardly calm but I see the shocked dismay in his eyes. He, apparently not over-fond of his relatives, is trying to cope with all the funeral arrangements by himself.

With some help from his friends!

Nali is a wonderful organiser, even when her cheeks are damp with tears. While a shattered and shaky looking Harith greets visitors and accepts their condolences, Nali works behind the scenes and orders her assistants about with grim efficiency.

Her assistants are Mithra and I.

*

It is late when the last visitor leaves. Harith turns down numerous offers from relatives to stay the night and ushers the stragglers out with barely concealed impatience. When we come to say goodbye he seems surprised.

'Where are you going?' he asks. 'Stay. Stay the night.'

'We'd be in the way,' Mithra says. 'We thought you might want to be alone.'

'No, no. I need you here … I need to talk with someone to keep from going mad.'

We freshen up and sit in the garden to talk. We talk of the future to keep the horror of the present away.

'I'll have to give up studies,' Harith tells us softly. 'There's no one else to take care of the business.'

'There must be managers, surely,' Mithra protests, 'can't they carry on till you finish your finals?'

'No. No, I don't think that will work,' Harith answers. 'My father was very involved in day-to-day running. You need that in the motor spares business.'

'What … what about his project,' Nali asks. I can sense the concern in her tone. 'You'll close that down, won't you?'

Harith's face is in shadow so I can't see his expression, but I notice that he sits straighter in his chair. His voice, when he finally answers, is unusually harsh.

'No. I most certainly won't close it down. That's the main reason I want to get involved straight away. I want to show these bastards that the Jayakody family can't be frightened off.'

'But Hari … it will be very dangerous, surely,' Nali wails. 'They'll try to kill you as well.'

'My father didn't take the threat seriously but I will. I'm hiring the best possible security; we have the resources,' Harith says calmly. 'Enough about my plans. Tell me what you will be doing after the finals.'

They look at me.

'I want to get a job as a trainee journalist,' I tell them shyly. 'If you know anyone in the business, now is the time to use your influence.'

'Aren't you planning to do a diploma course at the Open University?' Mithra asks.

'Well, yes. Miss Decima has agreed to pay my fees but I need a job to support myself.'

'OK, so we have one potentially famous journalist,' Mithra says mockingly. 'You Nali, what about you?'

'My father wants me to get a safe government job, preferably as a teacher,' Nali says with a grin. 'I suppose he thinks teachers are easy to marry off.'

'He'll still need a hefty dowry, won't he?' Mithra asks with a wicked grin. 'Even if you are a government teacher.'

'Oh shut up, Mithra,' I protest indignantly. 'Enough about us! What are you planning to do next year, apart from telling lies about girls?'

Mithra's mischievous grin vanishes.

'My mother's sister lives in Melbourne,' he says soberly. 'She's sponsoring me, you know, to do a masters at Monash.'

'That's wonderful, Mithra,' I say. 'How long will you be away?'

He looks at me for a moment before answering.

'My mother wants me to apply for resident status,' he says, his eyes now on the ground. 'She says the facilities are better there, you know, to cope with … my disability.'

Nali and I share a huge double bed in a guest room.

'I feel a bit depressed that Mithra is going away,' I say, looking up at the ceiling where a security light from the garden is making a curious pattern. 'I thought … I thought we'd all stay in touch afterwards.'

'Harith and I will be here, baba,' Nali says comfortingly. 'Anyway it's good for Mithra to get away from his awful father. That must be why he wants to go.'

'Mmm. I suppose we must be happy for him,' I say, 'but I'm going to miss his antics.'

'I'm still mad at him for saying I'll need a hefty dowry,' Nali says. 'Bloody cheek.'

'Yes, he's too much.'

'Let's teach him a good lesson,' Nali says, sitting up suddenly. 'Did you know he's sleeping in Sidath's room?'

'So?'

'Let's cover our heads with a sheet and creep into his room. When he sees a ghost hovering over the bed he'll think Sidath has come back.'

'Oh, he'll scream like a baby,' I clap my hands gleefully. 'Where is Sidath's room anyway?'

'Harith told me it's at the end of the corridor.'

'We'll give him a real send-off,' I say. 'Something to remind him of us when he's in Australia.'

Our bedroom opens directly into the foyer. A corridor leads off to the left, dark and deathly quiet.

Except for the giggles that we struggle vainly to suppress.

We walk side by side, each with an arm round the other's waist. The bed-sheet is draped across our heads with enough slack to pull down over our faces at the critical moment.

The foyer is dimly lit from the hall below but the corridor is black as tar. We feel our way forward gingerly till Nali stubs her toe on a chair and swears. Her moan of agony turns to fury when I start giggling again.

We reach the door at last.

Nali turns the handle and eases the door open. I can feel my heart thudding painfully as we peer into the room. A tiny night-lamp near the bathroom throws just enough light to make out the bed in the middle of the room, a pale covering sheet drawn up to the neck and a dark head against the pillow.

I feel a nervous giggle bubbling up; it ends in a gasp of pain when Nali pinches me.

We creep to the foot of the bed and, as we had done in rehearsal, lower the sheet over our faces to make a frightful, double headed apparition. I can't wait to hear Mithra's terrified scream.

'HARRH, HARRH, HARRH.' That's Nali growling.

'I'm Sidath. I'm Sidath,' I say, attempting a deep tone but ending in a giggly squeak.

'EEEEEEEEEEEEEEEEEEEEEH'

The scream is loud enough to raise the dead, loud enough, nearly, to stop my heart. The screamer is not Mithra.

A female voice!

We might argue about everything, Nali and I, but we are in full agreement at that moment. We need to be somewhere else, and right now.

We turn to run, trip over the sheet and go sprawling on the ground.

'DEIYANEY MAGEY PUTHA ÄVILLĀ. MAGEY PUTHA ÄVILLĀ.

Oh God, my son has come. My son has come.

We scramble out of the room on all fours, dragging the wretched bed-sheet behind us. Lights are coming on in the other rooms; we can hear feet thudding on the floor. Behind us the old lady is calling out again, and at the top of her voice:

'YANNA EPĀ PUTHEY. ANEY YANNA EPĀ.'

Don't go son. Please don't go.

Once in the corridor we are able to see well enough to run. I get the door of our room shut just before excited voices erupt in the corridor.

Running footsteps and shrill voices fill the house for a full ten minutes before the commotion tapers off. I am just beginning to think we have got away with it when I hear the door open. The lights come on.

We pretend to be asleep.

The next moment I am howling in pain and outrage as someone whacks me on the head with a pillow. Nali gets the next blow.

Harith stands by the bed, pillow in hand; a grinning Mithra sits at the foot of the bed.

'What are you doing in our room?' Nali yells, opting for attack. 'And why are you hitting us?'

'You two devils did something to frighten my mother, I'm sure of it,' Harith says grimly. 'Admit it.'

'Are you mad? How could we have done anything?' Nali responds gamely. 'We were fast asleep. Ask Suji if you don't believe me.'

'You're both liars,' he replies. 'If you had come out during the commotion I might have swallowed it but, like donkeys, you pretended to sleep through all that noise.'

Nali and I look at each other; I see her resigned shrug.

'We ... wanted to scare Mithra because he was mean to us,' I admit sheepishly. 'We covered ourselves with a bed-sheet and said ... and said it was Sidath.'

'So why did you idiots go to my mother's room?'

'You told me Mithra's room is the last one,' Nali complains crossly. 'It's all your fault.'

'Mithra is in the last room,' Harith says, 'on the other side.'

'Oh.'

'I'm so sorry, Harith, your mother is already suffering enough,' I say contritely. 'We didn't mean to frighten her. It was a terrible thing to do.'

'No harm done, actually,' Harith responds easily. 'I told old Maggie to sleep in her room. She's settled down now.'

'It must have been a severe shock. We must apologise in the morning.'

'Better not! She really believes Sidath visited her with a message. Now she'll spend her time offering poojas for his restless spirit.'

Harith grumbles that he is no longer sleepy. He suggests that we all go down and make coffee. Nali quickly shoots that idea down, knowing we are both wearing Harith's oversized t-shirts and are in no state to go roaming around the house. Even now we lie there awkwardly with the sheet pulled modestly up to our necks.

The boys don't seem concerned. They settle down for a chat.

I still feel bad about what we did to that poor lady. I must have dozed off soon afterwards but my sleep is uneasy. The box-spring mattress is soft and yields easily even under my slight weight; so different from the mattress on the boarded bunk in the hostel.

Unwanted memories flit through my mind like thieves in the night.

Kaneru seeds have a fleshy green covering that turns

black when the seeds mature. The seeds had been cracked open, white kernels collected in a coconut shell. He had mixed the pulp with sugar before eating it.

We found him sprawled on the kitchen floor when we came home, my little brother and I. Our screams brought neighbours who lifted him out of the pool of dried blood and vomit.

They said he was dead.

I had looked down at his lifeless body with relief … and confusion.

Then in my desperate need I ran to Yasawathi for help. Instead of helping she chose to accuse me. She said he had killed himself out of shame. Shame for what I had done, so it was entirely my fault. Then she had assaulted me almost to the point of death.

I had been twelve years old at the time.

I will always be twelve years old.

Terror fills my mind again, terror and despair. In need of reassurance, I reach out to touch Nali on her shoulder.

She's not there.

The door to the bathroom is open and the light is off, so she isn't there either. I carefully open the bedroom door and look along the corridor.

Too dark.

The stairs leading to the hall are on the far side of the foyer and there I see the silhouette of two heads. Unmistakably Harith and Nali seated on the steps, heads close together, speaking in whispers.

I step back into the room and shut the door. I cannot fully describe the feeling of wonder and delight that banishes, for a while, my dark memories.

I put my head down and fall asleep immediately.

20

My aunt is weeping so loudly I cannot make out what she is saying. I am frantic with worry that something has happened to one of the girls.

'Aney duwey, eyāta pihiyen änalā,' she says between sobs. *'Kāmarey hämathänama ley.'*

Oh daughter, he has been stabbed. There's blood all over the room.

'Kātada thuwāla, nändey, māmatada?'

Who has been hurt? Is it uncle?

More weeping. She must be holding the telephone awkwardly for her voice is faint and indistinct.

'Nähä nähä, māma nevei. … Father,' she wails. *'Father Basil wa thamai käpuwey.'*

No no, not uncle. Father. They have stabbed Father Basil.

I know my hand is shaking as I press the receiver against my ear. My chest is constricted, I cannot breathe.

'Fatherta hungak thuwālada? Kohetada genichchey?'

Is Father badly hurt? Where did they take him?

'Father ethanama malā.'

Father died on the spot.

No. No. No. No. No. No.

I feel my knees collapse under me as I sink to the ground. I know that my whole body is racked by convulsions. I grasp my knees and curl into a ball.

I hear the excited chatter of the office staff trying to

help me to my feet, then the Dean summoning a nurse from the infirmary. They take me away and give me some pills to swallow.

The pills make me drowsy but they don't take away the pain.

How am I to ease this agony? I had been traumatized to the point of madness when he met me for the first time. He, more than any other, had helped rebuild my life. He had given me hope and strength, shown me a future. How will I ever fill the void he has left behind?

*

I am still in the infirmary, unable to shake off my despair when Miss Decima comes to see me. When the nurse ushers her in, she doesn't say a word; just gathers me in her arms and hugs me.

And we cry and cry till there are no tears left.

'I want … I want to attend his funeral,' I tell her. 'Do you know where it will be?'

'When the police released the body, his order wanted him buried in Galle,' Miss Decima says gently. 'The funeral was yesterday, darling.'

There are more tears then but Miss Decima lets me cling to her and talk. Somehow it helps.

Just a little.

'Father Basil believed in you,' Miss Decima says, 'much more than you think.'

'What do you mean?'

'He admired your courage and your intelligence, of course,' Miss Decima says slowly, as if she is searching for words, 'but there was more. He thought you are a person of rare value. He felt the opportunity to help you was, for him, a special privilege.'

'Rare value? Oh madam, Father must have been joking,' I protest bitterly. 'If you knew the truth about me you will realise I'm worth nothing. Less than nothing.'

Miss Decima grasps me by the shoulders and looks into my eyes.

'Father Basil told me about it, child,' she says. 'You had a sad and terrible experience but it was not your fault. Surely you must see it does not make you worthless. Those of us who know the truth can see the opposite is true.'

If I had any value, why did she abandon me? Why did she go away and let me face that horror alone? I was worthless to the one person who mattered to me.

*

I wait till Kumudu is alone in his cubicle. He still uses the campus office although his work as national convenor takes him away most of the time.

I hear the crows squabbling for perches on the mara trees surrounding the union office as I climb the stairs. The office is dark except for the light in the far cubicle. I see his shaggy head bent over some papers on the table.

I wish I had an axe to split that head in two.

He looks up in surprise when I stand at the door.

'What is it?' he asks.

'You bastards killed him,' I find my voice rising. 'He was a good man. He was worth a thousand of you and … and …'

'I suppose you are talking about that priest,' he says calmly, leaning back in his chair.

'You know very well who I'm talking about,' I say sharply as tears begin to slide down my cheeks again.

'Why did you have to kill him? He was actually helping poor people; the same thing you say you want to do.'

'Sit down.'

'No. I don't want to sit down,' I scream. 'I want to know why you killed him. He was a saint, you are just a bunch of thugs and butchers.'

Kumudu jumps to his feet and I hear his chair crash to the ground behind him. He is a big man and his bushy beard and untidy shock of hair give him a bear-like quality. His eyes seem to flash as he glares at me.

'SIT DOWN,' he roars, 'before I come round this desk and twist your foolish neck for you.'

'No, I will NOT sit down,' I shout back. 'I am not a helpless old priest and I'm not afraid of you.'

We stare at each other angrily for a minute that seems to stretch into infinity. Finally Kumudu shrugs his shoulders, lifts the chair up and sits down.

'Please sit down, Sujatha,' he says quietly, 'there are so many things you do not understand.'

'So, explain them to me! Why have you killed that truly good man? What wrong did he do?'

Kumudu sighs.

'In the first place, I did not know anything about it till afterwards,' he says slowly, 'but I can understand why his … elimination was ordered.'

'Really? So your thugs could look like fearless warriors?'

Kumudu's eyes flash again but he controls himself with an effort.

'He might have been a good man, as you say, and he was trying to help the poor in his own way,' he replies. 'But his way is worse than no help at all; it is not in the interest of the poor.'

'How dare you say that?' I demand furiously. 'Did you bother to ask the people in the village what they thought?'

'They don't know what is good for them, only we do,' he answers with complete confidence. 'People like this priest give them a crust of bread for the day, satisfy their needs for the moment.'

'What's wrong with that?'

'It keeps the poor from rising up. In a way the priest was worse than the corrupt city folk. By helping the poor he was robbing them of their anger … of their will to fight.'

'Fight for what?' I am yelling again. 'The poor are suffering out there and you … you butchers want to kill the people who try to help them …'

'Listen to me Sujatha; this is not a time for foolish sentiment. You know that we have a plan. It will sweep away the corrupt cities and restore our rural poor to their rightful place. It is for the good of our people. Anything or anybody that threatens our plan must be ruthlessly crushed. Your priest was seen as a threat, he had to be removed.'

My fury is so great I am unable to speak for a minute. If I were a man I might have leapt across that table and strangled him. I don't speak till I have control.

'Father Basil said that I will find out, from some painful experience, that the end does NOT justify the means,' I say in a cold, measured tone. 'He was right; if the means are wicked, then the end is also wicked. If you are prepared to commit murder as a means; then your end is also murderous. I now know Kalinga's plan is not about helping the poor, it is to seize power for himself.'

I expect him to erupt in anger but he surprises me

by remaining calm.

'Your priest was wrong and you are wrong. Centuries of injustice can't be swept away by wearing a robe and preaching. Violence is necessary to topple the system, to crush the oppressors. You are also wrong about Kalinga. He is a true patriot who has committed his life to this great cause. One day, when the poor have their rightful place, you will realise that the means we used were justified.'

'I suppose Somasiri Jayakody was also an obstacle,' I say ironically, 'so he had to be killed?'

To my surprise Kumudu shrugs his shoulders.

'Yes, he was. We warned him but he didn't listen,' he says calmly.

'So your people killed him? Just like that?'

'Yes. People like him are doomed anyway,' he goes on callously. 'What does it matter if he dies now or a little later, when the wave strikes?'

'Wave? What wave?' I ask incredulously. 'Do you mean Ginirälla?'

'Of course.'

What have I got myself involved in? I had been working to uplift the poor but these people are talking casually about multiple murders. And it seems there are worse atrocities to come.

I want to get out of here.

'I don't believe in your cause any more. There are ways to help the poor without killing people,' I tell him, getting hurriedly to my feet. 'I am resigning from the union. I will expose your activities to everyone.'

I expect him to protest but find him staring at me; the expression in his eyes is strange, unnerving.

He speaks as I reach the door.

'Sujatha, I spared that Jayakody fellow's life because you begged me to do so,' he says. 'Do you remember?'

'Yes.'

'Well, now I want to ask a favour of you.'

You want something from me? The only thing I'd willingly give you is a spoonful of cyanide!

'What?' I ask, trying to hide my surprise. 'What do you want of me?'

'Don't resign from the union and don't speak against it,' he replies. 'There's only two weeks to your finals. Finish them and leave the campus. Do what you like after that.'

'What difference will it make if I resign now or later? And why should it matter to you?'

He studies me gravely before he speaks.

'If you resign and speak out, the others will see you as a traitor ... and a threat,' he says quietly.

'So?'

'They will want you eliminated and I ... I will be expected to give the order.'

JOURNAL IV

If you want a picture of the future,
imagine a boot stamping on a human face …
forever.

George Orwell

21

I feel dizzy when I look up. Mithra stands by the door of the cubicle looking down at me. My second reaction is fury.

'You miserable scoundrel,' I say nastily. 'A year and a half without even a postcard, and now you walk in as if nothing has happened.'

He just grins. The crooked smile is the same but almost everything else has changed. He's heavier and isn't wearing spectacles; walks with only a slight limp.

No crutches.

'My *gamey kella* looks very glamorous now, doesn't she? Let me see … she's cut her hair short and … isn't she using lipstick?' he drawls mockingly. 'Good heavens, she's even wearing jeans! What is the world coming to?'

He has always been able to make me squirm. Luckily Fazlia, the girl who shares my cubicle, is away on an assignment.

'Will you shut up about me?' I say testily. 'I want to know why you never wrote to anyone.'

'I was testing myself.'

'What do you mean?'

'You know my mother wanted me to apply for resident status. I could have done so, after my Masters. Well, I wanted to see if I could make a life out there, so I cut all … ties.'

'And?'

'It didn't work out,' he says with a wry smile. 'Something was missing, so I chucked it up.'

'You mean you're not going back?'

He shakes his head.

'No. No, I'm not going back.'

Mithra wants to know everything that's happened since he left for Australia soon after graduation.

'I was taken on as a trainee reporter while doing my diploma at the Open University. They assigned me to the political desk and that suited me just right.'

'So you finally left the JSP, did you?' he asks mockingly. 'You're not for the revolution?'

'I'm still for changing the system but not through the JSP. You were right about them and I was wrong,' I admit reluctantly, 'and if you mention that even once, I'll hit you with something.'

'Okay, okay, but what's been happening on the political front? You must know all the inside stuff.'

'I wish I did. The PF – JSP alliance is in place. There's infighting, of course, but the President still holds all the power and he has three more years to go.'

'And your friend Kalinga, what is he up to?'

'It's like one of those trick pictures. Look at it one way, he's just the Mahaweli Minister, going about his job and doing it well.'

'And from the other angle, what do you see?'

'Something frightening but shadowy, you know? Something so serious that killing is nothing. And Kalinga is at the bottom of it. Trouble is, I just can't get hold of the story.'

'Surely you can tap someone in the JSP? What about that bearded thug?'

'Kumudu? He's gone underground. I know he has formed cells in all the government schools. He's seems to have terrific power over the education system but he's chosen to be out of reach.'

'What about the other leaders?'

'I tried several sources in the JSP. It's quite strange, you know, but the leadership only talk about a scheme to organise students for political agitation. I suspect that Giniralla is a secret conspiracy within that scheme and known only to Kalinga's faithful.'

A telephone rings in the next cubicle.

'Sujatha, are you there? Call for you,' a man says, thrusting the receiver through a slot in the partition.

'Hullo. This is Sujatha.'

'Are you lady who write in Sunday paper?'

'Ye-es. Who is this?'

'Never mind name,' the man says. 'I can give informations about … about … *loku kumanthranayak thiyanawā.*'

A big conspiracy!

'You want to tell me about this?' I ask cautiously, for we get many crank calls. 'Will you be able to come to my office?'

'No, no, too dangerous. They are watching … watching,' the voice is agitated now. 'You must come here. I will tell … every information. You must promise … promise to … protection …'

'You will have to tell me your name and address if you want me to help you.'

'My house is 42/1, Angulana Station Road, Ratmalana.'

'And your name is?'

'Peiris. Sebastian Peiris.'

I return the receiver through the partition and stand for a moment chewing a fingernail.

Mithra asks:

'What is it? Who was that?'

'A man says he has information about something but I can't tell if it's a serious story or a crank call.'

'What are you going to do?'

I make a sour face.

'Go to Ratmalana, I suppose, and talk to the fellow,' I say with an exaggerated sigh. 'It's a hard life, being a reporter.'

'How will you travel?'

'Bus, of course,' I say. 'Did you think junior reporters are given limos?'

'I'll drive you down,' Mithra offers. 'I'm free this afternoon.'

I look with surprise at the mud spattered, but clearly new, Land Rover Discovery parked near the front gate. The words 'WORLD WATER AID' is painted on the doors.

'My employers,' Mithra explains shortly. 'It's a British NGO involved in constructing wells and restoring village tanks in the dry zone. I'm a field co-ordinator.'

I stop and turn on him furiously.

'How long have you been back?"

'Er ... three weeks,' he answers sheepishly.

'You mean rascal! Three weeks and you only came to see me today?'

'Well, I wanted to have a job in place and the vehicle, you know,' he says, 'to impress you.'

I look at him and find, to my surprise, that he is serious. Well partly anyway.

'You're such an idiot. I mean, I'm impressed all right but I'd have preferred to see you the day you came back.'

'Mm. Next time I'll remember.' The grin is infectious.

'Rubbish, there won't be another time. From now on I want a call from you every single day. Is that clear?'

'Yes ma'am,' he says with mock humility. 'The village girl has become very bossy, hasn't she?'

'Oh shut up! We'd better get going if we're to beat the office traffic.'

He uses a remote device to unlock the doors and another button on it to start the engine.

'All modern conveniences,' he says proudly. 'Automatic transmission as well.'

I don't know what that means; or care!

'Show off,' I say and he makes a face.

He drives confidently towards the Galle Road.

'Tell me about your crutches,' I ask diffidently. 'Did you pawn them during a pub crawl?'

'Donated to charity,' he answers gaily. 'They fitted me with a device called a caliper. Lengthens and supports the bad leg, you know. Allows me to walk almost normally.'

'It's wonderful,' I say, genuinely glad for him. 'Going to Australia had some benefits, I suppose.'

'Enough about me. What news of the others?'

'Nali is teaching at St. Bridget's. Harith is doing well in his business,' I tell him. 'Harith and Nali are getting engaged one of these days. Did you know?'

'Really? That's wonderful. I did wonder, in those days, if something was going on there.'

'Nonsense, you never had a clue.'

'And you? Is there anyone on the scene?'

'What?'

'Do you have some revolutionary reporter hanging around? Or maybe Miss Decima has found a mudalali's son for our gamey kella?'

'Knock it off! Marriage is not for me.'

Mithra has been silent for several minutes.

'Suji, I know you've had a bad experience,' he says softly. 'I want you to tell me about it.'

'You can't be serious,' I snap angrily. 'I've only told Father Basil and that was twelve years ago.'

'Now you can tell me.'

'Are you mad? How can I speak about such things?'

'I'm a friend and friends can make demands on each other. I want to know about this.'

I expect a mischievous grin but he is staring at the road; his jaw muscles are working. This is a new, and slightly disturbing, Mithra.

'I … I'll think about it,' I say in a small voice. The memories still have the power to make me feel wretched and helpless. I see the past as a dark, haunted room I dare not enter.

'You need to put this behind you, baba,' he says in a kindly voice. 'If Father Basil was alive he would have helped you, I am sure. Since he isn't here, it's up to me.'

'Are you planning to become a priest, then?'

'I might, if you drive me to it.'

'You will despise me when you know the truth.'

'In your own words, that's rubbish,' he says with a laugh. 'Isn't Angulana Road to the right somewhere here?'

*

Something is wrong. I sense it when people run in that particular way; when they have that look of ghoulish curiosity to observe, for instance, a pedestrian run over by a bus. Mithra parks by the side of the road and we push our way through the crowd of onlookers.

A woman is screaming. I should know it well, that

keening sound when hope is gone. I see her in the veranda, trying to struggle free and being restrained by another woman. Two small children with shock-frozen faces cling helplessly to her housecoat.

A man lies, face down, on the front steps.

Two men are bending over him, trying to turn him over. I see the blood dribbling down the steps and into the garden.

A wide-eyed man stands at the little gate trying to keep the crowd away. I wave my press card, hoping that something vaguely official will impress him.

'I'm from the Statesman newspaper. Is that Mr. Sebastian Peiris?'

'Yes, yes. I … I live next door. I heard gunshots and came … Seba is lying there … blood on the ground …'

'When did this happen?'

'Few minutes only …'

'Did you see who shot him? Did you see anyone?'

'No. No one here when I come. Only Seba … on the ground.'

'Why aren't they taking him to hospital?'

'Dr. Jegan from next house … he say Seba already … dead. Must wait for police.'

The police vehicle drives up just then and parks across the gate. A constable shoos the crowd away. A man with sergeant's stripes on his sleeve, tunic buttons straining against his belly, marches to the house. Bystanders trickle back to form a circle once again.

I grab Mithra by the arm.

'Start asking questions,' I whisper. 'Find out what you can about Peiris. A description of the attackers; anything! Let's get to them before the cops.'

'I don't know how to ask questions,' Mithra protests.

'I'd rather watch you at it.'

'Just do it,' I say, giving him a push. 'Hurry.'

He goes off grumbling once again about bossy women.

Headlights flash by us in an endless stream as we drive back to the city. The shock of the killing only hits me then. I can't dispel the image of those two little girls hanging on their mother's dress.

Adults play their games but it is little children who always pay the price.

'Was he killed to keep him from talking about something?' Mithra breaks the silence. 'I mean, could there be a connection, do you think?'

'It could be something else, I suppose,' I say, more to myself than to him, 'but that's not likely.'

'So will you try to find out what it was?'

'That's my job.'

'Will it be dangerous?' Mithra asks. 'For you, I mean.'

'If every reporter digging for a story is killed, there won't be any left. Don't worry about me.'

'Mm.'

'You spoke to some people, didn't you? Did you find out anything?'

'Most of them had arrived after the killing. One fellow had passed by earlier and seen Peiris in the garden, smoking a cigarette. The lane was deserted, he told me, except for some schoolboys on bicycles. They had stopped by the roadside to chat.'

'Schoolboys? Late in the day for them, isn't it?'

'Maybe they'd been to tuition class,' Mithra says.

'What did you get?'

'A neighbour told me Peiris was a site supervisor. He had worked for some big contractor but lost his job a few weeks ago.'

'Is that all?'

'Peiris had been well off while he had his job. He's been drinking heavily in recent weeks. All the neighbours seemed to know about that.'

22

News item
12th June

MAYA CITY PROJECT OPENS ON 7th JULY.

Contractors are working round the clock to complete the Maya City Project in time for the ceremonial opening on 7th July. A company spokesman said that, despite the huge number of tasks still to be carried out, he was confident it would be finished on schedule.

The Maya City project comprises a hotel, large shopping mall, restaurant complex and two wide-screen cinemas. An amusement park and apartment complex is planned for stage two of the development.

23

Sita Peiris refuses to speak to me till I tell her that Sebastian had called me just before he was shot. She looks puzzled and steps back, away from the door.

'I am so sorry about what happened … ' I start.

She interrupts me rudely.

'Yes, yes,' she says, clearly impatient. 'What's this about Seba calling you?'

I look closely at the woman's worry-lined face.

'He called the newsroom and asked for me; said he knew of a conspiracy.'

'Why he call you? He don't know you.'

'He had seen my name in the Sunday paper. That's why he asked for me.'

She seems slightly mollified, so I press on.

'Where was Mr. Peiris working?'

'He work for Milford Engineering. He was site supervisor.'

'What site was he assigned to?'

'Maya City site. He was there from beginning of project.'

'I heard that Mr. Peiris had lost his job. What happened?'

I see a change in her expression. She hesitates, then:

'Would you like cup of tea?' she asks abruptly.

'Yes, thank you.'

I take a moment to study the overcrowded room. The wide screen TV in a corner looks new, and expensive. The three-piece drawing room suite looks new too, and just a little too big for the narrow sitting area.

Eyes set in two curly heads look me over from behind a curtain. I beckon to them and, after some pushing and backing off, two little girls come forward. The taller girl tells me she is eight, two years older than the small botheration.

They are just beginning to open up when their mother returns. A quick frown darkens her face.

'Why you not doing homework?' she barks. 'Go and do. Go, go.'

She places the teacup and saucer on a stool by my chair without glancing at me and returns to her seat. I take a small sip and sigh with relief; she doesn't think much of me and so has put very little sugar in the tea. In our culture, tea served to an honoured guest is sweetened heavily enough to trigger a diabetic coma.

'You were telling me about his job …' I prompt her.

'They ask him to leave.' Her voice has a bitter edge. 'He work for twelve years. Many sites, suffering in sun and rain; then suddenly, before even project over, they say go home.'

'They must have a reason, surely. Why did they ask him to leave?'

She doesn't want to answer at first. I wait patiently till the silence gets to her.

'They say he was drinking … at work. They say they warned him but he … didn't stop.'

'Was Mr. Peiris a heavy drinker?'

'No, no. Only during parties and … and church feast.'

'So when did he start to drink heavily?'

'About two months.'

'Something must have been worrying him. Did he

tell you anything?'

'No, he don't tell. Get angry when I ask.'

'He told me about a *loku kumanthranayak.* A big conspiracy! Have you any idea what it might be?'

'What conspiracy for Seba,' she scoffs. 'He was building supervisor. How he can know about thing like that?'

'There must be something to make them shoot him,' I blurt out thoughtlessly. 'I'm sorry. I didn't mean to …'

'Can't be anything from here. Maybe at his workplace he hear something.'

'Nonā, Nonā.'

Lady, Lady.

Mrs. Peiris mutters something under her breath and lumbers to her feet. I follow her out of the house and see an unshaven lout leaning over a bicycle by the gate. A wooden box tied to the back, with a knife handle sticking out of it, tells the story.

Fish vendor.

'Honda thora peththak thiyāgatthā nonatama denna,' the fellow calls out.

I kept a good slice of seer fish just for you, lady.

'Keeyada ada?' Mrs. Peiris growls. *'Umba hari horā.'*

What's the price today? You are a big rogue.

'Nä nä, mama adu karalā denney.'

No no, I will reduce for you.

I wait impatiently while they haggle and finally agree on a price.

The man says:

'I saw master last week just before … before he is killed.'

'What?' Mrs Peiris snaps. 'Where were you? What did you see?"

The man is taken aback by the sharp reaction.

'Master is standing near gate when I pass. Have good seer. I ask if he want but he say no. I ride on but soon I hear gunshots. I didn't know master has been shot till next day.'

'Did you see anyone else near the gate?' I butt in, trying to control my excitement.

'Only two … no, three boys on bicycles. They are talking … roadside. No one else.'

'Maybe those boys saw the killer,' I say. 'We must try to find them. Do you know them?'

'No. Not from around here.'

'Can you describe them?'

'Cannot remember faces. White school clothes. All have book bags, I think.'

'Did you see them again?'

'Yes, yes. They … soon after gunshots, they ride past me towards station.'

I turn to Mrs. Peiris.

'I'm sure those boys saw something,' I say. 'Is there a school nearby or maybe a tuition class, do you know?'

The woman shakes her head, looking puzzled.

'No. No school and haven't heard of tuition class.'

'Can you make some enquiries? It will really help if we can question those boys.'

I leave a card and she promises to call if she gets any information.

*

Nali calls me at work. I had been trying, without success, to inject some life into a boring story on union activity at the Electricity Board. I'm happy to put it aside and chat for a while.

'So? So? What's our clever reporter up to these days?' she asks gaily. 'What's the latest scoop?"

'All dull stuff, Nala,' I reply, 'and I can't get to the bottom of the one story that's interesting.'

'What's it about? Some Minister caught with his hora woman?'

'That's not news. No, a man wanted to expose a conspiracy but was killed before he could speak to me.'

'Hmm. You'd better be careful, messing around with criminals,' she says. 'What news of Mithra?'

'He's digging wells in Tangalle or somewhere.'

'Let's have a reunion,' Nali suggests. 'What about Saturday? Will Mithra be here?'

'Lovely, let's do that,' I say enthusiastically. 'Mithra should be in Colombo for the weekend.'

'That's fixed then, we'll meet at Harith's and go out to dinner,' Nali says. 'Where's this new boarding of yours?'

'Hamer's Avenue in Wellawatte. I'm sharing a room with Fazlia, a girl who works with me.'

'We'll pick you up at about 7.30. Is that all right?'

'Fine. Are you getting engaged then? Is that what we're celebrating?'

'I'll tell you when we meet,' she says, but I sense the suppressed excitement in her. 'What about you, baba? Have you found yourself a kolla?"

'No kollas for me, Nala. You know that, surely.'

'Nonsense. I'm going to fix you up with one of Harith's friends. They are all mad about you.'

'Oh stop it.'

The boy in the next cubicle cries out.

'Call. Call for Sujatha.'

I pick up the receiver thinking it is Nali.

'Is this Sujatha Mallika?'

A gruff male voice.

'Yes. Who is calling?'

'Shut up and listen carefully. Sebastian Peiris was silenced because he wanted to betray us. We know that you went to his house on the day he died and again yesterday. Your investigations must stop now. Is that clear?'

'It is my job to report on these matters,' I say bravely, although there is a tremor in my voice. 'Who are you?"

'Shut up, bitch!' the man's voice is low but the menace comes through clearly. 'Just answer yes or no. Do you understand what I said?'

'Yes.'

'We will not warn you again. If you continue to meddle in this matter, we will kill you.'

He rings off. My hip knocks painfully against the edge of the desk as I stumble to my seat.

'What's the matter, Sujatha?' Fazlia asks. 'Who was that?"

'A man. He claims … they killed Peiris. They will kill me as well if I follow up the story.'

Fazlia's face goes still. She frequently reports on the Northern conflict and knows the risk of offending extremists.

It is the first time for me.

'What have you found out about the murder anyway?'

'Very little. He had started drinking heavily and lost his job. The wife doesn't know what was bothering him.'

'So you've no idea what it's all about, or who's behind it?'

'I don't know what it's about but now, after that call, I'm wondering …'

'What?'

'That warning, some people I knew were threatened in the same way ...'

'Did they listen?'

'No.'

'What happened to them?'

'They were killed. In both cases I know JSP activists were responsible.'

'Oh. Is that all you have to go on?'

'No-o. I've told you about their Ginirälla project. I hadn't been able to get any further with that. Now Peiris mentions a conspiracy and is killed immediately afterwards. I try to investigate and I am warned off in the same style. Can it be connected, do you think?'

'It's very thin ...'

'Then there are the boys.'

'What boys?'

'Three schoolboys on bicycles were at Peiris's gate. I thought they were witnesses but now I wonder ... what if they were the killers?'

'Rubbish. Why would schoolboys kill Peiris?'

'Ginirälla is about training students,' I say. 'I know it is more than indoctrination. What if they've been trained to kill?'

It is Mithra who picks me up on Saturday evening. Our landlady, Mrs. Blyth, looks him over suspiciously.

'Who this young fellow?' she demands from the depths of her settee.

'This is Mithra, aunty, an old friend from university.'

'Well Mithra fellow, you better bring this girl back safe,' she growls, rising to her feet like a whale coming ashore. She walks us up to the vehicle. 'And don't be late.'

'What's the matter with the old battery?' Mithra

demands as we drive away. 'Anyone would think you're some delicate little flower.'

'She's very protective; doesn't like me going out with strange men.' I say. 'And I am too, a delicate flower, so you'd better take good care of me.'

Mithra mumbles something under his breath.

'What was that?' I ask suspiciously.

'Nothing.'

I rap his head with a knuckle and draw an anguished howl.

'Admit that I'm a delicate flower, otherwise I'll give you another one.'

'You're a delicate *pol mala.*'

Pol mala is a coconut flower; not the most attractive bloom.

'Hey, stop it. You'll make me crash. Stop it!'

Nali runs towards me with a wordless cry of joy.

We hug each other in such haste, and so much enthusiasm that we trip and fall over. My knee is bruised and Nali scrapes her elbow. We lie on the ground nursing our injuries and crying out in pain; and having a fit of giggles. Harith yanks us unceremoniously to our feet; he tells us to behave because his mother is watching from an upstairs window.

'I want to know all the details, Nala,' I demand. 'How did Harith propose? I'd have died laughing – oh my little *poosi*, I can't live without you. Will you be my *kadala gotta?*'

'Can we have some decorum here? That's a private matter,' Harith groans, 'and we only just decided to get engaged …'

'Just decided? What rubbish,' I say scornfully. 'I saw the two of you on the staircase that night, after the funeral.....'

'Whaat? You little wretch,' Nali screams, 'you never said a word to me. Anyway we were only talking ...'

'Talking? More like lip-reading.'

'Will you two donkeys shut up,' Harith pleads. 'If my mother picks up what you're saying, I'll never hear the end of it. Even the neighbours can hear you ...'

Mithra asks: 'Does your mother know it was Nali who scared hell out of her that night?'

'No, not yet,' Harith says with a grin. 'I've promised Nali not to tell ... so long as she obeys me at all times.'

'Tell and see what happens,' Nali retorts gamely. 'She'll chase me off and you'll have to marry one of those creatures with rings in the *buriya*.'

'He'll never risk it, baba,' I say confidently. 'Harith is so lucky; he should kneel down and kiss your toes every morning.'

'This girl is loony. Kissing toes every day; can you imagine?' Mithra throws his hands up. 'No wonder she can't find a boy friend.'

'I'm going to fix her up with a nice boy,' Nali announces. 'There'll be plenty of them around during the wedding.'

'Don't waste your time, baba,' I say. 'I'm going to become a nun.'

We eat string hoppers with curried squid, sitting out there in the garden.

'How is the business going?' Mithra asks. 'Have you taken full control?'

'Oh yes. The motor spares business is very competitive but we're doing all right,' Harith says thoughtfully, 'it's the Goldwood project that's a mess.'

'What's happening?'

'We've spent too much money to abandon it but progress is slow,' he goes on. 'I'm spending a fortune on armed security. I've got a new manager, an ex-army man; he's done a good job so far. '

It is nearly midnight when Mithra pulls up outside my house. I'm pleased when he gets down, Lankan style, for a final chat near the gate.

'Well that couple is fixed up and I'm for the nunnery,' I say with a laugh. 'Now we have to get you settled. Have you anyone in mind?'

'Yes.'

'Really? You never told me. Is it someone you met in Australia?'

'No. Before I went.'

'Who is it? Not some awful creature, I hope,' I say. 'You'd better bring her to me for an interview.'

'She's an awful creature all right but there's no need for a interview.'

'You're not marrying anyone without my approval. What's this woman's name?'

Mithra is laughing.

'It's you, you idiot.'

'What? Are you crazy? You know very well I can never …'

I feel a thudding in my chest; and an emotion I have never experienced before. A sea of panic with an unfamiliar thread of exhilaration running through it!

'For an year and a half in Australia I tried to forget you,' he says simply. 'I realised then that I never could. I came back just to be near you.'

'Oh, Mithra, you know I have a … problem. I can't … if you know the truth you'll run away from me …'

'Hey, you'll get a thump on the ear if you go on like that. I'm not asking for a commitment from you. There's no pressure like that at all … just let me come and see you and we'll see what happens.'

'You'd better go … before I start crying,' I say.

'Good night then, little Suj,' he says easily. 'You told me to call you every day, remember? I shall do that.'

'All right.'

24

Site Manager Sarath Walpita is immensely pleased with himself. He has been in charge since the foundation stone was laid and is not shy to claim full credit for his achievement.

Justifiable pride, I have to admit, as he conducts me through the site. The hotel towers above us on my right, glass windows glinting in the morning sun. The cinema multiplex stands next to it with an independent car park. On the left is the centrepiece of the project, the sprawling shopping and restaurant complex. The site is like an ant heap, workers scurrying about endlessly.

I tell no lies, but I do let him think that I propose to write a feature on the project.

'This is the atrium of the shopping complex,' he says proudly, leading me through a set of immense glass doors.

I am not an admirer of opulence but the grandeur of the chamber takes my breath away. The black granite floor shines like a mirror under a glass roof that towers some six storeys above me. Transparent bubble elevators move up and down to serve the galleried floors above. A chandelier the size of a truck blazes in the centre of the atrium, competing with the sun above.

'Well, what do you think?' Walpita spreads his arms as if to embrace the scene.

'It is very grand,' I answer.

'This is where we'll have the opening ceremony on the 7th of July,' he rambles on with paternal pride. 'It will be a big show.'

'Today's the 20th, isn't it? You have just sixteen days. Can you finish the work in time?'

'There are dozens of subcontractors besides our own men; thousands of tasks in progress,' he says confidently. 'We are tracking every one of them. We'll be ready.'

I sit in his office patiently writing down more details of the project; mostly the heroic contribution Walpita himself has made to keep the work on schedule. After twenty minutes of monologue, and a nice cup of tea, I rise to leave.

'I saw a report about one of your employees who was murdered recently,' I say. 'Peiris. Sebastian Peiris wasn't it?'

'Yes, poor fellow,' he answers easily. 'He worked with us for many years but we had to let him go.'

'Really? Why was that?'

'Booze. He was found drunk on duty. We don't tolerate that kind of thing … had to sack him.'

'What kind of work did he do?'

'He was the chief civil supervisor for the shopping complex,' Walpita says. 'A very reliable fellow, been with us many years. Started hitting the bottle only recently.'

'Could anything related to his work have driven him to drink?"

'Plenty of stress, of course, for all of us but he was the only fellow who started drinking at work. Can't have that.'

Mithra calls and I feel my heart lurch.

'So, so? How is my little girlfriend keeping?'

'I'm not your girlfriend,' I rebuke him sharply. 'What makes you think it's so easy?'

'I gave up Australia to be near you,' he says. 'What more do you want? You have to be my girl now.'

'Nonsense. I've seen the tele-dramas. The boy has to cry and suffer for weeks and weeks. The girl makes up her mind only in the last episode.'

'But I wooed you for three years on campus,' he complains. 'Surely you don't want me to start again?"

'On campus you pretended to be a sheep … I thought of you as a friend. Now I find you've been a wolf all along,' I answer. 'Anyway you were bullying me most of the time. Is that your idea of wooing?'

'Oh all right, I'll start over again. What must I do then?'

'Call me twice a day from now on. You can bring me presents and, most important, I want to see you suffering.'

'Why on earth do you want me to suffer?'

'That's how it is in the tele-dramas.'

'All right then, I'll suffer,' he says. 'In fact I'm crying now.'

'You're such a liar. I think you're actually enjoying this.'

Five minutes after his cheerful goodbye the phone rings again. Mithra, I feel sure, trying to finish his obligation for the day.

'Is this Miss Sujatha?'

A woman's voice.

'Yes.'

'I am friend of Sebastian's,' she says. 'Before he was killed … Seba told me he wanted to speak to you.'

'Yes. What is your name?'

'Wilma Peters.'

'What was your relationship with Mr. Peiris?'

'We are … were close friends.'

'What did you want to speak to me about?'

'They made him do something … terrible,' she whispers. 'He regretted later, wanted to stop them. That's why they kill him.'

'Do you know what he had done? Did he tell you?'

'He say things … when he is drunk. He drink because he is frightened.'

'Can you come to my office? There will be a reward if your information is useful.'

'No. No. They might be watching.' The woman's voice has risen, she seems close to panic. 'They will kill me also.'

'Where can we meet then?'

'Can't today, my husband at home. You come to Wellawatta Food City tomorrow morning at eleven. I will meet there.'

'How will I know you?'

'Red handbag,' she says after a moment. 'I will stand near meat counter with red handbag.'

Mithra is on the phone again that evening. Mrs. Blyth guards her telephone like a mother hen but she doesn't mind incoming calls. I find it easy to speak to Mithra when he is safely miles away.

'These calls are going to finish my whole salary,' he complains. 'Can't I just write letters?'

'No, the calls are essential,' I say sternly. 'Good thing you mentioned writing. I want a letter from you every day … that's in addition to everything else.'

'Oh no,' he groans. 'Do you think I have nothing else to do? What if I write one and post a photocopy every day?'

After some minutes of frivolous talk he says

cautiously:

'My team has started work at a village called Medamulana. That was where you were born, wasn't it?'

I feel as if someone had thrown a bucket of iced water on me. I struggle to control my voice.

'Yes. What … what work are you doing there?'

'We are helping villagers build new wells. Water is a problem, you know, with the drought.'

'And are you going down there yourself?'

'Yes. In a few days,' he says. 'Would you like me to enquire after anyone there?'

'NO. NO. Oh, please don't talk to anyone about me. Don't ask any questions. Promise me.'

'Calm down, baba. I won't say anything, all right? Forget I mentioned it.'

'Mm.'

'What news of your cousins?' Mithra asks, trying clumsily to steer the conversation into calmer waters. 'Isn't the older one in University now?'

'Yes. Loku is at Sabaragamuwa; History degree. Punchi is sitting for her O Levels this year.'

'Sabaragamuwa is it? I drive past the campus sometimes. I might drop in and see her. You don't mind, do you?'

'No. I don't mind,' I say lightly, 'but don't try your larks with her. She's a tough one.'

'No larks, I promise,' he laughs. 'So what's happening to your investigation? Have you found the killer yet?'

'I'm meeting a witness tomorrow,' I tell him. 'Maybe I'll make some progress then.'

Mithra doesn't share my enthusiasm.

'Who's this witness?' he asks, serious now. 'Are you sure it's not a hoax … or a trap?'

'A woman; she might have been Sebastian's lady friend. Claims to know what was worrying him.'

'I don't like it. Where are you meeting her? Tell her to come to your office.'

'She refused. I'm meeting her at Wellawatte tomorrow morning.'

'Take someone with you,' he says, anxiety clear in his tone. 'Shall I call Harith?'

'No. I'll think of something.'

*

I'm quite sure this Wilma Peters woman is genuine but Mithra's doubts begin to work on my mind. By morning I'm feeling nervous but not fearful enough to worry Harith.

Fazlia offers to come with me but I dissuade her, knowing she faces a deadline and is already late. In the end I just borrow her abaya, that long black dress that conservative Moslem ladies favour. The hijab and veil, a head cover with only a narrow opening for the eyes completes my disguise. We are about the same size, Fazlia and I, and sometimes borrow clothes from each other. Fazlia wears shalwars to work and covers her head with a scarf; the formal black dress is reserved for family and religious functions.

I pick up Mrs. Blyth's plastic shopping basket from the kitchen and slip out of the house. A trishaw drops me outside Food City a few minutes before eleven.

Not many customers are in the shop at that time and assistants are busy restocking the racks. I drop my shopping basket into a trolley and push it down an aisle. I resist the temptation to look at the other shoppers, especially those at the meat counter.

I begin to move along the shelves, stopping to check the price of tinned pineapple. A loaf of bread goes in the cart. A quick glance reveals a young woman standing near the meat freezer; she clasps a red handbag across her waist. My elaborate disguise makes me feel foolish.

A man brushes against my trolley as he walks towards the checkout. My eyes flash across his face more out of annoyance than curiosity. Something cold touches the back of my neck.

I have seen that face before!

I dare not turn to look at him again so I try to picture that face. Heavy, handsome features under closely cropped hair; shirtsleeves rolled high display muscular arms. Where did I see bulging muscles shown off like that?

It hits me. On the bus going home after my first semester on campus, this was the scoundrel who sat next to me and tried to fondle my breast. What is he doing here? The little girl, his sister, told me he had planned to enter university the following year. If he had, he would be in his final year now.

Is it merely a coincidence? Then the informant is genuine and this fellow, Nishantha, is there for some unconnected purpose.

What if the explanation is sinister?

Someone called to say I would be killed if I pursued the investigation. I had ignored the threat and gone to the Maya City site. If this is a trap and they mean to kill me, then it confirms that there is a plot involving the Maya City project. Does the presence of a student-thug like Nishantha mean it is connected to Giniràlla?

Has he recognised me? If he hasn't, I still have a

chance. I add a tin of mackerel to the loaf and push my trolley towards the checkout. There is a heavy woman with a load of groceries ahead of me. I look around casually expecting to see Nishantha near the entrance.

He's gone.

Could I have imagined all this? Should I go back and interview the woman waiting for me by the meat counter?

The street door is pushed open and another young fellow comes in; white clothes and a knapsack across his shoulders. I feel his eyes pass over me. Then, one by one, he looks over the other customers. He pulls out a trolley and pushes it down an aisle.

I haven't imagined it.

I pay for my purchases and walk into the street. Sure enough, I see the back of Nishantha's bristly head. He's standing on the pavement appearing to look at the traffic passing by, but every time the door opens his head swings around.

I want to hurry away but a small voice inside my head tells me that it is safer to remain standing next to him, pretending to be unaware of the danger. Nishantha might have seen me arrive in a trishaw so it is best to leave in one. Galle road is buzzing with traffic. I move to the edge of the pavement and wave at every passing three-wheeler. I feel his eyes boring into the back of my head.

Where are the trishaws when you need one urgently?

One driver finally swerves to the side of the road. I don't realise that I had stopped breathing till the trishaw moves out and I draw a deep, relieved breath.

25

News item
26th June

MINISTER LOKUGE ON MYSTERIOUS OVERSEAS JAUNT

Mahaweli Minister Kalinga Lokuge has caused a stir in government circles by going overseas without cabinet sanction. A spokesman for the Presidential Secretariat stated that permission has not been granted for the Minister to leave the country. A reliable source within the JSP revealed that Lokuge had failed to obtain clearance from the party politburo as well.

It is known that Minister Lokuge has a great interest in and affinity for Kampuchea, having made several visits there in the recent past. He is believed to have travelled to that country once again. Lokuge was accompanied by JSP student convenor, the elusive Kumudu Prasanna.

Insiders say that Minister Lokuge will be called upon to explain his conduct to cabinet when he returns to the country tomorrow.

26

'Akki, I'm at the Museum,' a voice shrills over the telephone, 'can you come and meet me?'

My cousin Loku.

'What are you doing in Colombo, nangi?' I ask, completely taken aback. 'How did you come?'

'Our professor arranged a trip. I wanted to surprise you,' she says. 'Will you come soon?'

'Yes, yes I'll come. From where are you calling?'

'I'm using a friend's mobile and he's grumbling about his bill already,' she says gaily. 'Come soon.'

I have been taking extra precautions when leaving the office. We'd wait, Fazlia and I, for some of the boys to leave and follow them to the bus stand. There's no one to come with me at this time so I hail a trishaw and go directly to the Museum.

I catch up with a group of students crowding noisily around King Rajasinghe's throne and regalia. I try to work my way through the mob but find the smell of perspiration overpowering.

Am I getting too finicky in my old age?

I stand near the door and wait. The boys study me appraisingly as they file past me into the next chamber. I'm used to that now; I'm even used to the smutty comments they whisper to each other.

'Akki.'

My baby sister is getting to be a proper young lady. Her arms twitch as if to reach out and hug me but then fall back to her sides.

She smiles shyly.

'Baba, you should have told me you were coming,' I say as I walk beside her, following the others. 'When are you getting back?'

'I didn't have the money to join but at the last minute a friend gave me a loan,' she says. 'I was hoping you … can give …'

'How much is it?'

'Two hundred.'

'Yes, of course I'll give it to you,' I say. 'But tell me. How are nända and Punchi? I haven't been home for ages.'

'I haven't gone home either,' she says, looking away uneasily. 'I have been very busy.'

I resist the temptation to question her about that. We chat about her studies and health. Too soon we are standing by the hired bus with the boys pushing their way forward unceremoniously. I hurriedly pick out all the crumpled notes in my bag, relieved to make the two hundred; just! I will need to skip a few lunches this month.

I give her the parcel I had brought along from the office.

'What's this?'

'Some notes for a book I'm hoping to write one day,' I say. 'I want you to keep it very carefully. Can you do that for me?'

'Really? You're going to write a book?' She looks at the brown paper parcel with amusement. 'Sure. I'll keep it for you.'

'Nangi, please be careful with it,' I say earnestly, wondering if I am making a mistake. 'It really is important …'

'Don't fuss. I'll take care of it,' she responds casually and steps into the bus.

One wave and she's gone.

Mithra calls in the evening, lifting my spirits immediately.

'How is *gamey kella* doing?' he asks. 'Has she spent the day thinking about her boyfriend?'

'What boyfriend?' I shoot back. 'You are still on probation. Anyway I'm too busy to think about boys.'

'Girls shouldn't be allowed to work. They should stay at home and think about their men.'

'Dream on.'

We tease each other for a while. Then:

'Loku came to town today. Some kind of field trip,' I say. 'I gave her my diaries for safekeeping.'

'What diaries? I didn't know you had any.'

'From the first days on campus, I kept a record of the rag and union activities … also about this Ginirälla project.'

'You are a secretive devil, aren't you? In future you have to tell your lord and master everything.'

'I was reading about the French revolution the other day,' I say. 'It describes how lords lost their heads.'

'You were such a sweet, submissive village girl. What has happened to you?'

'Be serious for a moment. Don't get upset that I say this, but if anything should happen to me, I want you to get my diaries from Loku and give them to my editor. Will you do that?'

'Of course I will. But baba, has there been another threat? Why are you saying this?'

I hear the concern in Mithra's voice and find some comfort there. I decide not to tell him about the incident at Food City just yet.

'No, it's just a precaution. Kalinga Lokuge has been abroad and is returning tomorrow. His supporters, the student wing I suppose, have arranged a meeting to welcome him at the airport. I want to be there.'

'Don't go, Suji. It's far too dangerous,' he says with quiet intensity. 'Please don't go.'

'I'm going with another reporter and a photographer. I'll be all right, really,' I say reassuringly. 'I'll call you as soon as I get back.'

*

They have cleared the airport car park for the meeting. Young men and women with red armbands control the crowd with practised ease. And the crowd is a sizeable one, enough to fill the car park and overflow into the open area outside.

Our press credentials earn us a prominent position in front of the stage.

Kalinga keeps us waiting for nearly an hour. He finally enters through a side gate and is escorted to the stage. The bear-like figure of Kumudu follows close behind him.

I remember that Kalinga had not accepted the customary security detail drawn from the police, preferring instead to be protected by cadres from his own youth corps. They surround the stage now.

There is no introduction.

Kalinga walks up to the microphone and acknowledges the thunderous roar by raising one clenched fist above his head. The cheer goes on and on till he opens his fist and stretches his fingers, showing an open palm. The cheering stops abruptly.

'I thank you for coming here today not only to

greet me but also to show your support,' he says in his distinctive hoarse voice. 'I will need all your strength and your courage in the next few days, for I am surrounded by enemies who want to pull me down; who want to divert me from the great task I have set for myself.

'The pygmies in government want to know why I left the country without their permission. My answer is that I travel in the service of my people. I travel to further our great struggle to restore the poor to their rightful place. I travel to find the means to crush the oppressors and robbers who keep our people in misery.

'So my answer to the pygmy people in government is this. To serve the poor of my motherland, I need permission from no one.'

Sunil, the reporter who has accompanied me, whispers in my ear.

'I never thought he'd challenge the government like this. This bugger is up to something.'

I just nod, not wanting to miss any of this. Kalinga is heavier and better groomed now but the intensity and raw power is still there; I feel the impact just as much as I did four years ago. But now there is something new in his demeanour, something unpleasant, even dangerous. I can't quite pin it down.

He rants on about all governments that have, since independence, worked to protect the rich and suppress the poor. To tumultuous cheers he lashes out at the current government of which he is a part, declaring that it is as bad as the others.

When the meeting is over, and the crowd is being ushered out, Kalinga surprises us by inviting members of the press for a brief conference. Kalinga and Kumudu draw their chairs to the edge of the platform and sit directly above us.

The questions pour in.

'Which countries did you visit?'

'Thailand and Kampuchea.'

'Why have you visited these particular countries so often?'

'There are important lessons to be learnt there.'

'Why did you go abroad without cabinet approval?'

'I don't need approval to work for the poor.'

'You have, in addition, severely criticised the government today. Won't they take action against you?'

'Let them try.'

I only get a chance to speak towards the end.

'What is your special interest in Kampuchea?'

'I said before, we can learn from their experience.'

'Are you talking about the programs of the current regime there,' I ask diffidently, 'or those of the previous one? Pol Pot's regime?'

Kalinga goes very still. I can feel his eyes on me, cold and watchful.

'I will answer that question later.'

I go on recklessly.

'Can you then tell us the object of your Ginirälla program?'

I draw some puzzled looks from the reporters around me. Kalinga stares at me again and now his eyes are blazing. I see Kumudu lean over and whisper in his ear.

'I will respond to that later,' Kalinga says tightly.

A few minutes later Kumudu stands up to terminate the conference. Someone taps me on the shoulder. I turn to find a young woman wearing an organiser's armband standing behind me.

'The Honourable Minister will answer your questions

in private,' she says impassively. 'Come with me.'

I look helplessly at Sunil but he only shrugs his shoulders. I follow the woman and feel my knees tremble as I climb the steps to the stage. They have moved the chairs to the back of the stage, away from the reporters who are being escorted out.

Kalinga is seated, while Kumudu stands behind him. I realise that the man has changed, or perhaps I am seeing him with adult eyes for the first time. There is something brutally vicious about him, a mindless arrogance. My fear intensifies when I realise he has no intention of answering questions. His body seems to vibrate with rage, keeping everyone around him very still.

'You stupid little bitch,' he says. 'You were with us once. Now you have chosen to work against us.'

'I also want to help the poor,' I respond, recklessness overpowering my fear for that moment, 'but I don't agree with the way you do it. The means you use are inherently evil.'

Kalinga springs to his feet and steps closer. Fury seems to radiate from his eyes. I raise my hands thinking he will strike me.

He controls himself with a visible effort.

'I know you've been digging into my affairs. Don't think your puny efforts are a threat to me. Nothing can stop my victory,' he says, his voice strangled by the strength of his anger. 'I have tolerated your impudence so far, but not any more. You are a piece of filth, a worm I can step on at anytime. I will make you realise that.'

Kalinga stalks away.

Kumudu's eyes rest on me for a moment and they seem to be filled with regret. He turns to follow his leader. I stand there shivering, unable to move. I shudder when I feel a hand on my arm but turn to find my colleague

Sunil standing there. I might have fallen if he had not helped me down the steps.

It was the mention of Pol Pot that had triggered Kalinga's fury. What had that brutal regime done that can serve as a lesson for our country? What connection does Giniràlla have with that?

For his recent conduct, Kalinga might well be sacked from the government. So what great victory is he talking about?

Mithra must have been asleep when I call him.

'Hullo. Suji? What's the matter? Are you all right?'

'I'm all right now and safely at home,' I say unsteadily. 'I just wanted to talk for a minute. Do you mind?'

'No, of course not.' he answers. 'What happened? What upset you?'

'I attended Kalinga's meeting. During question time I asked him about Kampuchea and Giniràlla. He didn't answer but called me up for a private meeting afterwards. He was angry. So angry it was very frightening. He said he had tolerated my meddling up to now but not … not any more.'

'Honey, I told you not to push these people. They're dangerous.'

'I don't know what to do. I can't stay in hiding.'

'Yes, you can. Come down to Tangalle with me. Stay out of sight for a few days.'

'I can't. These people are going to do something very serious, something affecting the country. I feel I'm the only one who even suspects anything. I can't go and hide.'

'I'm frightened for you, baba. Shall I ask for leave and stay in Colombo for a few days?'

'No. I'll call you if I see any sign of trouble.'

'Please be careful. I will not be able to bear it if ...'

'Yes, darling, I know.'

'What? What's that word you used?'

'Nothing. The connection must be bad.'

*

I spend a good part of the next day in the library. I look with numb horror at the notes I have culled from the books spread out before me.

The purge of Phnom Penh

On 17th April 1975 an army of young peasant boys marched into Phnom Penh. The war in Cambodia was over.

One week later Phnom Penh was empty.

The Khmer Rouge had, at gunpoint, driven three million people out of the city. They were forced to march hundreds of kilometres in burning dry-season heat. Hundreds of thousands, including sick people chased out of hospitals, old folk and little children, perished on the way. The peasant soldiers' casual brutality brought death to thousands more.

A human flood poured out of the city. People carried their most precious belongings in homemade carts, on bicycles or on their heads. People were executed for the slightest reason, mothers in childbirth left to die by the roadside. Piles of rotting corpses lined the highway.

Survivors of the march were put to backbreaking work in farms. Others were condemned to a slow death in special camps.

About 600,000 people had lost their lives in the Cambodian War. Between 1.4 million and 2.5 million people were brutally put to death in the ensuing 'peace'.

To the revolutionary leader Pol Pot, city life represented the corruption of man. He believed that people could be reformed ... but not cities. He was not concerned with the number of people who perished in the cleansing process. One or two million young people were enough, he believed, to make the new Kampuchea.

The Khmers believed that, if a basket is known to contain even a few rotten fruit, it is a waste of time to identify and select the bad ones. It is so much easier to throw the whole basket in the river!

My head swims as I read through the notes once again. A feeling of unreality seems to grip my mind.

I take a sheet of paper and make a list of facts, and educated guesses, relating to Kalinga Lokuge:

1. He believes that the poor can take their rightful place only when the cities, and the corruption they represent, are crushed. I've heard him say it myself.
2. He has personally formulated a plan to achieve this aim. He told us about it but never revealed the details.
3. He has visited Kampuchea several times but has never given a satisfactory reason for his interest in that country.
4. He flew into a rage when I mentioned Pol Pot.
5. His own party seems to be unaware of any conspiracy so he must be working independently.
6. He openly criticised and defied his own government; he is not afraid of being sacked from the cabinet. This must mean that he is ready to launch his strike.

It lacks substance when I put it down on paper. I don't even have enough to go to my own editor. There are many unanswered questions too.

I take another sheet and make a second list.

1. The Khmer Rouge had a peasant army. Has Kalinga trained a student militia under his Ginirälla program?
2. The Khmers fought and won a war to take power. Kalinga's militia is clearly incapable of waging war. How will he seize power?
3. What is the conspiracy Sebastian Peiris knew about? Is it linked to Ginirälla? How?
4. What can I, a woman without resources or influence, do about all this?

27

They have killed Fazlia.

Mithra had turned up unexpectedly on Thursday afternoon. I could tell he was really worried because he barged into the office without calling first.

'Have you had any trouble?' he asked as soon as he saw me. 'Phone calls? Anything?'

'No. Nothing at all,' I had answered easily. 'I'm being very careful and Fazlia is keeping an eye on me.'

'Don't worry, Mr. Mithra,' Fazlia had laughed. 'The boys in the next cubicle escort us to the bus stand. We are taking good care of this girl.'

'I'm taking you out today,' he told me firmly. 'I'll drop you back after dinner.'

'Ahh Mithra, I want to shower and change before going out,' I had protested. 'Take me home first.'

'No time for that; I have to get back to Tangalle tonight. I only drove up to talk to you.'

He had gone through my notes with rising alarm.

'Baba, this is frightening. It's far too serious for us to handle,' he had said. 'We must go to the authorities with it.'

'Whom could we go to? The man is a Minister and all I have is guesswork. No criminal act can be traced to him. What can anyone do?'

We argued all through dinner.

Mithra wanted me to get out of Colombo for a few

days to let things cool down. I was convinced that some awful catastrophe was about to overtake the nation and I had a duty to do something, however futile and hopeless that was.

It is late when we finish.

'Why don't you stay the night and leave early morning?' I ask. 'It's a very long drive, isn't it? You must be tired.'

Mithra looks at me speculatively and hesitates.

'There's something … I have to attend to in the morning,' he says finally. 'It's no problem, really. I enjoy driving late at night.'

The moment Mithra turns into the lane I sense that something is very wrong. The house is ablaze with lights and there is a crowd of loiterers outside.

Oh no. Something has happened to poor Mrs. Blyth!

Mithra parks the vehicle and we hurry forward, only to stop abruptly when we see the police jeep.

I spot old Mr. Burrel from the house across the street. He is leaning heavily on his walking stick, trying to peer over the crowd.

'Uncle, what has happened?' I ask. 'Is anyone hurt?'

'T … terrible thing, child' he quavers. 'Some men … broke into house. They locked aunty in her room … then they shot that Moslem girl … your friend.'

'Oh no. Is Fazlia badly hurt? Where is she?'

'I'm sorry child,' he says gently. 'Ambulance came but they say … no use. She's dead.'

'No. No. No. No.'

I feel hot tears scalding my eyes. I turn away blindly and try to push my way through the crowd.

How can sensible, laughing Fazlia be dead? It must be some mistake. I must get to her.

Mithra grasps my arm and hauls me to a side.

'You can't go in there, baba,' he whispers. 'We must get out of here.'

'No. No. I must find Fazlia.'

I am dazed and disoriented, shattered by sorrow. Mithra holds me by the shoulders; I can feel his fingers digging painfully into my back.

'Listen to me. Listen,' he says harshly. 'She must have been asleep. They came for you and shot her by mistake. Do you understand?'

'No. No.'

Mithra shakes me, trying to make me focus.

'They might still be here, in the crowd. You are in danger even now. We must get out of here.'

He lets me cry.

I crouch in a corner of the seat. My eyes are shut but tears keep slipping through, down my chin and onto my chest. My wispy little handkerchief is soaked and useless; I need a towel. I hear a keening wail go on and on, like a distant siren. I realise only later that it is coming from somewhere deep inside me.

It is well past midnight when Mithra pulls off the deserted highway at Kalutara. The tar-black coffee scalds my lips but helps me to steady myself. When we get underway again I am able to make some conversation.

'Where are we going?'

'To Tangalle,' he says. 'I've rented a small annexe. You can stay there till we make some other arrangement.'

'What about my job? I can't just stay away.'

'Don't you think you should tell your editor the

whole story?'

'I … I don't know. He'll ask me to go to the police, won't he? They'll question me for days and it'll still come to nothing.'

'Well tomorrow's Friday. Call your editor and ask for the day off,' he tells me. 'We'll decide what to do over the weekend.'

The headlights make twin tunnels in the gloom and the leather seats are warm and comfortable.

'Go to sleep if you like,' Mithra says kindly. 'I'll wake you up when we're close.'

He's trying to change from teaser to protector. At any other time I would have found the effort amusing.

But not now.

'Then you'll fall asleep at the wheel and kill us both,' I say. 'Let's talk about something … anything but politics.'

'Well if you want to keep me awake, this is a good chance to tell me about your childhood … problem.'

I look at him angrily. The faint glow of the dash lights show him calmly studying the road before him.

'You will despise me when you know the truth.'

'Goes to show how little you know me,' he replies calmly.

I stare at the road ahead and don't say anything.

'My mother abandoned me when I was twelve years old. They said she ran away with a man from Giriulla. My little brother and I were left alone. She … never came back; never wrote. Never sent one message to find out how we were.

'She pretended to love us. She seemed to dote on us … till one day, without a word, she went away. She …

forgot about us.'

I thought I had finished my tears but they start again, in a flood now. I begin to squirm in my seat, straining against the seat belt. I want to jump out of the vehicle; do something drastic to ease the pain.

Mithra swerves to the edge of the road and stops the vehicle. He flicks off my seat belt and draws me closer to him. I struggle for a moment and then give up. I allow my head to rest against his shoulder.

'He pierced me then,' I whisper into his shirtsleeve, 'the very night she went away.'

'Shit, you were only a child. Who? Who raped you?'

I push myself away from him, squeezing myself once again into the far edge of the seat.

'My f … father.'

Mithra is shocked into silence. I'm glad I'm not able to see the revulsion that must be on his face now.

'Come over here.'

'What for? Are you stupid? Haven't you been listening? I'm soiled … I warned you. You despise me now and I don't blame you.'

'Will you shut up and come here?' Mithra roars, his voice booming inside the close confines of the vehicle. He grabs my arm and drags me to his side. I feel his arms go round me as he pushes my face into the hollow below his chin.

'It's no use Mithra, there are more horrors. You can't change …'

'Did you hear me tell you to shut up?'

'I …'

'Not a word.'

'Mm.'

'You are a very rare and wonderful person. To me, you

are life itself. Nothing that has happened in the past can change that. I now know you've had a terrible experience as a child. But listen carefully. If you say one more word about being soiled or worthless I'll give you such a smack it'll rattle your teeth.'

This is a new Mithra, strangely comforting.

'Go on then.'

'Are you sure you want to hear the rest of the story? Sordid doesn't even begin to describe it.'

'Just tell me everything.'

'He'd come home drunk and drag me to his mat. He'd keep mumbling how lovely I was. My own … father … doing that awful t … thing because I was lovely. I … only remember the pain as if I was being stabbed, the stink of arrack and sweat, and … shame.

'Night after night after night!

'What hurt more than all the abuse was the knowledge that my mother had gone away … and left me. I had to face that unspeakable … horror alone.

'She could have protected me … she preferred to abandon me for some man. If she had loved me even a little bit, she could have taken me with her. That was what broke my heart. It made me realise that I had no value.'

I am crying again, moaning as I relive the despair I had felt in those awful days. A sorrow, like a tumour, that will never leave me. I feel Mithra's arm tighten across my shoulder and try to control myself.

'It went on till one day he asked me if … my period had come. I said no, barely understanding what it meant. He asked me every day, screaming at me, as though it was my fault.

'A few weeks later he killed himself by eating Kaneru

seed. I didn't know what to do; I had no one to turn to … so I went to Yasawathi.

'She is my father's older sister; her husband is the village headman. They have no children.

'She was alone in her kitchen when I told her. She flew into a rage; I have never seen anyone so angry, so frightening. She said I was a slut who had given myself to some boy in the village and now, when I got into trouble, I was trying to disgrace my dead father.

'She picked up a piece of firewood and attacked me. I ran out of her kitchen but she caught me in the garden. She was a big, strong woman; she … caught my wrists in one hand … lifted me up and … and beat me and beat me on my stomach with the f … firewood.

'She kept repeating two words as she beat me.

'Vesa bälli, vesa bälli.

'Prostitute bitch. I suppose I've always thought of myself as that.'

Mithra tries to comfort me by rocking me from side to side. I feel one hand stroking my hair.

'You know that's not true, baba; a child abused by someone she trusted. How could it possibly have been the child's fault? Yasawathi must be a devilish woman to have assaulted you like that.'

'I was barely conscious when she dropped me in the tall grass and went back to the house. I was terrified that she would return to kill me so I tried to crawl away but couldn't straighten my body. My stomach hurt so much.

'It was only then that I realised I was bleeding. My dress and …my lower body were soaked in blood. I didn't know it then but I lost my baby in the weeds and rubbish behind my aunt's house.

'I thought I would die too. I wanted to.'

'Yasawathi's husband came and carried me into the house. I suppose he was afraid I would die out there. He helped me to clean myself but they wouldn't let me go back home. Instead they locked me in a tiny windowless room they used for storing paddy.

'It was dark and musty in there and I was terrified. I was frightened to breathe thinking the air would finish and I would suffocate.

'They kept me locked up during the funeral. Through it all I had only one thought going round and round in my head.'

'Oh mother, why did you go away and abandon me? Did I mean so little to you?'

'My mother's sister Seela came for the funeral. When she found that I was ill she offered to take me away to Angunuwewa. I think Yasawathi was glad to get rid of me so she agreed immediately. Seela looked after me as though I was one of her own but it was really Father Basil who helped me to recover my sanity.'

There is a light under the porch but Mithra parks by the side of the old house. A weathered door in the wing leads to the little apartment. What might once have been an office room is now converted for sitting and dining.

Mithra leads me through a door on the left into an untidy bedroom.

'Don't you make your bed up in the morning?' I ask to cover my nervousness.

'What's the point? I'll only disturb it again in the night,' he responds lightly, sensing my mood. 'Easier this way.'

'You need a nanny, not a girl friend.'

'Same thing,' he laughs.

Then:

'You can sleep in this room; I'll try the sofa in the hall. I'll give you a T-shirt to wear. That ok?'

'Mm.'

'There's a spare toothbrush somewhere. The bathroom's through that door.'

'Is it in better condition than the bed?'

'Yes.'

'All right then.'

28

Mithra is still asleep, feet hanging over the armrest of the sofa, the metal calliper on the floor below. The door at the opposite end of the sitting room leads to a tiny kitchenette. I find some Nescafè and sugar and make two cups. Mithra opens his eyes when I prod him in the ribs with my toe.

'Mmmm. This is what I like,' he says, stretching his arms. 'Room service.'

'There's only stale bread,' I say. 'What do you eat for breakfast?'

'Buttered toast. You can make some.'

'Sounds awful. Don't you have anything else?'

'I'm sure there's a packet of biscuits somewhere.' he says. 'Let me look.'

Mithra follows me to the kitchen.

'Hmm. Nice legs.'

'What? What … did … you … say?'

'Nice if we had eggs.'

'You're such a liar.'

We are eating toast when Mithra takes my hand.

'Suji, I told you I had to come back last night. I meant to bring you back with me anyway.'

'You needed someone to arrange your bed and make your toast?'

He doesn't laugh.

'I told you didn't I, that my crew was at Medamulana. They are constructing new wells, deepening existing wells.'

My throat is dry. I stop eating.

'Who is Sujith Kumara?'

'My b … brother.'

'His well had run dry. He is one of those we are helping.'

'So?'

'There is an abandoned well in his garden, filled with earth and rocks. Can you remember it?'

'Yes, I think so.'

'The old well seems to be in a better spot. My crew tried to restore it. When they were digging, they found … something in the well.'

'What?'

'A body … a skeleton really, at the bottom.'

I jump to my feet and hear the crash as the chair falls over behind me.

'What are you saying? Whose body is it?'

'They don't know.'

'Why are you telling me this?'

Mithra walks round the table and puts his arm round my shoulders.

'It's a woman,' he says gently. 'She might have been killed and her body thrown in the well.'

'You think it's my mother? It can't be. She went away with someone. Everyone in the village knew that.'

'We have to go there,' Mithra says.

'No. No. How can you ask me to go back there? I never want to see that place again.'

'Your brother can't help. Maybe he was too young at the time,' he goes on. 'It is up to you. There are some scraps of fabric … you might remember something.'

I keep wiping my hands.

The orange Land Rover floats through a browned-out landscape. Failure of the monsoon has left the rice fields with sun-scorched stubble from the last harvest. The only green I can see is in the crowns of large, deep-rooted trees lining the road. Cattle stand listlessly in the shade, waiting till nightfall brings some relief from the searing heat.

Mithra knows the way. He turns off the main road before we reach Wiraketiya. The signpost pointing the way to Medamulana is new, I'm sure, but the track hasn't changed very much. White dust billows from the unsealed surface as we pass by.

'Have you seen your brother since you left?' Mithra asks. 'It's been twelve years, hasn't it?'

'I haven't seen him.'

'Any special reason?'

'He was being brought up by Yasawathi … and you know about her,' I answer.

Mithra doesn't say anything.

'He hated me anyway; thought I was taking his mother's place,' I say bitterly. 'I can't blame him for that.'

The village has grown. Houses nestle between banana and coconut trees, some thatched, and others with red tiled roofs. Passers-by stop and stare as the Rover grinds its way along the narrow track.

I see Keera's shop at the junction and my heart begins to pound. I know what's round the next bend and squeeze myself into the seat hoping the leather will cover and hide me.

I can't face this.

Mithra brings the vehicle to a halt and gets down. I raise my eyes and stare with disbelief at the crowd gathered outside my old home. A police jeep has been parked further up the track. I see a policeman walking towards our vehicle.

Mithra opens my door and takes me by the hand.

'You should have … warned me …'

'You wouldn't have come then,' he says gently. 'This needs to be done and I'll be with you every minute. You can do it, I know.'

The uniformed man addresses Mithra.

'Is this the girl?'

'This is the lady, yes.'

The man turns to me.

'I am Sergeant Somasiri. Please come with me.'

The crowd press in from the sides but Somasiri goes ahead and makes room for us to follow. I keep my eyes on the ground and hold my hands together to conceal my trembling fingers.

It takes a moment for my eyes to adjust to the relative gloom inside the house. A harassed looking man with thin grey hair is seated behind a table on my left. Standing by the side of the table is another middle-aged man in spectacles who seems to be giving evidence. The space on my right as well as the front veranda behind me is crowded with onlookers.

On a mat on the floor before the table is a loose collection of bones. I can see a skull and a ribcage.

I catch some of the words of the spectacled man.

'… woman … about thirty years …'

'Can you tell me when she died?' the man behind the table asks.

'I cannot say accurately with the means at my disposal. More than ten years, I'd surmise.'

'Can you determine the cause of death?'

'There is a severe depression at the back of her skull. She appears to have been killed by a blow to the head.'

'Thank you, doctor.'

The policeman walks up and whispers in the ear of the seated man. Grey hair looks up and gestures to me.

My feet carry me forward while my mind is running away.

'You are Sujatha Mallika?'

'Yes.'

A murmur runs through the room but grey hair quells it with an angry stare.

'You are the sister of Sujith Kumara who lives in this house?'

'Y … yes.'

Grey hair takes time to write down each question and answer.

'I understand you left this village twelve years ago. Is that correct?'

'Yes.'

'Do you remember the well at the back of the garden?'

'Yes.'

'Was it in use when you were taken away?'

'No. My father filled it up; he said the water had gone bad. He dug another well on the other side.'

'Can you tell us when this happened?'

'No … No, I can't remember.'

'I know this will be painful for you,' grey hair says kindly, 'but I want you to examine the remains on the mat here. Is it possible for you to tell us who that is?'

I had kept my eyes turned firmly away but now I have no choice. I take a hesitant step and then kneel before the pitiful remains. The bones are tiny, making it hard to imagine they once supported a human frame. A few scraps of wispy material are arranged at one corner of the mat.

I leave the skull for the last, hating every moment. I stare at it for a long time before getting to my feet.

'Well?'

'This is my mother, Ran Manika.'

I hear gasps of surprise behind me.

'How are you able to identify her?'

'She had a broken front tooth, exactly like that.'

'Are you certain?'

'Yes.'

'How did she break her tooth? Do you remember?'

'My father threw a clay pot at her. It hit her on the face, broke her tooth.'

He is standing near the gate, a short, thickset man in a white sarong. He looks at me uncertainly.

'Chooti malli.'

Small brother.

'Akki.'

Sister.

I had wondered if he still despised me. The relief is so overwhelming that I ignore the crowd and wrap my arms around him. He looks startled by my demonstration of affection but, after a moment's hesitation, I feel his fingers grasp my shoulders.

'Malli dakkinna thiyana satuta kiyanna bähä.'

I can't tell you how happy I am to see you.

'Api nitharama akki gäna kathakaranawā. Priyāth ähuwā akki gäna.'

We talk about you often, sister. Priya also asks about you.

'Priya?'

Sujith pushes a blushing girl in a loose blue dress towards me: thin and pretty and hugely pregnant.

I hold her hands as Sujith looks on with an air of pride.

I try to put the thoughts tumbling through my head into some order. Mithra concentrates on the road, avoiding the worst of the potholes and corrugations. When we reach the main road he turns his head briefly:

'Are you angry then, that I took you there?'

'I want to be but I can't just now,' I tell him. 'I'll punish you for it later.'

He laughs. Mithra always laughs.

'I don't see why. Your brother was happy to see you, wasn't he?'

'Mm. That was wonderful,' I say very softly, treasuring the memory. 'I can't believe the little fellow has got himself a wife as well. They look a nice couple; makes me feel old.'

'You're becoming an old maid all right,' Mithra says. 'I'm trying to save you from that fate; you should be grateful.'

'Oh shut up.'

'The old woman who was staring at you and muttering, was that …'

'Yes, that was Yasawathi.'

'She looks a vicious old witch.'

'That she is,' I say with feeling. 'I suppose, at the time, she was desperate to cover up the scandal. She did manage that, when you think about it.'

'Must have been quite a shock for her though, to see you come back there like a princess.'

'What princess?' I ask irritably. 'Don't talk rubbish.'

'You don't realise the impact you have, baba,' Mithra says simply. 'Everyone was surprised, even that coroner fellow. I could see it.'

'Don't talk about my … appearance,' I say sharply. 'You know I don't like to talk about that.'

Mithra pats me on the knee.

'I wasn't speaking about your appearance, honey. Really I wasn't,' he says gently. 'There is something about you that makes people stop and … stare.'

We stop at the market. Mithra can't make up his mind about what he'd like for dinner. He objects to everything I select till I realise that he's just trying to annoy me. I give him a thump on his ear and pick what I fancy.

We potter about the apartment all evening and then Mithra sits on a stool watching me prepare dinner. He offers useless suggestions from time to time.

'Don't you believe in helping out?' I ask finally. 'Or is criticism the only skill you have?'

'In Australia they taught me that there is management and there is labour. The job of management is to tell labour what to do and point out its mistakes …'

I hold a frying pan over his head.

'And what did your professor say about this?'

'That when labour gets violent, the only thing management can do is to submit completely. What do you want done?'

'Peel these potatoes.'

'Yes, ma'am,' he says, 'right away, ma'am.'

Sleep won't come.

The enormity of what has taken place is too much. I have spent the day in denial, trying to avoid thinking about it. My mother is dead; has been dead for a long time. The structure of my life has now been turned on its head.

What does it mean?

Mithra has sensed my confusion and avoided the subject. I have managed to suppress it too, while we chatted about everything else. Now I'm alone and the memories are flooding my mind.

'Mithra,' I call out softly through the half open door. 'Mithra, are you asleep'

'Not any more.'

'I can't sleep. Can you bring your stuff and come here?'

'To your bed?'

'Of course not! Can't you sleep on the floor, near my bed?' I ask. 'Or I can sleep on the floor and you can have the bed.'

'Yeah, that'll be good,' he laughs.

He comes limping into the room carrying his pillow. He rummages in a cupboard and pulls out what appears to be some heavy material and throws it on the floor by the side of my bed.

'My mum won't be happy if she knows that her quilted bedspread is being put on the floor,' he says.

'She won't be happy to hear that you have a girl in your bed either.'

'She'll be more upset to know that the girl has taken my bed and put me on the floor.'

It makes me feel bad, really it does. I lean over the edge of the bed and see the outline of his head below me. I let my hand brush against his cheek.

'Oh Mithra, I don't know what I'd do without you.'

He puts his hand over mine, holding it against his cheek.

'Does it bother you when I do that?'

'No,' I say softly, 'and I'll tell you something else if you promise not to let it upset you.'

'Sure.'

'You know I could never stand having men come close to me. I never felt threatened by you because …'

'Because of my leg?' he starts laughing. 'This is the first time in my life that I have something to thank polio for.'

'You're not angry I said that?'

'Nothing you say to me could make me angry.'

He places his hand on my cheek. I'm surprised to find it far more pleasant than I had expected. I let my own fingers run through his hair.

Why am I short of breath?

'You can't say you're worthless now, can you?' Mithra asks.

'What do you mean?'

'You thought she had abandoned you,' he goes on, 'but she didn't, did she? She must have loved you very much.'

'How can you know that?'

'She wouldn't let him harm you. That has to be why he killed her.'

'My poor mother. How awful that she had to die because of me.'

'She died because your father was a murderous criminal. How can you possibly blame yourself for that?'

'It was because of my … appearance,' I moan, feeling tearful again. 'It is my curse. All these horrors took place because of that.'

'It is a gift, my love,' he says. 'It is part of you. How can you blame yourself for what others do because of that?'

'It has brought me so much sorrow and trouble,' I tell him. 'Once, during the rag, I picked up a razor. I thought if I … slash my face, the interest in me will end.'

'Oh Lord!'

'Nali came in at that moment and took the razor from my hand ….'

'I can't discuss this while you're hanging over me like a bat,' Mithra says firmly. 'Come down here.'

I'm not sure this is a good idea but Mithra just pulls my arm and I tumble on to the quilt. I had been holding a pillow and it falls with me. I let it lie between us, stretching from chest to knee.

'What's this?'

'Safety barrier.'

'The things you put me through would drive any other man insane,' he groans.

'Nothing to drive! I knew you were insane from the day you did that … awful thing on the VC's chair.'

'Well you jumped in front of his car to save me, remember? You must have been eyeing me from that time.'

'Oh shut up.'

Near panic keeps me chattering. Mithra's face is very close; there's fresh mint in his breath. I feel his lips brush my forehead, then my ear and cheek. I had braced myself, digging my fingers into the pillow, biting my lip to keep from crying out.

Without conscious effort on my part I find the tension slipping away. There is no attack on my person, no disgusting smell of arrack.

And no fear!

I feel his lips moving slowly to the edge of my mouth. They brush my lips lightly at first, like the touch of a feather. He catches my lower lip between his and I feel his tongue running along it.

I should have been repelled but, to my surprise, find it pleasant.

More than pleasant.

Without my realising it, my right hand has released the pillow and is now clutching the back of his head. I hear a moaning sound.

I know it's me!

Mithra says:

'You kiss like a puppy. Don't you know how?'

'How can I? I've never been kissed on the mouth before.'

'Haven't you seen it in movies?'

'There's no kissing in Sinhala movies. They only hold hands.'

'I'll have to teach you, I suppose.'

'Are you sure this is hygienic?'

'Of course it is, sugar. All lovers do it.'

'Mm. All right then.'

'Throw this damn pillow away, will you?'

What else could I do?

'I didn't know it would be like this,' I murmur into his chest.

'Aha! I think someone has had a good time,' he answers, teasing me again.

'Oh shut up,' I say. 'Anyway you should have told me.'

His fingers had been stroking my hair. He grips a handful playfully.

'If I even mentioned the subject, you would have run away,' he says gently. 'As it is, it took me more than four years to get you into my bed.'

'All these years … and this was what you wanted?'

'Of course.'

'I thought you were such a gentleman, now I find you're a real wretch,' I tell him severely. 'Anyway, what will happen if I get pregnant?'

'Well if it's a boy, you can call him Mithra. If it's a girl, name her Maithri.'

He howls when I pinch his stomach.

'Oh, all right then,' he says. 'If you're going to torture me I suppose I'll have to marry you.'

'Are you sure you want to?'

I feel his arms tighten across my shoulders.

'Surer than anything else in my life.'

'What about your parents? I've no dowry to bring.'

'You really are an idiot,' he laughs. 'Everyone who sees you will wonder what on earth made you select me. They'll think I'm the luckiest man in the world.'

'You're lucky all right,' I say. 'Even just now, I had to do all the work.'

'That's what happens when you pick a man with a bad leg,' he murmurs. 'Anyway I didn't hear you grumbling at the time.'

29

There's a sharp rap on the door.

'Answering the door is a wife's job,' Mithra mumbles, his mouth full of roti. 'Rule 23 in the marriage manual.'

'I'm not your wife as yet,' I call from the kitchen. 'What are the husband's duties anyway?'

'I've performed them last night, don't you remember?' he laughs. 'That's all. Everything else is yours.'

'I have a feeling you are going to have a very short marriage.'

The rap is repeated, more loudly this time.

I suppose it is some tradesman. I smack Mithra's head as I walk towards the entrance. The night latch turns easily and I throw the door open.

Kumudu towers above me, shutting out the sunlight; his eyes above the wild beard are blazing.

I'm unable to move … or speak. I hear Mithra's footsteps as he comes up and stands beside me. Kumudu brushes past us and enters the sitting room.

The tranquillity we had enjoyed, Mithra and I, was only a bubble; like a marauder, terror has entered our sanctuary. If Kumudu is here, his killers must already be outside. I hope they will end it quickly.

'Mithra has nothing to do with this,' I say desperately. 'Let him go.'

'Shut the door, sit down over there,' Kumudu snarls, 'and shut up.'

Wordlessly we obey him, sitting side by side on the

sofa. Kumudu remains standing in the centre of the room.

'Is there anyone else here?'

'No, we're alone,' I reply. 'How did you find us?'

At first I think he isn't going to answer, then he looks at Mithra:

'We were not happy with your employer so we've kept a close watch on their staff. I saw in a report that you joined them,' he says. 'When Sujatha disappeared, I guessed that she'd come to you for help.'

'Kumudu,' Mithra says calmly, 'Why this campaign against Sujatha? Why are you trying to harm her?'

'Our leader has decided that she is a threat to our movement. The order has gone out that she is to be eliminated.'

'I've seen Sujatha's notes,' Mithra replies mildly. 'There's nothing there that even remotely threatens your movement. Surely you must know that.'

Some of the tension seems to drain out of Kumudu. He walks to the window, pulls the curtain aside and looks at the road.

'Oh, I know that. The trouble is this fool offended our leader. He's given the order now so only he can withdraw it. And he won't …'

'So you're here to carry out your brave leader's instructions?' I ask. I hope he can detect the contempt in my tone.

Kumudu's stare is withering.

'If I'd come to kill you, you'd be dead by now.'

'Why are you here then?'

Kumudu sits down.

'To warn you,' he says simply. 'You have no idea with what determination my people are hunting you.'

'Surely she'll be safe here,' Mithra says, 'unless you

inform on us.'

'There are others from our time on campus that know who Sujatha's friends were,' he answers roughly. 'They'll trace you, just as I did. They might be on their way even now.'

The room goes quiet as we assess this new threat.

Kumudu gets to his feet.

'Pack up and leave this place,' he says grimly as he turns to leave. 'Do it soon.'

I follow him to the door.

'Kumudu,' I call out, 'what's this secret that justifies so much killing? Why did Kalinga get so angry when I asked him about Kampuchea? What are you people up to?'

'Your foolish tongue has already placed you under a death sentence,' he growls. 'Don't you understand that this is something far bigger than you can even dream of? Leave it at that, use this chance I'm giving you to save your life.'

'No,' I say recklessly, 'no. Your project is wicked. I'm going to find out what it is and expose it.'

Kumudu turns round. I brace myself thinking he'll attack me; instead he looks exasperated, like a parent with a dim-witted child.

He ignores me and speaks to Mithra.

'Our struggle is a noble one. All disadvantaged and marginalized people will bless us for it. Kalinga is a man of destiny. His vision will change this land and bring about a glorious future. No one can stop our victory now.'

'Kalinga is a madman. I saw it in his eyes,' I blurt out rashly. 'He will lead this country to ruin.'

'That's not true. I believe in him. He will save the country,' Kumudu replies, his voice calm and confident.

'You come from a poor family; you should have been with us. You have compassion without intellect. Your silly sentimentality turned you against us.'

'Well, you're influenced by sentiment too, aren't you?' Mithra says quietly. 'Isn't that why you're here?'

Kumudu stares at me without speaking, then he turns to Mithra.

'Dias.'

'Yes?'

'This girl is a stubborn fool! She'll try to meddle and get herself killed,' he says softly. 'Take her out of the country.'

'What?'

'If you want to save her, take her abroad. That's the only sure way.'

'I'll try …'

'Do it,' he snarls roughly, 'and do it within five days. After that … it will be too late.'

'Where are we going?'

'I'm still trying to figure it out,' Mithra says as he swerves to allow an inter-city bus to blast past. 'I have to remain in the area, for my work.'

'Can't we find another place close by?'

'They'll expect that and check around,' Mithra says. 'If they know so much about us, they'll know that I cover the area up to Ambalantota. A fellow called Abeynaike is responsible for the villages from there to Kataragama.'

'So?'

'I thought of going to Hambantota. It's in Abey's area but close enough for me to handle my work.'

'All right.'

Mithra is silent for some time, concentrating on the road.

'Baba.'

'Hmm?'

'We can't ignore Kumudu's warning. I'll feel happier if you went out of the country for a while.'

'Where can I go? I have no money and no visa. I can't just pack up and leave.'

'I can arrange for the funds and Singapore doesn't require a visa.'

'No. I think he's still worried about what I might find out. Anyway I'm not leaving you. We'll face this thing together.'

'He said there's only five days …'

'I can't imagine what that means. Let's wait and see.'

The clerk at the reception desk keeps glancing at me. I'm sure he suspects something and feel my cheeks grow warm. I ignore him and walk to the veranda to admire the view.

The rest house has been built on a bluff overlooking the bay. A small pier juts into the water and, further out, fishing boats keep bobbing in the swell. The sea in the wide bay is a startling aquamarine, jewel bright in the midday sun.

Mithra has parked the orange Land Rover by the side of the building nearly, but not completely, hidden from the road. He comes out with a boy who carries our luggage to a room on the first floor. The fellow fusses around with the air conditioner and TV till Mithra gives him a small tip and gets rid of him.

The click of the lock releases the tension I had felt since Kumudu left and we had hurried out of Mithra's apartment. It seems natural for Mithra to put his arms around me and for me to rest my forehead in the hollow of his neck.

'The shower made my neck sting,' Mithra drawls as we come downstairs for breakfast. 'Know what I found? A perfect set of teeth marks.'

'What?'

'You bit my neck,' Mithra says pulling his collar aside. 'Here, you can see the mark.'

'Keep your voice down, you idiot,' I whisper, looking around nervously, 'people will hear you. Anyway I never bit you; you must have dreamt it.'

'Yes, you did and it hurt too,' Mithra goes on with a laugh. 'I never thought the *gamey kella* will turn into a tigress after just one night.'

I feel my cheeks burning.

'Will you stop it? I'll never do anything if you start talking like this.'

I feel his arm tighten affectionately across my shoulders.

'Oh all right, I won't tell anyone then,' he says, 'but for a shy girl, I mean …'

'Shut up, shut up.'

Mithra's phone rings. It startles me because no one has called since we left Colombo. Mithra lifts the little instrument to his ear and listens for a moment. I see his eyes open wide.

'Oh Lord, when did this happen? … Where? … Are they all right? … Oh no … both of them? … What do the police say? … OK, thanks for calling me.'

Mithra puts the phone in his pocket; he looks shattered.

'What is it? What's happened?'

'That was my office in Colombo. My colleague Abey and his wife were shot and killed last night.'

'Who did it? How did it happen?'

'They were driving to Tissa; the vehicle was found by the roadside. The police have no ideas.'

'Do … do you think it is connected with us?'

'Abey was driving an orange Land Rover,' Mithra says, 'just like mine.'

My sense of wellbeing is blighted in a flash. We look towards the road fearfully wondering if they have spotted us already.

Mithra says: 'Let's go to the room. We need to decide what to do.'

'Oh Mithra, all this is because of me,' I say, trying to hold back my tears. 'Your friend lost his life because of me; I don't want to lose you as well. Put me on a bus. I can disappear for a while.'

'No,' he answers firmly. 'I'm with you till the end.'

'But …'

'No.'

'Then we have to get out of this area, don't we?'

'Yes.'

The new road from Hambantota to Suriyawewa is broad and straight. It is also the quickest route out of the areas where Mithra's employer, World Water, has ongoing programs. Mithra has decided to take refuge in the hill country where the JSP strength is less overwhelming.

We both agree that the first priority is a safe hiding place. It is only then that we can even think of what to do next.

We reach Suriyawewa without incident. Mithra turns left towards Embilipitiya. The Rover is flying and each kilometre, even each spin of the tyre, brings an infinitesimal measure of relief.

Mithra's phone shatters our tranquillity once again. He catches my eye as he puts it to his ear.

'Hullo. Ah, Harith … you're looking for Suji? She's with me. Yes, right here … hold on.'

I put the phone to my ear.

'Yes, Harith.'

'Where are you guys?'

'Are you alone?'

'Yes. Why do you ask?'

'We're on the road, going towards Embilipitiya.'

'The security manager from my site called; he's an ex-army chap called Marasinghe. Says he's discovered why they want our project stopped; why they killed my father.'

'Did he explain?'

'Something about a massive facility in Block III of Yala.'

'What on earth is Block III?"

'It's a forest reserve south of the land given for our project. No visitors are allowed there.'

'So what is this facility?"

'Said it is like a … prison camp, all barbed wire and sentry towers.'

A trickle of iced water seems to run down my back.

Who would want to build a prison camp? Who are the intended inmates?

'What are you going to do?'

'Marasinghe is a bit of a poacher and stumbled on this place during one of his hunts. Says he can take me there.'

'Are you going?'

'Yes. That's why I called you,' Harith says. 'Do you want to come?'

'When?'

'Tomorrow morning.'

'I'd like to Hari, but there are some complications. Can I talk to Mithra and call you back?'

'Sure.'

Mithra is not happy.

'I just don't think you should risk going there. I'll go with Harith and see what it's all about.'

'No. Kumudu admitted they had Somasiri Jayakody killed, so this prison camp must be the reason. This is part of Kalinga's plot and it's something really terrible. We must stop them.'

'How can we do that?'

'Only by exposure in a newspaper, but I need some solid evidence for the story. Photographs of the camp might be enough. Once that comes out the authorities will be forced to investigate.'

Mithra sighs.

'Call Harith then.'

'You don't have to come, honey,' I say. 'I'll go along with Harith, then come and pick you up.'

'Whither thou goest, I will go.'

'What's all that about?'

'Passage from the Bible; it's called the Song of Ruth.'

'I like the tune.'

Harith is to leave early next morning. He's coming along the coast and wants to pick us up at Tissa. Mithra parks by the side of the road to discuss our options.

'It means going back,' Mithra says. 'It's a big risk.'

'Do we have to go back the same way?'

'No-o, we can go to Tanamalwila and then on to Tissa. I don't think they will expect us to return to the area.'

'We'll be going past my village.'

'Do you want to visit your aunt?'

'I'd love to but they'll be on the look out for me there, won't they?'

'Yes.'

'Where can we stay then?'

'Harith has made reservations at Tissa Resort. We can go in after dark,' Mithra says. 'It should be safe enough for one night.'

The reservation is for Mr. Nimal Perera. When the clerk picks up the registration form and turns to fetch the key, Mithra leans over.

'Shall I ask for a isolated room?' he whispers. 'Your moaning might disturb the other guests.'

'Will you stop it?'

I kick him in the shin and draw a satisfying gasp.

They give us a room on the first floor with a balcony overlooking the Tissa Wäwa. Headlights of vehicles moving on the bund on the far side throw ghostly shadows across the water and a tree filled island some hundred metres off shore.

We take time to shower and change and go down for dinner when most of the other guests have finished. Curries and surprisingly crisp hoppers are still on offer at the buffet table.

We walk down to the garden afterwards. The area beyond the swimming pool has been terraced with steps leading down to the wäwa and ending in a short pier. The weathered planks creak and sway when we step on them. We walk gingerly to the end and sit with our feet hanging over the edge.

'It's so peaceful here,' Mithra murmurs, 'like another

world. I can't believe that, out there, killers are searching for us.'

'What are we going to do?'

'Stay hidden, I suppose. What else can we do?'

'We might save our own lives,' I say, 'but what about the others? What about the country?'

'I still can't believe that something really bad will happen. It's mostly guesswork, isn't it?'

'It's more than that. Kalinga is a madman. He wants to cleanse the cities of corruption; I'm sure now he's planning to follow the Kampuchean model. That means he'll put every man, woman and child out of their homes and on to the road. He means to purge Colombo.'

'And do what?'

'He's built a prison camp, hasn't he? Why else would he go to the enormous expense and effort to set it up?'

'How can they force people to leave their homes and go to a prison camp hundreds of kilometres away? Surely they'd resist?'

'In just a few days, an army of peasant boys emptied Phnom Penh of three million people. They just shot a few hundred and the rest fell in line like … like chickens. Kalinga has recruited a student army; he's trained them for four years. He means to do this.'

'But he can't just send an army of unarmed students to take over a country,' Mithra objects.

'Did you know that the Mahaweli ministry has a big armoury? And who's the Mahaweli minister? Kalinga Lokuge.'

'But there's a president and a prime minister … the armed forces,' Mithra says doubtfully. 'They are not going to hand the country over to a bunch of students, even if they're armed.'

'Kalinga's not about to start a civil war; he means to

take power first. As leader of the country he'll unleash his student militia against the civilian population.'

'So that's what it comes down to, doesn't it? Can he seize power? How will he do it?'

'I have no idea.'

'Kumudu told me to get you out of the country in five days,' Mithra says thoughtfully. 'We've already used up two of them.'

I want the air conditioner switched off and the windows open. Mithra grumbles about *godayas* not being able to appreciate modern conveniences. He humours me just the same when I remind him he's still under probation.

A gentle breeze flutters the curtains. It is quiet now except for an infrequent squawk of a night heron from the water's edge.

And Mithra trying to get his breath back, as he rests his head on my chest.

'I don't know how this will end, honey,' I tell him. 'My only regret is that I dragged you into this.'

'Do you regret anything else?'

'No. I've never been happier in my whole life,' I say. 'If I die tomorrow, I'd have no regrets.'

I feel his arms around my waist.

'You are life to me. I can't let anything happen to you.'

30

The blast lifts us off our feet and flings us to the ground.

Mithra has parked the Land Rover at the far end of the garden, screened from the road by an untidy bougainvillea shrub. I have seen him testing his remote ignition device from various distances over the last two days. This morning he tries it from the porch in front of the reception. I see the yellow lights flash as the locks fly open; Mithra extends his arm and clicks the device again to start the engine.

The Rover blows up in a flash of intense orange-white flame that scorches a mango tree and knocks down the boundary wall. I have an impression of flying dèbris and shattering glass before the blast hits me and flings me away like a rag doll.

People are running in all directions. A security guard is holding his leg and screaming for a doctor. Mithra crawls over to me and runs his hand over my face.

'Are you all right, baba? Are you hurt?'

My throat aches when I try to speak.

'I'm … don't think … are you ok?'

'Hurt my hip but … I'm all right. We have to leave this place,' he says shakily. 'They might be watching us even now.'

We climb laboriously to our feet and recover our bags. We limp, arm in arm, into the empty foyer as curious guests and staff hurry past us to gape at the scene of the explosion. There is an awe-induced chatter in the garden.

Mithra asks:

'Should I get the key? We can hide in our room for the moment.'

'No. They'll soon know we were not in the Rover. They'll come looking for us.'

'How do we get out then?'

'Let's try the back.'

High walls on either side separate the resort from the adjoining properties. There is no escape over those walls or along the edge of the wäwa. I try to control the turmoil in my mind.

Get hold of yourself. Think.

I notice that Mithra is moving gingerly, placing his feet with extra care.

'Darling, are you all right? Why are you walking like that?'

'Say it again?'

'What?'

'That word! Repeat it.'

'Oh stop it.' I stamp my foot in exasperation. 'This is not a time for your jokes.'

'Hit my hip on the ground. I'll manage, don't worry,' he says with a strained smile. 'That's the second time you've called me darling.'

'Stop making fun of me. Let's get to the pier.'

'Why? Is there a boat there?'

'No, but I think we can call one up.'

I'd seen them from the balcony, boatmen taking visitors for rides around the island. The trees on the little island are covered with nesting birds, grey herons, pelicans and ibis. The explosion has frightened them into the air but, as we reach the pier, we see them settling down again.

The boats are tied up by the bund waiting for customers, mainly holidaymakers passing along the main road. One boat had come down this morning to collect a family from the resort.

We stand on the pier and wave.

A boat filled with noisy children putters past, circles the island and goes back towards the bund. The other boatmen have either failed to notice us or have decided we are not worth the trouble.

We can hear voices in the terrace behind us.

Come on. Come on.

One boat finally detaches itself from the bund and comes in our direction.

Crawling.

An unshaven man with a straw hat and three-quarter trousers slouches at the rear, a calloused hand on the throttle.

'Kurullo doopatha balanna dāhai.'

Thousand to see the bird island.

'Dāha dennang. Apiwa bund eka langata geniyanna.'

We'll pay the thousand. Take us to the bund.

The man looks puzzled when we throw our travelling bags aboard. He seems about to ask a question, then shrugs and gestures to us to climb in. The boatman pushes the tiny craft away from the pier and turns up the throttle but the tiny craft responds with agonizing slowness.

There is an angry yell from the terrace behind us. Mithra and I ignore it and keep looking at the bund, willing the boat forward. The boatman must have turned to look for he calls out to us uncertainly.

'Apita enna kiyanawā.'

They want us to go back.

'Härunoth apeng salli nähä,' Mithra says.

If you turn back, there'll be no money from us.

It seems like hours but it is only a few minutes later that we climb awkwardly out of the boat and up the sloping face of the bund.

The main road from Hambantota comes to a junction at the end of the bund. The road to the left runs past Tissa Resort and then to Kataragama while a right turn takes one to Tissa town and Kirinda.

The bund is crowded with holidaymakers. Buses and vans are parked in a row on the landside. People are milling about, some running across the road towards the water, others straggling back to their vehicles.

Mithra grasps my hand.

'They'll come after us by road. Let's get into the crowd.'

I have to grit my teeth to make the effort. My body aches as if it has been beaten on a rock, the way we wash clothes in the village. I can see, from the set of his features, that Mithra is also in severe pain.

We keep to the landside and move through the mob. We pass a vehicle disgorging a throng of people carrying parcels of food and bottles of water. The next group have finished their meal and are climbing the bund with their utensils. Some of them are already seated in their bus, others are milling around the footboard. A silver haired man in national dress is attempting a head count.

We stop to rest and look back just in time to see a white van screech to a halt some fifty metres away. Two men jump out of the vehicle and shout something to a boatman. They walk along the edge of the road, questioning each boatman in turn. Our man in his three-quarter pants climbs up the bund; we see him pointing down the road in our direction.

I feel tendrils of panic touch my mind.

They'll be on us in a minute. We'll be forced into the van, taken to a quiet spot and shot. There will be no escape.

I don't want to die. I don't want Mithra to die.

Mithra murmurs:

'There's a trishaw coming. Let's get on it. It's our only chance.'

'No. They'll see it stopping and chase us down,' I say, fighting to stay calm. 'Give me a moment.'

I go up to silver hair who is still trying to complete his head count.

'Māmey. Magey aiyage kakula thuwāla wunā,' I say dolefully. *'Aney, apiwa handiya langa bassanna puluwanda?'*

Uncle, my brother has injured his foot. Please, can you drop us near the junction?

The old man looks annoyed.

'Api wanndanāwe yanney. Methana hitiyoth bus ekak ēvi.'

We are on pilgrimage. If you wait here, a bus will come.

'Aiyata polio nisā kakula durwalai. Dämmama beheth dānna oney,' I go on pleading. *'Aney. Methana handiyata witharai.'*

My brother's leg is weak because of polio. He needs treatment urgently. Please, it is only up to the junction.

The old man is not convinced. I allow my fingers to touch his forearm lightly as I watch him wrestle with the problem.

'Ahh hondai, naginna ehenang.'

Oh all right, get in then.

I have to help Mithra up the steps. We move to the back, ignoring the surprised looks of the other pilgrims.

The van is just yards away. I can see one of the men, a young fellow wearing a black cap speak to people from the bus next to ours.

Tell the driver to start off. Tell him now!

White hair insists on taking another head count. I want to smack the old fool when he misses the count halfway and starts over again.

Please get it right this time. Please ask the driver to take off.

He's finally satisfied. He waves his hand and the driver engages first gear with a frightful crash.

Too late!

Black cap has his hand on the railing, ready to climb in.

Horns blasting at full volume make him look over his shoulder. I see a heavy truck and a passenger bus attempt, at great speed, to pass each other on the road beside us. Black cap releases the railing and flattens himself against the side of our vehicle to avoid being hit. Our driver, not having seen him at all, pulls on to the road and roars away.

We stand under a tree as though waiting for a bus. I can feel tremors pass through my body and try to still my shaking fingers.

'We can't stay here. They might turn back at any time,' I say, 'or there might be others.'

'We can go to town … hire a vehicle.'

'No. They'll expect us to do that, won't they? Isn't it

better to hide somewhere and ask Harith to come pick us up?'

'There's another small hotel called Priyankara up the road,' Mithra says. 'We have to pass Tissa Resort again to get there.'

'That's good. They won't expect us to come back this way.'

We hope for a trishaw but what turns up first is a ramshackle bus, crowded to the roof and listing sharply to one side. Passengers clinging to the footboard grudgingly allow us toe-space. We might easily have fallen off if not for the chivalry of a grinning lout who hooks a log-like arm around us.

Wedged in as I am, I'm only able to steal a quick glance at the scene of the explosion as we race past it. A sizeable crowd of loiterers still hangs around the collapsed wall and a black police vehicle now stands under the porch. The Rover is a gutted wreck, unrecognisable except for the orange paint at the back.

Priyankara turns out to be a comfortable guesthouse with some twenty rooms. We use the lobby toilet to clean ourselves up, move to the tiny lounge and order tea.

'Is your mobile still working?' I ask.

Mithra takes it out of his pocket, fiddles with it and then punches a number.

'Harith?'

'Yes.'

'Hi, where are you? … Where? Oh Koslanda. I thought you were coming along the coast. Oh. We're stuck in Tissa and the Rover is … busted. Can you come and pick us up?'

I hear yelling from the other end and grab the phone.

'… about to call you. Had to come the other way. Can't you just hire a car and meet us at the site?'

'Harith listen, things have become very dangerous,' I say, trying hard to remain calm. 'They wired a bomb to the Rover; it went off when Mithra used his remote to start it. They've been chasing us … we're afraid to get on the road.'

'Suji, I didn't know. Of course I'll come and collect you. Where are you?'

'Place called Priyankara Hotel, close to the Tissa Resort,' I say. 'Hari?'

'Yes?'

'These people are killers. You'll be taking a … big risk in coming for us. We'll try to find our way if you think it's better.'

'Don't talk rot. Of course I'll come for you,' Harith says stoutly. *'Āvey näththang Nali magey oluwa kāvi.'*

If I don't come for you, Nali will eat my head.

I feel a trace of warmth, and normality, for the first time.

'How long will you be?'

'Two hours at most. Stay hidden till we get there.'

The hands of the clock are nearly vertical when Nali rushes into the lounge with Harith following close behind. Her eyes are bright with affection; her smile warms me like a fire. We hug each other with comforting murmurs.

'Are you all right, baba? Are you hurt in any way?' I feel Nali's fingers stroking my cheeks. 'This is awful. They can't murder people like this. Can't we go to the police?'

Everyone starts speaking at once. Harith takes charge.

'Let's discuss this later. We have to get out of here,' he says firmly. 'Mithra, what about your vehicle?'

'It's a total wreck.'

'Don't you have to make a police entry, at least? They'll be looking for you.'

'No-o I don't think that's a good idea. The cops can't do anything and we'll be exposing ourselves.'

'All right, let's go then,' Harith says. 'If we can get to the site, we'll be safe.'

Harith decides to get to Buttala through Kataragama and Galge. Fear and tension keeps us quiet till we reach Kataragama. The road thereafter runs along the western border of Yala, mile upon mile of scrub jungle on either side. It might have been the distance we had already covered or the lack of traffic on the road but the feeling of imminent death, of tensing one's body to receive a hail of bullets, gradually eases off.

Maybe we have fooled them for the moment; maybe we have got away.

I tell them about my strange interview with Kalinga, of his fury when I question him about Kampuchea and my research on the genocidal cleansing of Phnom Penh by the Khmer Rouge.

'Do you really think Kalinga is planning a bloodbath like that?' Harith asks. 'They massacred millions of people; took that country back to the stone-age.'

'I keep telling myself it's incredible but everything points to some conspiracy like that. How else can you explain his fury when I ask a simple question? I mean, he promptly orders my death.'

'Are you sure that it's you they are trying to kill?'

'They killed my room mate Fazlia thinking it was me. They killed Mithra's colleague because he was in an orange Land Rover. Then they wired a bomb to Mithra's vehicle, ' I say hopelessly. 'Anyway Kumudu told us that Kalinga has ordered it.'

'Kumudu? How did you meet Kumudu?' Nali asks, turning her head.

'He found us. Told us to leave Mithra's place. He … he wanted Mithra to take me out of the country. Said it was the only sure way to save … my life.'

Nali kneels on the front seat and leans over it.

'Do you mean he came all the way to warn you that his people are trying to kill you?'

'Yes. I suppose so.'

'That thug had his eye on you, didn't he? Even when we were on campus.'

'Nonsense,' I reply firmly. 'We were colleagues in the union, nothing more.'

'Oh I see,' Nali jeers. 'Just because you worked together once, this murderer risks his position to come and warn you. Sure, that seems reasonable.'

When I look out of the window and don't respond she turns and slips back into her seat.

The interior of the Prado goes silent; the others appear to be digesting what they had heard. We cross some trucks going the other way but, for the moment, there is no vehicle creeping up on us from behind. I stare at the arid scrub and try once again to form some coherent plan.

Nali asks:

'Mithra?'

'Hmm?'

'You brought Suji to Tangalle on Thursday, didn't you?'

'Friday morning when we got in,' Mithra answers easily. 'Yes.'

'Today's Monday, so you've been with her for three

nights. Right?'

'Yes, sure.'

Nali scrambles around on her seat again. Her frowning face comes over the headrest.

'Suji,' she says suspiciously, 'Suji, look at me.'

'What? Is there a problem?'

'You're hiding something from me,' she says with a frown. 'There's some change in you. I can tell. What have you been up to?'

Mithra laughs.

I feel my cheeks getting warm and cover them with my hands. Nali reaches out and tries to pull my hands away.

'Take your hands off. What are you hiding?'

'Nothing. Nothing. What's there to hide?'

Mithra says:

'What's the fuss about? I looked after her as if she was a nun.'

Nali tugs at my wrists, trying to uncover my face. She drags herself over the backrest till she overbalances and lands on top of me with a thud.

Everyone starts yelling as if a murder is taking place; the vehicle veers dangerously across the road as Harith turns to see what the commotion is about. Nali and I wrestle each other and land on Mithra's lap.

'This wretch has been up to something and she's hiding it from me,' Nali pants.

'Ow! Get off me, you mutts.' Mithra yells, pushing us away from his side of the vehicle.

'You shut up,' Nali snaps back. 'You're the cause of the trouble.'

'It's … all … in …your … mind, Nala,' I say, panting from my exertions. 'Nothing happened. Will you get off me … I can't breathe.'

'Show me your face then,' she gasps, still tugging at my hands. 'Why are you covering it?'

'Will you two stop shouting?' Harith roars. 'I can't drive with all this noise.'

'It's this Suji,' Nali complains bitterly. 'She's been up something but won't admit.'

'Mithra, is this true?' Harith asks.

'Of course not; Nali is mad,' Mithra answers calmly. 'How on earth do you put up with her?'

A man in a tight-fitting black uniform stands by the side of the road. He raises his hand and Harith eases the vehicle over to park behind an open-sided Land Rover. There are more uniformed men seated inside; armed men.

'These men are from my site security,' Harith tells us.

'Is he the man who found the camp?' I ask softly as the tall man walks round the Prado towards Harith's door.

'Yes, Captain Marasinghe,' he replies. 'Get down, I'll introduce you.'

The Captain is about Harith's height but heavier. He smiles easily when he greets Nali, white teeth flashing under a thin moustache. His left arm is slightly bent and appears to be frozen at the elbow.

'Captain, this is Mr. Dias and this is the journalist, Miss Sujatha Mallika,' Harith says formally and then turning to us. 'The Captain keeps our site under tight control. We've not had any trouble since he took charge.'

'I've brought an escort for you, sir,' the man says confidently. 'No one will interfere with us.'

'Good. Let's get going then.'

The Defender leads the way, taking a right turn on to a gravel track before Buttala town. We travel through small villages and brown-dry patches of cultivation, passing an occasional hand tractor or bullock cart. Villagers cover their faces for protection against the cloud of dust raised by the two vehicles. Soon there are no more habitations, just scrub jungle shimmering in the afternoon heat.

Twenty minutes later we are at the gate.

I had known that the Goldwood project was an ambitious enterprise but had not expected such elaboration in the middle of the forest. The gate itself is a heavy steel affair that slides along the tall boundary wall. An elegant single storey building stretches along the right hand side of the road that bisects the enclosure. A warehouse towers over us on the left as Harith drives through to the compound behind. A small bungalow sits in the centre of a manicured lawn. Harith drives directly to the porch.

The heat hits me like a hammer as we get down. It is unnaturally quiet except for a generator thudding in the distance.

'We'll be safe here,' Harith says. 'I've got to go to the office for a while. Why don't you have a shower and get some rest. I'll ask Marasinghe to come over in the evening; we'll have him tell us about his discovery.'

Nali says:

'We've only got two rooms so Suji will share with me. Mithra, you're with Harith.'

'Fine.'

'You sure that's not a problem?'

'Why should it be a problem?' Mithra asks innocently. 'Does Harith snore?'

'Of course he doesn't,' Nali snaps.

'So tell me, Nala,' Mithra asks with a wicked smile. 'How do you know that?'

'Shut up and go in there,' Nali says, pushing Mithra to the door of the first room; then to me:

'Däng, magey podi horā, umbata magen berenna bähä. Mata ättha kiyanakang umbey bella mirikanawā.'

Now, my little rogue, you can't escape me. I shall throttle you till you tell me the truth.

JOURNAL V

*The terrible thing is that everyone
has his reasons.*

Jean Renoir

31

The sun has dipped below the trees and I see their dark outline against the purple-red sky. Marasinghe comes striding towards the veranda. There is a competence in the way he carries himself; a self-sufficiency that borders on arrogance. I wonder if we have, at last, found a man who might stand up to the thugs who are pursuing us.

For the first time in many days I feel a sense of security that is not entirely dependent on staying hidden.

'Sit down, Captain,' Harith says easily. 'Will you have some tea?'

'I've just had some, sir,' he replies. 'Thank you.'

'My friends would like to hear, in your own words, what you told me over the phone.'

'When you recruited me after your father's death, the men were afraid to go to the work sites. It took me several months to recruit and train a good security detail. Although we also received threats, we were able to protect the men and make sure the work continued on schedule.

'One rule I made was that no one was to cross the boundary into Block III. I had a suspicion that whoever was trying to stop our project was up to something in that part of the forest.

'It seemed to work well because the threats died down and we were able to work in relative peace.'

Marasinghe pauses as if to measure his words.

'Go on,' Harith says.

'I broke my own rule and went into Block III …'

'You were poaching, weren't you?'

'Well sir, it's hard to get beef in Buttala sometimes, so I thought I'd whack a deer or pig …'

'And …'

'I stumbled on this place I told you about. The buildings are all of similar size, long dormitories. Only the roofing is different, some have green sheets but mostly they are of cadjan or straw. They've preserved the trees but the clearing still is incredibly large … buildings stretching as far as we could see. But all of it is surrounded by razor wire fences with watch towers every hundred yards or so.'

'Do you know who is responsible for setting this up?'

'No sir,' the big man says with a hint of a smile, 'and we didn't stop to ask.'

'Have you any idea what all this is for?' Harith asks.

'No sir,' Marasinghe replies, 'but I've seen places like that in movies.'

'What do you mean?'

'War movies about concentration camps. This is very much like that.'

We sit in silence, too overwhelmed to put our thoughts into words. Hearing about it from an eyewitness makes it more real, more deadly.

'How far is it, to this place?' Harith asks.

'We can get to our boundary in the Rover. There are no roads in that part of Block III so we have to follow game trails. It'll take about three hours to get there.'

Harith turns to the rest of us.

'OK. Must we inspect this personally or should we just convey what the Captain has seen?'

'The authorities will never act quickly enough on a hearsay report,' I say slowly. 'I must be able to say I've seen it myself ... and have photographs.'

'If Suji goes, I'm going too,' Nali says.

'Are you sure you want to do this, Nala?' Harith reaches across and touches her hand. 'It can be very dangerous -'

'I'm not letting Suji go alone.'

'All right then, Captain,' Harith says, 'there'll be three of us.'

'Four.'

Harith turns to Mithra in surprise.

'What?'

'If she goes, I go.'

'I'll take care of her, machang,' Harith says gently. 'You know that.'

'I know that, but you see ... I'm the one who has to look after her.'

Harith looks at Nali. 'Ahh, so you were right, after all.'

'Of course I'm right,' Nali turns on me, pretending to be furious. 'I knew you were hiding something from me. I -'

'We'll go into that later,' Harith says hastily, cutting Nali off. 'What do you think, Captain? My friend has a bad leg. Will he be able to make it?'

'If he's fairly fit, I don't see a problem,' the man says confidently. 'We'll be able to help him along.'

'Harith, something very big is due to take place in three days time,' I say hesitantly. 'If we wait to find out everything, it might be too late.'

'What do you want to do?'

'I have prepared a package of documents. It includes my current journal,' I tell him. 'We need a reliable man to leave tonight and take it to my editor.'

Harith looks at Marasinghe.

'You want to send a messenger to Colombo?' Marasinghe asks and goes on easily. 'Certainly. I can drop him in Buttala tonight. There are buses every hour or so.'

'He has to get off at Belihul Oya and collect another parcel of documents,' I say. 'They are with my cousin. There's a letter to her with the address of her boarding house.'

'I have a good man, Mr. Harith,' the Captain says. 'I'll go and tell him to get ready.'

'Yes, do that,' Harith says. 'What time should we leave tomorrow?'

'Soon after an early breakfast,' Marasinghe replies. 'We'll have to carry some food and water with us. I'll arrange it.'

We had been quiet at dinner except for a mumbled 'pass the string hoppers' from one of us. We are washing our fingers in the little pantry when Marasinghe returns with another man, a young fellow with close-cropped hair and a badly pitted face.

I give him the letter to Loku and directions to get to her boarding house. He will have no difficulty in catching her before she leaves for lectures at the Sabaragamuwa campus. I also give him the sealed package that contains my current diary, my notes on Kampuchea and a letter to my editor outlining my suspicions and urging immediate action. I tell the messenger, Premasiri, that he is to deliver both packages to the newspaper office not later than noon on the next day.

Marasinghe leaves us, saying he will drop his man in Buttala. We hear a vehicle start with a roar and then watch the headlights recede into the night.

We sit in the veranda and listen to the forest sounds. A peacock calls from a treetop and tiny bats flit in and out of the house snapping at insects on the wing.

Nali asks: 'When did you start these journals of yours?'

'On campus, soon after the rag.'

'We're in this now, up to our eyebrows,' she says, 'so you'd better tell us the whole story.'

I try to throw my mind back; there are so many fragments.

'Kalinga addressed us during the rag. Remember?'

'Load of rubbish about historic wrongs and cities being full of corruption,' Nali says with a sneer. 'Yes, I remember.'

'It wasn't rubbish at all,' I respond warmly. 'The colonial powers certainly rewarded traitors and minorities while loyal Sinhalese villagers were kept in poverty. All the post-independence governments sustained the system to keep the ruling class in control. The rich need the poor to remain poor.'

Nali looks surprised.

'You really believe this stuff, don't you?'

'It isn't stuff, it's the plain truth and -'

'Oh, all right, calm down, will you.' Nali says. 'Get on with the story.'

'I joined the SSU because I believed in their cause. Kumudu was the union leader and Kalinga was the national convenor for the student wing. I worked in their projects, wherever I was sent.

'I learned about a secret program called Ginirälla. During the vacations, the best cadres were selected and sent for intensive training.

'I wanted to be part of it, so I volunteered. I was selected but Kumudu crossed out my name. When I protested he told me that once in the program, no one would be allowed to leave. He thought I would try to.'

'He had more sense than you seem to have, thank God,' Nali murmurs. 'Go on.'

'I continued to work with the party. I tried to find out more about Ginirälla but never got a word out of any of those who had been taken in. I also listened to Kalinga many times; there is no doubt that he is a true visionary. He is convinced that eliminating poverty by gradual change is not possible. Those with power don't want that change and will not allow it.

'To Kalinga, the establishment and the city are the same thing. He kept telling us that change is possible only after we crush the cities; destroy them utterly. He never explained how that was to be done.'

I stare into the darkness for a while trying to collect my thoughts.

'You remember Palitha, that boy from my village? He was in Ginirälla but he must have discovered something that frightened him. He wanted to leave the program. He asked me to appeal to the leadership to let him go; he promised never to reveal what he knew.

'I think he was coming to you, Harith, to ask for protection when they killed him and tried to blame it on you. I began to have doubts about the movement then; not about the objectives but about the methods they were prepared to use.

'Then they killed Father Basil. I was almost insane with grief when I confronted Kumudu. He swore that he had not known about it but he did try to justify the killing. His explanation was … obscene.

'They believe that the poor must be helped only after the revolution, after the ruling class has been crushed. Until then the poor must be kept hungry! Those who succour the poor now do them a great disservice by dampening their anger. Kumudu told me that only his cadres will be allowed to help the poor; all others must be chased away or killed.'

They all start speaking at the same time.

'What a vile policy! There will be a special hell for these animals.'

'I can't believe anyone can be so callous.'

'I told Kumudu that I was leaving the union; I told him that I would expose their ... wickedness,' I go on, 'but he said it was dangerous; the others would denounce me as a traitor, demand extreme action against me. He persuaded me to sit for the finals and just ... fade away.'

'The JSP formed an alliance with the Peoples Front and came to power. Kalinga became a Minister and Kumudu was appointed the national convenor for the student unions.

'I interviewed a number of JSP stalwarts on behalf of the newspaper. They seemed to know nothing of the Giniràlla project and assured me that they only wanted to organise the students for political activities.'

'They were lying?'

'It's hard to be sure, you know,' I reply, 'but I think the leadership of the JSP are not involved in this conspiracy. Kalinga and Kumudu have hijacked a legitimate party program. I don't think the other leaders know about the military training.'

'You mean Kalinga is planning to take power on his own?' Harith asks, surprised.

'Ye-es. Yes, I think so.'

'Go on with the rest of it.'

'You know most of it. Your father was killed. Do you remember Sena, the tracker? He mentioned that outsiders were coming into block III to construct buildings. That must have been the time they were starting their work on their prison camp.'

There've been a spate of unsolved bank and payroll robberies in the outstations, rumours of training camps; killing of aid workers in many remote areas.

'Then Sebastian Peiris called. He wanted to report a conspiracy but he was killed just before Mithra and I got there. I am convinced that the killers were those three boys in school uniforms. I had a call warning me that I would be killed if I investigated the Peiris case. When I ignored it and visited the Maya City site, they tried to lure me into a trap. I escaped because I was wearing an abaya and hijab, but I identified the killers; in fact I had met one of them before.'

'Did you find out why Peiris was killed?' Harith asks. 'What was the conspiracy?'

'I don't know. I haven't found anything.'

'Go on then.'

'When I interviewed Kalinga at the airport, I asked if his interest in Kampuchea had to do with Pol Pot and the Khmer Rouge. If he had just said no, it would have ended there but he went completely berserk; it was frightening to see. He called me a slut he had tolerated up to then but wouldn't anymore. That very night he ordered my execution.'

'Do you know that for sure?'

'Kumudu told us.'

'I never thought there was any significance in Kalinga's visits to Kampuchea till I saw his reaction. It was so extreme, so … out of proportion. And the man has changed.'

'Changed? How?'

'He was like a … a prophet. When he spoke of the poor and their suffering, his sincerity was clear. Anyone would have been convinced; anyone would have followed him. He still might be sincere about that - I don't know. I do know that his ego has grown - now he has the appearance of a megalomaniac. It's terrifying.'

The veranda is quiet as the others try to come to terms with what I have told them. Mithra breaks the silence.

'Kalinga needs to take power to put his plans into action. His student militia can't take over the country. The armed forces will crush them in no time.'

'You're quite right,' I say. 'His militia might be suitable for terrorising the population, not for seizing power. He has some other plan for that.'

'He's just a cabinet minister,' Harith says reflectively. 'Even in his own politburo, he's ranked third or fourth. How can he hope to take control of the government?'

'We don't know, and have no hope of finding out,' I say. 'If we can take some photographs tomorrow and get them to the authorities, they'll investigate and get at the truth.'

'I certainly hope so,' Harith says, yawning and stretching his arms. 'Let's get some sleep. We have a long day tomorrow.'

I am busy making notes when Nali comes out of the shower.

'What are you up to now, baba?' she asks, wiping her hair and looking over my shoulder.

'I sent my journal to Colombo,' I say with a shy grin.

'I'm using this little notebook to continue the saga.'

'How many books did you have?'

'Three with my cousin and the current one; that's four I've sent to my editor.'

'Did you really keep notes of our time on campus? The rag and everything?'

'Yes.'

'Sneaky little devil, aren't you?'

'Sure. '

'Never mind that then,' she says, 'tell me about Mithra.'

'Nothing much to tell,' I answer, getting to my feet hastily. 'I need to take a shower.'

'You have to come out sometime, and I'll be waiting,' she says. 'Don't think you can escape me.'

I take my time in the shower. The room is dark when I come out, so I slip under the covers as quietly as I can. Nali isn't asleep though; I feel her take hold of my hand.

'Is Mithra the one then?' she asks gently. 'You're sure about this?'

'Yes. Yes I'm sure.'

'I'm happy for you, nanga. I used to worry, you know,' she whispers, 'thinking you'd get entangled with someone who'd hurt you. In all the world, I can't think of anyone who'd take better care of you than Mithra.'

'And you, baba? Is Harith good to you? Are you happy?'

'Yes, we're very happy,' Nali says, 'but I don't like his mother. She's a crazy old bat and she hates me.'

'Ahh you'll get round her. Don't worry.'

'Tell you what; let's have a double wedding. That'll be fun.'

'Mithra hasn't asked me yet. His parents might object

when they find out I have no money.'

'Rubbish. They'll love you. Anyone would.'

'They may not get the chance if Kalinga's plan goes through. We might all be in a labour camp … or dead.'

'Those books you sent. Is there enough evidence there for your editor to do something?'

'I don't know. They were personal diaries. I found some release from my own fears and … and demons by writing; putting my thoughts on paper. I never intended to have someone else read them.'

'But you did write about Kalinga's activities?'

'Yes. Yes but I don't know if it will be enough.'

32

There are six of us in the party. Marasinghe leads the way with one of his men bringing up the rear. Both men carry shotguns. The Land Rover had turned back after dropping us by the boundary of Block III. It is the best time to be out in the forest with the sun just peeping over the trees and the air filled with birdsong.

Despite the tension, I feel my spirits lift just a little when I breathe jungle air and hear its much-loved sounds. Barbets, bulbuls, robins and orioles perch on the crowns of trees and shrubs to soak up the sunlight and preen their feathers.

Marasinghe takes us in a southerly direction, sometimes over open ground and at others, twisting and turning to avoid tracts of thorn or muddy hollows. The sun gets uncomfortably warm and we are soon bathed in perspiration. Mithra struggles along but I can see that he is distressed.

'Are you all right?' I ask worriedly. 'Can you carry on?'

'Sure,' he says with a grin. 'I just pretend to limp so you can fuss over me.'

'Liar.'

'I can manage. Don't worry.'

'If you're in pain, you can find a place for you to wait,' I say. 'You can get some rest and we'll collect you on the way back.'

'Are you going on?'

'You know that I must.'

'Then I will too.'

'Let's take a water break,' Marasinghe says. 'There's a shade tree in the clearing.'

The water, still cold from the refrigerator, puts new life into us but the captain insists on a full, military style, fifteen-minute break. Almost by force of habit I take out my little book and make some notes.

Marasinghe looks amused.

'Have you started another journal, Miss Sujatha?' he asks.

'Yes.'

'Your four diaries should be reaching Colombo any time now,' he says confidently. 'I hope your editor takes some action immediately.'

'He has to read and understand them first, and then decide if he is to take the matter seriously,' I say, voicing my own fears. 'I don't know how long that will take.'

'If we can show him some photographs of the prison camp, he'll have to take it seriously.'

'We'd better get them quickly then, hadn't we?'

Marasinghe glances at his watch and signals to the others.

The sun falls on us with punishing strength. A little moth seems to be fluttering at the back of my brain, some worrying morsel of information that I have overlooked. I try to pin it down but as I focus on it, the moth slips away.

Marasinghe still leads the way and we persuade Mithra to go next, allowing him to set the pace. The captain is forced to stop from time to time for the rest of us to catch up.

Harith, walking directly behind me says:

'You haven't forgotten your old habits, have you?'

'What?'

'You're still snapping twigs and dropping leaves to mark the way.'

'Oh,' I say in surprise, 'I didn't realise I was doing that. Just a habit, I guess.'

'Well, it saved us once so I'm not grumbling.'

The buffalo hold us up.

The track has led us to a hollow filled with murky green water - and wallowing buffalo. The captain holds his hand up but it is too late. We hear the grunts of alarm and the splashing, squelching sound of heavy bodies rising out of the mire.

The buffalo have all turned to stare at us; the bigger animals toss their horns. Shouts and rocks have little effect except to make some of them advance aggressively. The buffalo are not ready to abandon their comfortable wallow in this noonday heat. The vegetation on either side of the pool is too dense to force our way through so we have no choice but to go back and swing round the pool in a wide circle.

The air seems to scorch the lining of my nose and throat.

Mithra is in pain; I can tell from the way he holds his head.

'Captain,' I call out. 'I think we need a break.'

Marasinghe glances at Mithra's face and gestures to the rest of the party.

'We might as well have some food and rest a bit,' he says. 'Let's use that shade over there.'

The others clean the area of dried dung and leaf litter. I help Mithra to lower himself to the ground. He grimaces in relief and still manages a strained smile.

'I hope you noticed I wasn't the one to call for rest.'

'This is not a contest,' I say in exasperation. 'You should have told me you were in pain.'

'Then you'd have thought I was a wimp.'

'I would not,' I snap. 'Let me see your leg.'

'No. Don't fuss,' he says dismissively. 'I can manage.'

'Darling, you must let me look at it.'

'Mithra, is this woman bossing you already?' Nali asks as she strolls over. 'Take my advice. Don't tolerate any nonsense from her.'

She helps me, though, once she realises what I'm trying to do. We ignore Mithra's protests and roll up his pants. I barely manage to suppress my gasp of alarm when I see the condition of his wasted leg.

Despite the padding at the clamps, the metal caliper has rubbed his skin raw, leaving it red and inflamed. Each step must have been agonising. Strangely, I feel his pain like a stab wound in my own side.

Is love like this, that I feel your slightest pain?

'You can't go on,' I say. 'Stop here. I'll stay with you.'

'No Suji,' Mithra says seriously. 'To convince your editor to take action, you must be able to say you've seen this yourself.'

'And if I go, you're going too, right?'

'Yes,' he grins, 'even on my knees.'

Is love like this, that I delight in your faintest smile?

Marasinghe has walked up to us.

'It's only a short distance from here. If we can find some material to wrap around his leg where it's sore, he'll be able to make it.'

'I don't know,' I say uncertainly. 'He's in pain…'

'We mustn't split up,' Marasinghe says firmly. 'We might have to use another route to get away.'

We decide to have our lunch before moving on. Marasinghe distributes the packets of rice and we sit in a circle to eat. Mithra has his back against the bole of a tree, with his leg stretched out before him. He grins when Nali tells him that the strips of cloth for binding his leg had come from my underskirt.

The rice has been packed in foil and then wrapped in sheets of newsprint. I spread the paper and open the packet but find it difficult to eat. Knowing I will need the energy, however, I force some food down my throat. I'm about to rewrap the parcel when a headline in the newspaper catches my eye.

I look at the date, and then carry it to where Mithra is sitting.

'Will all of you come here?'

'What?'

'What's this girl up to now?'

'Read this.'

4th July

PRESIDENT TO OPEN MAYA CITY PROJECT ON 7th JULY

Presidential advisor Suraj Pinto confirmed that, in view of the project size, and his own role in securing this massive investment for the country, His Excellency The President has accepted an invitation to open the project. The Prime Minister and several Cabinet Ministers are expected to attend the ceremony. Agriculture Minister and leader of the JSP, Mihindu Wanasinghe, has also confirmed that he will be present.

The Maya City project comprises a hotel, large shopping mall, restaurant complex and two wide-screen cinemas.

A spokesman for the developer announced that the opening ceremony would take place at the auspicious time of 11.07 a.m. on 7th July.

Harith looks at me with a frown.

'We've all heard about that project,' he says. 'Have I missed something?'

Instead of answering him, I turn to Mithra.

'When did Kumudu meet us?'

'Saturday.'

'What was the date?'

'Uh, the 2nd I guess.'

'He told you to get me out of the country in five days, didn't he? He said it'll be too late after that.'

Mithra has his eyes on the newspaper again.

'They are all together, aren't they?' he whispers. 'If they are killed, there will be no government.'

'An armed attack is out of the question, so it must be some … bomb,' Nali says fearfully. 'But surely security checks will prevent that?'

'Of course they will,' Harith says. 'There's no way anyone can plant an explosive; security is simply too tight.'

'I … I have an idea,' I say hesitantly.

They look at me.

'The promoter of the project was that Pinto fellow. He is known to be a close associate of the President, isn't he?'

'So?'

'So, given that and the size of the project, the President was sure to come for the opening, wasn't he?'

'Yes, yes. So what's your point?'

'Kalinga knew that when the project started three years ago,' I say slowly. 'What if they simply placed a … a device inside the structure of the wall or the floor, when they started construction? No security check will discover it.'

'You're crazy. How would they have known where to put it?'

'The atrium of the shopping complex is a stunning location. They're sure to have the ceremony there.'

No one speaks for a while, trying to come to terms with the idea. Mithra nods his head in agreement but the other two are far from convinced.

Nali looks up.

'I just can't see these student cadres placing explosives in building sites. Come on!'

'There are plenty of army deserters who have experience with explosives,' Mithra murmurs. 'No problem finding a competent mercenary to provide technical knowledge.'

'But you can't just walk into a construction site and plant a bomb …'

'Sebastian Peiris,' I say softly.

'What?'

'Peiris was the supervisor for the civil contractor. He would have had no problem organising it.'

'But how do we know he actually did what you say?' Nali asks.

'It explains everything else,' I say, trying to put my thoughts in order. 'Assume that he took a bribe to allow them to place the device. Assume also that he suspected they were JSP. OK?'

'Go on.'

'Now his conscience starts bothering him. He starts drinking heavily and is fired from his job. He sees my article criticising the JSP in the newspaper and calls me; says he is aware of a conspiracy and wants to tell me the story. They kill him and warn me not to investigate. When I persist, they set a trap for me in the supermarket.'

'What's the line of succession? Doesn't the Chief Justice come into it?' Mithra asks. 'They must have a plan for that.'

'I'm sure they have. Some cadres must be assigned to capture or … or kill him at the same time.'

'My God, this is serious.' Harith is convinced at last; and stunned by the implications. He bursts out: 'We have to inform the authorities straight away.'

'Does your phone have coverage?' Nali asks.

'No. No chance.'

'You're right, Harith. There's no time to waste,' I say. 'We'd better get back as soon as we can.'

Marasinghe has been standing behind Harith, listening to our conversation. His face is grave.

'We can be at the camp in fifteen minutes, sir,' he says to Harith. 'Why not take the photographs as well? It will help to convince the authorities.'

'Mithra …?'

'I'll cut a walking stick for him,' Marasinghe replies. 'That will help keep the weight off his leg.'

We argue back and forth. It is hard to dispute Marasinghe's position that, having come so far, turning back to save just half an hour doesn't make sense. We decide to go on.

I keep my eyes on Mithra, alert for any sign that he is in serious pain. The bandages and the wooden staff Marasinghe has given him seem to help, for he is managing for the moment.

As my concern for Mithra eases the moth comes back. I know there is something important that I have missed, some vital piece of information that is eluding me. I still can't pin it down.

Marasinghe holds his hand up and the column stops. He walks back and speaks to Harith.

'Sir, the clearing is just ahead. We can't all go up, we'll be spotted. Why don't you take Miss Sujatha and crawl up to the edge of the clearing?'

Harith thinks for a moment and nods. He takes a camera out of his knapsack and checks it.

'Sir, the clearing begins about fifty yards ahead,' Marasinghe goes on. 'Get on all fours and stay behind the undergrowth when you get close to the edge. There are watch towers and we don't know if they are manned.'

Marasinghe makes the mutinous looking Nali sit next to Mithra. Harith leads the way and I follow close behind him. I turn just before we step out of sight and am touched to see the captain salute us, palm forward and four fingers stretched out.

At one moment we are surrounded by thick foliage, then we walk round a heavy thicket, and we see the clearing stretching out before us. We drop clumsily to our knees and take shelter behind another clump of thorn bush. I feel the powdery leaf dèbris of the forest floor tickle my nostrils. Ants sting my fingers as fear stabs at my heart.

Gigantic.

This is the one word that springs to my mind. The

cleared area is filled with rectangular buildings, each perhaps twenty feet across and a hundred feet long. The roofing is either constructed of straw or sheets painted with some camouflage design. The block-work walls of each building go up to the roof with ventilation grills at intervals. No windows. The buildings have been arranged in rows and stretch as far as the eye can see. There are two perimeter fences; chain link on the inside and along the outer edge are rolls of barbed wire that glint in the sun. Razor wire, I think they call it.

There is a gap of about twenty feet between the fences.

Watch towers have been placed at intervals along the perimeter. The main entrance to the camp is situated about half a kilometre from where we are. There appear to be two large buildings just outside the entrance. Some heavy equipment, including a bulldozer, is being used to construct or repair a road leading from the gate.

The immense camp sits brooding in the sunlight like some monstrous beast, waiting to be fed. It isn't an ordinary predator that will pursue its prey; it is more like an ancient deity who must be propitiated by human sacrifice. I know who will be sacrificed to satisfy this beast's thirst for blood.

The citizens of Colombo.

Harith is busy with his little digital camera but I can't stand it any more. I feel my mind being engulfed in terror; I know I must fly away from this evil presence. I want to get back to Mithra and the comforting competence of Captain Marasinghe.

For some reason the memory of his four-fingered salute flits through my mind.

In a flash I realise that this was the thought that had been bothering me all morning. Marasinghe had told me that he had not heard from his man but that my four diaries should be in Colombo by now.

I bite my hand till pain overrides the panic I feel.

I had never mentioned the number of books that my cousin Loku is holding for me. How does Marasinghe know there are four journals in all?

Think. Don't panic. Think.

They must have taken the first three journals from Loku. Oh God, I hope they haven't harmed her. And for Marasinghe to know that, he must be in with them.

He has lured us into a trap.

I grab Harith by the arm; whisper urgently into his ear.

'Harith, Harith, we've made a terrible mistake. Marasinghe has betrayed us …'

Harith turns towards me with a surprised frown but his eyes flick away, looking at something over my shoulder. When I turn I see Marasinghe standing there, a mocking smile on his face. He holds the gun across his waist, the barrel resting on his stiff elbow and his finger on the trigger.

'I knew I made a mistake about the books.' His voice is easy, casual. 'I wondered how long it would take you to work it out.'

'Captain, I can't believe this. I trusted you …' Harith says in a strangled voice but Marasinghe cuts him off.

'We'll discuss that later.' The man's speech is crisp now, no longer deferential. 'I must ask you to come over and join the others.'

The barrel of the shotgun swings round till it is

pointing at Harith. We get to our feet and walk past him. Nali and Mithra are seated on the ground with the other man pointing a gun at them. They struggle to their feet when we appear. The shock is still stamped on their faces.

'Let's all walk away,' I say in desperation. 'Let them shoot us if they want. Come on, Mithra.'

Marasinghe doesn't say anything till I take Mithra's hand and turn around. He is smiling.

'I won't shoot you, miss, because they want you delivered … intact,' he says easily. 'But if you don't do exactly as I say, I'll shoot your friend through his knee - the good one. He'll never walk again.'

I have a bitter yellow taste in my mouth and want to throw up. I look at Mithra, feeling desperately sorry I have dragged him into this mess. Harith and Nali too, they would not be here if not for my obsession.

33

There is a desk by the window. A man is seated with his back to the light studying a file. He raises his head when we shuffle into the room but his features are still obscured by the sun-glare behind his shoulder.

He gets up and walks round the table. There is a smile on his face, but I see it is by no means a pleasant one.

'Well, well. So Sujatha Mallika has finally come home.'

I know that voice … and that face. Ranjit, the boy from my village.

Marasinghe addresses Ranjit respectfully.

'They took the bait, sir, just as we hoped. I had no trouble bringing them here.'

'Well done, Captain,' Ranjit says dismissively without looking at him. 'You can get back now. We'll look after our guests.'

A clearly disappointed Marasinghe seems about to say something, changes his mind and turns to leave. I hear the door close behind us. Ranjit turns to me again.

'You managed to escape our people by running and hiding,' he says with a sneer, 'so we baited a trap with offal. Sure enough, the shit fly has come to feed.'

'Why do you speak like that, Ranjit?' I ask, hurt rising above fear. 'We were friends at one time.'

I didn't see the hand move, just the clap of sound that fills my ear.

The impact swings me round; Mithra catches me as I stagger away. The sting of the blow has made my eyes water.

'Friends?' he snarls, his voice higher now. 'What friends? You thought you were too good for a man like me.'

I can feel his anger spreading through the room, like heat radiating from a fire.

'You went to the city to suck up to the rich, leaving me to rot in that village,' he goes on, 'and now you speak of friendship?'

'I struggled for what little I've achieved,' I'm stung into replying. 'You could have done the same.'

'Shit lies!' he snaps, very angry now. 'That bastard-priest chose to help you … and he chose not to help me. That was the difference.'

Ranjit is leaning over me with bared teeth; I feel drops of spittle strike my face.

'Is that why you killed him?'

Ranjit steps back. He seems to have suddenly controlled his anger.

'Yes,' he says calmly, 'and I'm glad I did it.'

'He was such a good, kind man. He helped so many people.' I am angry now. 'How can you boast about it? Have you no heart?'

'You are the heartless one, you selfish little bitch,' Ranjit says, his voice now icy. 'You call him a good man because he helped you. The dozens he chose not to help became more desperate. Our struggle is to help all the poor, at one time. We will not tolerate people like your bastard-priest who select a few favourites.'

The cells are underground, like dungeons.

We are in one of the two buildings outside the prison compound, on either side of the main gate. The corridors are bustling with young people walking about purposefully, some carrying files and documents, others talking animatedly and waving their arms. There is a sense of urgency, of expectation. Something momentous is about to happen and they are preparing for it.

They are all so young.

We follow two guards, sullen teenagers, to the end of the corridor. My heart sinks when we come to a flight of steps leading down.

Oh please, no. Don't put us underground. I won't be able to breathe.

Mithra takes hold of my hand.

'It's all right, baba,' he whispers. 'I'm here. We'll make it together.'

The fear will not subside. I have to make a conscious effort to breathe.

Breathe in, breathe out!

A long corridor stretches before us; it seems to run the entire length of the building above. Naked electric bulbs hang in a row from the concrete ceiling. The guard flicks a switch; the dim glow reveals rows of steel barred doors on either side.

Windowless dungeons, all empty now, all waiting impatiently for prisoners.

One guard unhooks a hefty ring of keys from his belt and opens the padlock securing a barred gate. With a flick of his fingers he gestures to us to get inside. The door slams and the click of the padlock seems to echo in the silence.

My lungs hold no air and the pain in my belly is unbearable. I feel a blackness descending and my knees lose their strength. I collapse on the floor.

I'm in Yasawathi's storeroom once again; the musty smell of paddy is strong in my nose. There is so little air to breathe. Soon the air will be finished and I will suffocate.

I hear a burst of laughter.

'Gäänita dhän thamai teyrilā thiyenney,' one of the guards says as they walk away.

It is only now the woman has understood her position.

Harith and Mithra carry me to the far end of the cell where the floor has been raised to form a step. Mithra wraps his arms around me.

'I know this terrifies you, love, but you must fight it,' he whispers in my ear. 'They are planning to house hundreds of prisoners here so there must be a ventilation system. Come on now, you can do it.'

It takes time and a supreme effort of will. Mithra's presence and encouragement is the crucial factor. My breathing eases and I am able to control the panic that had overwhelmed me. I open my eyes and survey my surroundings.

The cell is about twelve feet long and ten across. We are seated on a raised section of the floor adjacent to the rear wall. There is no light in the cell except for what filters through the bars.

I see the faces of my friends leaning over me, anxiety stamped on their features. I know I have to pull myself together at least for their sake.

'I'm sorry – so sorry about that,' I say, still gasping for breath. 'I'm better now.'

'I'm glad you've recovered, nanga,' Nali says, touching my bruised cheek with her fingertips. 'We were frightened for you. If we survive this I'll see that bastard skinned for slapping you.'

I feel ashamed of my weakness, touched too by their

concern for me when we are all in such grave danger. I pull away from Mithra and sit up.

'I'm all right now. Really,' I say. 'What are we going to do? We can't just sit here.'

We look at each other hopefully. It is hard to believe we are really prisoners. It seems more like a game that will end soon allowing us to go free.

'This Ranjit fellow,' Harith asks, 'Why is he so angry?'

'I never realised that he hated me so much, for getting ahead while he was stuck in the village,' I say slowly.

'We have to get out of here,' Mithra says. 'He means to harm Suji. I'm sure of it.'

'That padlock is solid,' Harith says. 'We can't force it open without some heavy tools.'

'Maybe we can surprise them when they bring our food,' Mithra suggests quietly. 'They may not expect serious resistance from us.'

'Ye-es,' Harith says doubtfully. 'Do we have anything we can use as a weapon?'

We search through our pockets, knowing it is a futile effort. Even Harith's small penknife and Nali's nail file have been taken away. They had ignored the little notebook in my pocket but that is no weapon. We look at each other, still trying to keep fear at bay.

'Harith,' Mithra says steadily, 'I can suggest something - if you promise to follow my wishes exactly.'

'What's the idea?'

'Do you promise?'

'I don't like the sound of this,' Harith replies. 'Tell me the idea first.'

'The only thing we can use as a weapon is the caliper on my leg. You can use it as a club,' Mithra says. His voice is a monotone, his eyes are on the floor. 'If only one guard comes with our food, and you're able to get behind him, you might be able to knock him unconscious.'

'That brace will be damaged if I hit someone with it,' Harith says. 'You won't be able to wear it again.'

'If there's a chance to escape to the forest, I won't be able to take it anyway,' Mithra says gravely. 'With or without the brace, I'll slow you down and we'll all be caught.'

'But …'

'That's what I want you to do for me. If there's a chance of escape, I want you to take Suji with you, by force if necessary. I'm staying here.'

Emotions flit through my mind in a confusing whirl.

'No,' I say firmly. 'I'm not leaving you behind. Whatever gives you that silly notion?'

'You must be sensible, baba. You are in great danger,' he replies earnestly. 'If you escape, you can come back with the police.'

'Harith and Nali can do that. I stay with you,' I say firmly, feeling more like myself at last, 'and if I hear one more word on the subject I'll whack you with that calliper thing.'

We can't tell night from day but it's seven thirty by Harith's wristwatch when we hear footsteps on the stairs. Harith stands by the side of the door with the metal brace hidden awkwardly inside his trouser leg. The rest of us are seated on the step at the far end of the cell.

I can hear my heart thudding as the footsteps draw nearer; then I see the shadows on the floor of the corridor. There are at least two of them. Harith has seen it too. He catches my eye and shrugs his shoulders.

One guard fiddles with the padlock and, in a moment, the door swings open. He stands outside and gestures to Harith to move away from the door. The second guard follows with a wooden tray, four tin plates of rice, a jug of water and an enamel mug. He dumps the tray on the floor nearly toppling the jug. A third man walks in behind him. I recognise the silhouette.

Ranjit.

He stands silently for a moment, staring at us. I can see that he has something under his arm. The guards gesture to Harith to join us at the back of the cell allowing Ranjit to stand at the centre. With a sinking heart I make out what he is carrying.

'I have read your first three journals, Sujatha,' Ranjit says with a tight smile. 'We were very amused at your efforts to hinder our struggle.'

'How did you get those journals?' I ask. Fear tightens my chest. 'I hope you didn't harm my cousin. She is only a child.'

Ranjit is taken aback for a moment; then laughs with genuine amusement.

'You really are naïve, Sujatha,' he says. 'Your little cousin has joined our struggle. She brought the journals to us as soon as you gave them to her.'

I step back. It is as if he has slapped me again.

'I don't believe you. Loku would never do that.'

'Believe what you wish, but the kinship of poverty is stronger than ties of blood,' Ranjit says. 'She will play her part when the time comes. Sadly you will not be there to witness it.'

I remain silent.

'I have just read the fourth journal and your notes.' The laughter has faded away now and the voice is menacing. 'Have you discussed your suspicions about the Maya City project with anyone else?'

'No.'

'What about the notes you've made about the Khmer Rouge and the purge of Phnom Penh? Did you show that to anyone?'

'No.'

'Is there a copy anywhere?'

'No.'

The eyes are shadowed but I know he is studying my face with deadly intensity. When he speaks finally his voice is very soft but strangely impersonal, as though he is a doctor discussing a patient's symptoms.

'It is important for us to know the truth about this and we can only find it out from you. You might be telling the truth, but then again you might be lying. The only way we can be sure is to take you over the edge.'

He leans closer and I see his eyes now. There is a kind of hunger there, of anticipated pleasure. He goes on.

'When the pain is beyond bearing, when the damage is irreparable, then what we hear is bound to be the truth. Only then can we be sure.'

My throat is frozen. I can feel my fingers shaking and clasp my hands together. Ranjit stares broodingly at me for a long minute.

'I will consult my superiors on this matter,' he tells me, as if he plans to discuss my illness with another doctor. 'If they agree that we require your answer urgently, I will send for you during the night.'

34

If terror alone can kill someone, I shall certainly die tonight. We are unable to speak, struck dumb by the horror to come.

An icy chill has taken hold of my body; I am shaken by spasm after spasm of shivering. Mithra holds me tight and the others sit close to me, making comforting sounds that bring no solace.

Sleep is out of the question. We wait for them to come.

Once every hour we hear heavy footsteps on the stairs and then we see the long shadow on the floor of the corridor, like an evil spirit. Every time I say to myself, this time they have come for you. This time it is the end.

What abominations has he in store for me? Removing my fingernails with pliers? Electric shocks? I have read about these loathsome practices but they have never seemed real. They do now.

Each time the guard shines his flashlight through the bars, then turns and walks away. I let my breath out after each inspection, knowing I have a reprieve and can live for a few more minutes. Then in the grey, hopeless hours before dawn, I feel the tension beyond bearing. I want them to take me away; I want them to kill me and bring this to an end. Anything seems better than this endless suspense.

I die many times in the night.

We have been let out to use the toilets. I splash water on my face trying, without success, to rinse away the horror of those dark hours. Nali grips my arm.

'Listen. What's that noise?'

I turn the tap off.

WHAP WHAP WHAP WHAP.

'It sounds like a helicopter,' I tell her listlessly, my mind still focussed on Ranjit and his threat.

Will they come for me in the morning?

'Do you think the air force is attacking the camp?'

'There'll be shooting then,' I say without interest, twisting my hair to squeeze the water out. 'No Nali, no one's coming to rescue us.'

The guard raps on the door.

'Time's up. Get back in the cell.'

They bring us boiled manioc and grated coconut on the same tin plates. I try to eat but when I raise a mouthful to my lips I want to throw up. I ignore Mithra's entreaties and push the plate away.

I hear footsteps on the stairs; I know it is too early for the guard to collect the plates.

Is this it?

I feel my body start to tremble again and clench my teeth to stop them chattering.

The guard fumbles with the lock, throws the door open and stands aside. Kumudu walks in and stands in the middle of the cell. It takes me a moment to realise that he is very angry. His voice, when he finally speaks, seems to vibrate with suppressed fury.

'Once!' he roars through gritted teeth. 'Just once in your life, you bloody woman, couldn't you do what you've been told?'

I open my mouth to speak but the words don't come

out. I have been hanging on to my sanity by a thread, balancing on the edge. The angry eyes and the bristling beard, the snarling voice, are just enough to tip me into the abyss.

I am rolling on the floor, howling and screaming like a soul in agony. It seems as if I have split in two, with my spirit standing in one corner of the cell watching a demented woman writhing on the floor.

'SHUT UP!' Kumudu yells. 'You, Nalini, help her up and stop her howling.'

Nali tells me later that while they clustered round me, trying to calm me down, Kumudu had turned and kicked the tray with the remains of our breakfast. The tray and tin plates had slammed into the wall with a crash.

Kumudu had yelled at the guard.

'What are you staring at? Clean that up and get out of here.'

When I finally manage to control myself and take note of my surroundings, I see that the cell is locked and we are alone once more.

Kumudu has disappeared.

The day seems endless. We sit in the twilight cell and measure time only by Harith's wristwatch. Nali forces me to eat some of the rice and dhal they send us at midday.

Mithra sits by my side as he has done throughout the previous night. Once again I find solace in his rocklike calm. He keeps saying things like,

'It's all right.' 'Don't be afraid.' 'Everything will work out.'

Stupid things that sometimes make me angry enough to lash out at him:

'Are you mad? How can you say everything is all right?' I cry out tearfully. 'Don't you realise our position?'

Mithra only smiles.

I try, perversely, to make him admit that he's lying just to keep my spirits up.

Mithra answers:

'No, I'm not lying. I prayed.'

I look at him in surprise.

'I didn't know you were religious.'

'I am now.'

I manage, step by painful step, to climb out of the well of my despair.

It is night when we hear footsteps again. If they have come for me, I tell myself that I will be ready. I have been to the bottom and clambered up again; I can manage my fear.

The jailer unlocks the door and stands aside for another guard carrying a chair. Kumudu comes in, sits in the centre of the cell and instructs a guard to fix a brighter bulb in the corridor.

He gestures to the guards to leave.

'That was quite a performance, Sujatha' he says with a ghost of a smile. 'Are you better now?'

'Can't you murderous bastards leave her alone?' Harith asks wearily. 'She can't take much more of this.'

'Shut up, you,' Kumudu snaps dismissively. 'If not for her tears, you'd have been dead a long time ago. '

'What the hell are you talking about?'

'You didn't know?' Kumudu seems amused. 'Well, don't worry about it then.'

He turns back to me. I'm relieved to see that he is no longer angry.

'What am I to do with you, Sujatha?'

'After you take power tomorrow I don't suppose it

matters,' I answer calmly. 'So long as you don't hand me over to that Ranjit.'

Kumudu stares at me for a moment. There is a strange expression in his eyes.

'He was very anxious to … interrogate you,' Kumudu says softly. 'You are fortunate that he asked for my permission and that I refused it.'

'He is a psychopath,' I snap, injecting into my tone some of the revulsion I feel. 'Is that the type of cadre you have trained?'

'We make the best use of each one's talents,' he replies sardonically, not at all put out. 'The interrogation chambers are in the other building and have been equipped with great imagination. The facility is for the robber barons. We will have to persuade them, won't we, to tell us where their wealth in hidden? Ranjit has an anger that makes him ideal for this work.'

'Are you really going to purge Colombo?' Mithra asks. 'Was Sujatha's guess correct? Will it be like Phnom Penh?'

'Yes,' Kumudu looks surprised at the question. 'Of course. Our cadres are poised to take control. Giniràlla will start as soon as we secure the city.'

'But there are hundreds of thousands, women and children, the old and the sick. You can't really mean everyone? You want to march them here? They'll all die on the road.'

There is a faint frown line on Kumudu's forehead.

'Have you seen a village cow during a drought? It is just skin and bone, hovering forever on the verge of death. It survives on a few blades of dried grass,' Kumudu says patiently. 'If you look closely you will see that it is covered with ticks, black and round … and healthy. However much the cow starves, the parasites never suffer; they are always filled with blood. The starving cow's blood.

'The people of Colombo are those bloated ticks. Parasites who live off the sufferings of the poor … they have done so for generations. So the question I have for you is this. Does it matter how these parasites die? Some will die of thirst or exhaustion on the road, some by a bullet in the back of the head. Some, of course, will be sent to Ranjit for special attention. The cow only wants to be rid of the ticks; it doesn't care how they die.'

The cell feels cold; it is as if a draft of chilled air has drifted in without our knowledge. We have been able to cope with our suspicions so long as they were unproven. Hearing Kumudu speak so casually about exterminating thousands and thousands of people strikes us dumb.

'The police and the army will never let you do this,' Harith says bravely. 'Your Ginirälla cadres will be chased away.'

'We will be the legitimate government. The police and army will take orders from our leader … otherwise their own generals will be caught up in the Ginirälla.'

'Blowing up the President and a few Ministers will not give you power,' Harith scoffs. 'You will just create chaos in the country, nothing more.'

Kumudu looks at Harith disdainfully for a moment, and then shrugs his shoulders.

'I don't have to explain anything to you. You'll see all this take place, if you live long enough.'

'I'd like to know,' I say carefully. 'Since we are to be killed anyway, there's no harm in telling us, is there?'

Kumudu looks at me with the faintest glint of amusement in his eyes.

'So you're ready to die, are you?'

'I'm not ready,' I answer steadily, 'but if that is my

karma, so be it.'

'You know the persons scheduled to attend the opening? We have positioned a device in the room where the ceremony will be held. The bomb is powerful enough to obliterate every person there.

'Article 40 of the constitution specifies that, if the president dies, power passes to the prime minister and then to the speaker. When all three, and several senior ministers are lost at the same moment, there is no clear provision for succession.

'Within minutes of the incident our cadres will take selected senior officials like the chief justice into custody, for their own protection, of course. Within an hour our minister Kalinga Lokuge will accuse the northern separatists of the atrocity, declare a state of emergency and himself temporary head of state.'

Kumudu looks at us sombrely.

'The shock of the disaster will be so great that the entire country will greet this announcement with relief. They'll want someone to take charge. That's enough for us. Within twenty-four hours our cadres will be in place and we'll have control.'

'You buggers are dreamers,' Harith scoffs. 'Do you think the service chiefs and heads of departments will take orders from some donkey, just because he declares himself head of state?'

I expect an explosion of fury from Kumudu; instead he merely looks disdainful.

'You people don't realise what's happened to this country. Most officials and public servants are now so politicised, they are no more than a bunch of cocksuckers,' he says with an ugly smile. 'That's why it will be easy. When a strong leader announces that he has control, do you think any of them will have the balls to stand up and object?'

Kumudu stares at Harith for a moment, and then shakes his head.

'No. They'll rush to kneel and be first in line,' he says with searing contempt. 'And they'll have their mouths open.'

'Where have you hidden your bomb?' I ask desperately. 'Surely security will be very tight?'

Kumudu laughs.

'Our little reporter never gives up hope, does she?' he asks with a sneer. 'She still thinks she'll be rescued so she can save her precious leaders.'

'You know we can't escape,' I answer steadily, 'so why not tell us?'

'The device is in the wall right behind the plaque the President will unveil. Security will never find it.'

'How will you trigger it?'

He stares at me for a moment and then shrugs his shoulders.

'Two wires connected to the device are inside the wall; they lead to a plug base in an office on another floor. Yesterday one of our cadres connected a mobile phone to that plug through what looks like a battery charger. When that phone rings, the circuit is completed and the bomb will go off.'

'So someone in the crowd is supposed to watch the ceremony and make the call at the right time, is that it?'

'Oh no. That will not satisfy us at all,' Kumudu says, smiling broadly. 'My leader wants to make this important call himself.'

'How?'

Kumudu takes an oversized mobile phone from his pocket.

'Satellite phone,' he says with quiet pride. 'I will punch out the numbers and he will press the green button. BOOM.'

'Kalinga's here?'

'Of course! All our leaders are here for a final briefing … and to watch the grand exit of the present regime,' he goes on. 'We'll fly to Colombo as soon as the bomb goes off.'

'How on earth will you know when to make the call? These ceremonies don't go exactly to time, surely?'

'The ceremony is being shown live on Rupavahini. We'll know exactly when she reaches out to unveil the plaque,' Kumudu is bubbling with suppressed excitement. 'With our leader, we'll see the launch of Ginirälla on national television. Isn't it beautiful?'

'Beautiful for you, not for the poor people who will die,' I say. 'Not beautiful for the people of Colombo.'

The smile fades away; Kumudu looks at me with an expression of regret.

'You know what it is to be poor; so poor you have to watch children starve, get sick and die. You know what it is to be without work or to work endlessly for a pittance. You know what it is to live without hope. You know how this intolerable injustice has gone on, generation after generation.

'You were with us. You know this is all true, don't you? Don't you?'

'I suppose so.'

'We can lift this yoke. We can give these suffering millions their place in the sun.'

'But -'

'But … I know! Your stupid sentimentality will not permit killing of a few miserable ticks in order to save the cow. That's your problem, isn't it?'

'The end … doesn't justify the means,' I murmur.

'That's the shit with which that priest filled your head. Listen to me. Nothing worthwhile can ever be achieved by means that everyone agrees is justifiable. That's why no one has done anything at all to uplift the poor. If you think I'm wrong, name something … anything that's been done since independence to really uplift the poor.'

The others seem to have receded to the background. This is between him and me.

'What you say is true, Kumudu, but how can you justify genocide as a means of helping the poor?'

His eyes acquire a fanatical glow; his body seems to vibrate with suppressed excitement.

'What terrible words you use. How can you call this genocide? It's more like cleaning a toilet. A little unpleasantness, and then the air will be clean. Forever.'

'Colombo is the economic hub of the country. If you remove all its people, the country will collapse.'

'That's what they teach you to believe,' he scoffs. 'When the chena cultivator burns the forest, you think only ashes remain. Yet, with the first rain, the plants spring up again.'

Kumudu stands up.

'You'll want to watch the ceremony tomorrow morning, won't you? Mustn't miss the climax,' he says with a laugh. 'I'll tell them to fix a TV down here.'

'The leader of your party is also due to be present at the opening, isn't he?' I ask casually. 'I suppose you've advised him to arrive a little late.'

'Of course not,' Kumudu says. His smile now has

a wolfish quality. 'It is very necessary for him to be a prominent victim. Then there will be no suspicion that we had a hand in the attack. Besides, if he is alive, he might have the notion that he's the logical choice to lead the nation.'

'What about the other ministers who don't attend the ceremony?'

'Oh, they've all grown fat on the perks of office. They'll need re-education, won't they? Ranjit and his crew will enjoy that.'

'So Kalinga will have absolute power in the country?'

'Yes. It is his vision and his plan.'

'The man has changed, Kumudu,' I say slowly. 'He is no longer the visionary we knew. I think he is very dangerous. No one will be safe, not even you.'

'No, you are wrong about him,' Kumudu replies confidently. 'We will build a new Lanka where there is justice and equity. You'll see.'

'No,' I reply. 'We'll be the first to be killed, won't we?'

'I will speak to my leader,' he responds sombrely. 'I will try to persuade him to let you go … after we've taken control.'

Kumudu turns at the door and looks at me.

'Try to get some sleep,' he says. 'I will see that you're not disturbed tonight.'

35

There is a slight, yet distinct, change in Kumudu's appearance when he comes through the door. His eyes have certain wariness; the easy confidence of the previous day is missing.

No smile.

We have slept well, as well as we can anyway, on that cold cement bench. The clang of the metal door wakes us but it is only the guard with our breakfast of boiled sweet potato and ground chilli.

Nali tries the TV set afterwards and finds a religious program on Rupavahini. There is no coverage from any of the other channels. She lets it run with the sound turned down.

A guard has followed Kumudu and stands behind him, leaning against the doorframe. He holds an automatic rifle across his chest.

Kumudu doesn't speak for a while, seeming to search for appropriate words. I feel my stomach tighten. Something is wrong.

'I am sorry, Sujatha,' he says at last. 'I pleaded your case with my leader but he refuses to pardon you. It seems that Ranjit has shown him your journals, especially your notes on Kampuchea. He is very angry, not so much for what you've written but that you had the audacity to think of thwarting him.'

'I … what will happen?'

Kumudu keeps his head still but his eyes swing sharply to one side.

'Be careful with your words,' he goes on softly. 'My plea for your release has damaged my standing to some extent. A guard has been sent to … keep me company.'

'I warned you to be careful,' I say, 'he's a madman.'

'Don't worry about me,' Kumudu goes on quietly. 'It's you I am concerned about. He wants all of you to be interrogated before you are … eliminated. Ranjit has been instructed to pay special attention to you, Sujatha. Our leader has ordered that your end must not be quick or … easy.'

I feel the room getting dark and closing in on me; my knees are giving way. I feel Mithra's arm go round my waist and I struggle to stay upright.

This is worse than my most awful nightmare, endless torture with nothing but death at the end. How can I bear this? Can I kill myself before they come for me?

Kumudu speaks again but my mind is spinning. I struggle to focus on his words.

'It will be wonderful when the poor are finally free. They will take their rightful place, won't they? They will be compensated for all the wrongs they've suffered.'

Kumudu's words are very faint, as if he's speaking to himself.

'The bloodsuckers will all be destroyed. There will be no more exploitation. Corruption will be gone forever. This is what we have worked so hard for.'

Have you lost your mind? Are you trying to convince yourself that the glorious future justifies one more atrocity?

Despite my terror and desperation I feel a twinge of concern for him.

He reaches into his pocket and takes out a tiny brown package. Over his shoulder I see the guard straighten up and look intently at it.

Kumudu extends his hand and in it, almost obscene in its incongruity, is an ordinary Mars bar. I hear a shocked whisper from Nali.

'Is this bastard mad?' she demands tearfully of Harith. 'They're planning to torture us to death and he gives her a chocolate?'

The guard had looked puzzled and seemed about to intervene; he shrugs his shoulders at Nali's words and leans once more against the doorpost.

As if in a dream I reach out and take the chocolate in its brown cellophane wrapper.

'You can secure your release with that,' Kumudu says very softly. 'Your friends too! You will know when to use it.'

I stare at him in confusion.

'Watch the program,' he murmurs. 'The auspicious time is 11.07 … unless the President is late.'

He pauses, then adds:

'I've failed. Now it is up to you.'

In a daze, I just nod my head. The guard coughs.

Kumudu comes up to me and for a moment it seems that he is about to embrace me. I raise my hand instinctively, to ward him off.

He stops when my palm touches his chest.

'Goodbye Sujatha,' he says. 'Perhaps in another life...'

'Yes, perhaps …'

The door slams shut and we hear the click of the

padlock.

'The man's insane,' Nali says with a puzzled frown. 'How can a bar of chocolate get us out of this mess?'

'He must have laced it with some poison,' Harith answers quietly. 'Cyanide maybe, if it's enough for all of us.'

'My God! Is that the release he's planned for us? To kill ourselves?'

'We are to be killed anyway,' Harith says. 'This way, we can avoid being tortured by that sadistic bastard. It is a release, I suppose.'

'This must be a dream,' Nali wails, tears pouring down her cheeks. 'We can't be sitting here calmly discussing suicide.'

We fail to pick up the footsteps, just the snap of the padlock and the door crashing open. Ranjit walks in followed by a short, heavily built man with a shaven head. They stand side by side near the door and their eyes move slowly over us. There is something impersonal about their gaze; it is as though they are inspecting cattle.

I feel a hollow sensation in my stomach when I see that Ranjit's companion is almost quivering with excitement.

'Ahh Sena, you wanted to go to medical college, didn't you?' Ranjit says with a smile. 'Instead of dissecting dead frogs, you can practice on these … animals; live ones.'

'When do we start work?' Sena asks, looking anxiously at him.

'After the ceremony,' Ranjit replies casually. 'After the leaders have left.'

Sena'a eyes are feverish; they return to me.

'Can I … attend to her?'

'No,' Ranjit laughs. 'Our leader wants her to be given

… special attention. Besides I have a personal interest in seeing to her needs.'

'I'll take the other one then.'

'All right.'

'How long do we have?'

'It'll be a week at least before our other guests start arriving,' Ranjit says. 'There's plenty of time.'

They turn to leave.

Sena says dreamily:

'I wonder how long it takes to make a proud one beg … Even when they know it's no use. That'll be the best moment.'

Ranjit turns at the door and looks at me.

'Take their clothes away,' he says with a wolfish smile. 'That's a good way to start with the high and mighty.'

The silence descends on us like a mist, threatening to separate us into our private hells. I reach out to Mithra but now I have no hope. I notice that his eyes are moist although his face is still calm.

He puts his arms around me. I feel chills running through me once again.

'It's all right,' he murmurs. 'It will be all right, I promise.'

I hear Harith trying to console Nali but she's having none of it.

'Harith, Mithra, listen to me,' she says firmly. 'We don't have much time. Listen.'

'Yes. What is it?'

'You must make sure that Suji and I are not handed over to those perverts,' Nali says through her tears. 'Are you clear on that?'

'Yes, the chocolate …' Harith's face is drawn; there is now a harshness about his mouth.

'Suji and I will take our share first,' she goes on grimly. 'You must make sure we're gone before you take yours.'

Harith looks shattered; Mithra's face is expressionless.

'If the chocolate doesn't work ...' Nali goes on remorselessly, 'you must find another way to kill us.'

'This is obscene,' Harith protests. 'How can I do a thing like that?'

'You must.'

'What - what do you want me to do?'

'We have arteries in our wrists,' Nali says quietly. 'I want you to puncture them so badly, no one can stop the bleeding.'

'No. No.'

'Darling, you must be strong,' Nali's voice is implacable. 'Can you imagine what those animals will do to us? You have the power to save us from that, so you must. This is a peaceful, easy death.'

"How can I cut your arteries? They even took my pen knife away.'

'Use your teeth.'

'You mean bite your wrist?'

'Yes.'

There is silence in the cell as we come to terms with Nali's demand, the finality of it.

Nali takes Harith's face in her hands and looks into his eyes.

'Will you do it? Will you save me?'

I know Harith is weeping. His voice, when he speaks, is hoarse and strangled.

'Yes. Yes I'll do it.'

'Promise me.'

'I promise.'

Nali turns to Mithra who has been watching silently.

'You, Mithra,' Nali says softly. 'Will you do the same for Suji?'

I look at Mithra and find his eyes filled with anguish.

'No.'

'My God, Mithra,' Nali says. 'How can you refuse? He will do unspeakable things to her - that Ranjit is a psychopath ...'

'No,' he says stubbornly. 'It won't come to that.'

Mithra raises his hand.

'The program has started.'

The site looks magnificent on camera, glass-fronted towers shining brightly in the sunshine. The car park is full, with more vehicles streaming in. The pattern is the same, with security escorts peeling off just before the main entrance. The VIP guests are being greeted and escorted inside by company officials.

The camera moves inside and we see the vast atrium of the shopping complex glowing like the interior of a spacecraft. The chandelier sparkles like a sunrise and is clearly reflected in the polished granite floor.

Guests are seated on chairs arranged in a semicircle around the daïs at the end. A two-tiered head table has been built for the most important guests; many are already in their seats. Security personnel stand at the front door and at the various exits; others stand along the walls gazing suspiciously at the seated guests.

Mithra grips my hand and points at the screen. On the wall, by the side of the head table is a drape with a tasselled cord attached.

It has to be the plaque the President will unveil. It is ominously close to the head table.

He is late, but only by a few minutes. The studio cuts to an exterior camera showing the Presidential motorcade turning into the complex. Three identical limousines, all of them with deeply tinted shutters, follow the security vehicles. They stop at the front entrance and the President steps out of the first vehicle.

The Prime Minister and other VIPs have come out to greet the President. JSP leader Wanasinghe is also there. They smile and bow; they hold their hands together in traditional greeting; then they follow the President into the atrium.

The speeches take forever. We sit on the shelf with our arms around each other, the two couples. We watch the screen as though mesmerised by it. We want the speeches to go on, for when they end, our lives will end too.

The chairman of the owning company, Lee Kwok Swee, invites the President to unveil the plaque. He smiles and rises to his feet. The Chairman gallantly helps him to step down from the daïs. The President has the cord in his hand and turns to the camera with a brilliant smile.

I feel my fingernails digging into my palms.

This is it!

KRAAANGGG.

The explosion is deafening. The building we are in shudders and pieces of plaster from the ceiling crash to the floor of the cell. I feel the tremor beneath my feet.

Nali screams. Harith is shouting something. The cloud of fine dust is so dense that I can barely see the TV screen. I stare at it in disbelief.

Has the shock affected my vision?

The President has unveiled the plaque and is

acknowledging the applause of the crowd.

I scream at Mithra.

'Quick. Open the chocolate. This is what he meant.'

I see in his eyes that he understands. He uses his teeth to rip open the cellophane wrapper. I help him pull the sticky bar apart and there it is, in the yellow caramel centre. I pick it up and clean it by inserting it in my mouth. Nali cries out in horror but Mithra gestures to her that it is all right.

The corridor outside the cell is filled with suspended dust; it shows like a halo round the bulb hanging from the ceiling. The dust has an acrid taste and catches in my throat as I breathe. The guards have gone.

I try the key and the padlock clicks open.

We creep up the stairs at the end of the corridor. The dust is more intense in the sunlight and seems to hang unmoving in the air. We hear confused shouting outside the building; from further away come the screams and wails of the injured.

The floor is strewn with broken glass and some roofing sheets have been blown off, parts of the block work wall facing the other building have been demolished.

Through a gap in the wall we see the building on the other side; what remains of it. There is a gaping hole with charred edges where the roof had been. A column of black smoke rises from the centre, channelling through the cloud of dust that floats over the area. Parts of the roof lean inward at an angle; another section collapses as we watch.

We see a man being led away with blood streaming down his face and the front of his shirt. An injured man lies on the ground calling for help; four others emerge from the building carrying a door with a mangled body on it. A panic-driven chatter fills the air.

'Let's look for a door at the back,' Harith whispers. 'There must be a way out on that side.'

There is no door. The corridor leads only to a row of rooms overlooking the rear compound. We squeeze through a narrow window and move towards the forest using the building as cover. We can still be plainly seen from the rest of the complex. We can't help looking over our shoulders, expecting a shout of alarm at any moment.

Mithra urges us to run, promising to follow at his own pace. Nali uses her favourite swear word while telling him to shut up. That helps to ease the tension for a moment.

The focus of all the surviving cadres must have been on the explosion and helping the injured, for we manage to reach the forest without being spotted. I feel as if I'm floating; I had been expecting to be killed in the most horrible way imaginable and here I am, still alive. We stop to look at each other in wonder and disbelief.

'Will someone explain what the hell happened?' Nali demands breathlessly. 'One moment we're contemplating torture and suicide, at the next we're free and running away.'

'Kumudu knew, didn't he?' Mithra asks, looking at me. 'He had prepared the chocolate … with the key.'

'Mm.'

'I was horrified when you put that wretched chocolate in your mouth, nanga. I thought you were doing it, killing yourself before me,' Nali says wonderingly. 'How did you know?'

'My hand touched his chest when he was saying goodbye,' I say slowly. 'I felt something strapped across it, under the shirt.'

'So?'

'When the explosion took place here, and not in Colombo, I knew what he had done. Then our release had to mean something … different.'

'Do you think he just blew himself up, to create a diversion, I mean?' Harith asks.

'No-o. The explosion took place at the precise moment when the President unveiled the plaque. Remember the plan Kumudu described? He was going to dial the number on a satellite phone and give it to Kalinga to press the send button,' I explain haltingly. 'I am only just beginning to understand what Kumudu has done. I think he had another phone wired to the device on his chest. Then he only needed to dial a different number.'

'Do you think Kalinga is dead then?' Nali asks.

'I'm pretty sure.'

'Why do you say that?'

'Kalinga wanted us dead. If Kalinga escaped, he would have hunted us down,' I say sadly. 'No, Kumudu would have made sure that Kalinga didn't survive; Ranjit too.'

'He really believed in this revolution; he sincerely wanted to help the poor, didn't he?' Nali murmurs in a tone of wonder. 'He destroyed it all - and gave his own life.'

'Mm.'

'He did it for you, didn't he?'

We work our way slowly along the edge of the clearing, taking care to stay in the tree line.

Harith asks. 'Are you sure you can find the markings you left, Suji?'

'I … I think so. It's only been two days. The leaves

would have withered. We can find them.'

'We've no water,' Nali says, 'and it's a long way.'

'We'll manage,' Mithra response confidently. 'After what we've been through, we can manage anything.'

Harith and Nali lead the way, casting around for the markers I had left during the outward journey. I keep pace with Mithra who still finds my concern amusing.

'What about your cousin?' he asks suddenly. 'I was shocked to hear of her treachery.'

'Hm.'

'What are you going to do?'

'One good smack … and one good hug. That'll settle it,' I say calmly. 'Ranjit was wrong, you know. The kinship of blood is far stronger than the kinship of penury.'

'Do you think Giniralla will fizzle out now?'

'Kumudu told us that their top leaders had gathered together to watch the assassination, didn't he? In that case, all of them would have been wiped out.'

We stop to rest; Mithra has more questions.

'What did Kumudu mean,' he asks with a slight frown, 'when he said it is up to you now. Was he talking about opening the cell door and getting out of there? I thought there was more to it.'

'Kumudu was really sincere about helping the poor.'

'Hm.'

'He also believed in the Giniralla program. He thought it was the only way to put things right.'

'So?'

'When he aborted the assassinations and killed all the leaders, he ended Giniralla, didn't he?'

'Yes.'

'This is not a victory, you know. It is one more

shattered dream.'

'What are you talking about?'

'Stopping Giniralla doesn't help our rural poor; nothing has changed for them,' I say. 'So there will be other plots, other Kalingas! Every maniac who wants to grab power will do it in the name of the poor.'

'Ye-es. Yes, I suppose that's true.'

'I think Kumudu was telling me that I have the responsibility now,' I say slowly. 'I have to do something to help them.'

'Help their wretched party?'

'No. The poor,' I say slowly. 'Alone, I can't do much, but … I must do what I can. Perhaps there will be others. If there are enough others we might make an impact.'

Mithra is silent for a while, lost in thought.

'You're planning to give up your job, aren't you?'

'Yes.'

'I'll join you then,' he says quietly. 'We'll do this together.'

As we get to our feet to resume our journey, Mithra puts his hands on my shoulders and studies my face for a long moment.

'He loved you so much,' he says. 'I hope I can love you as well.'

I look back at him, glad to see laughter in his eyes again.

'Just let me love you,' I reply joyfully. 'That's enough for me.'

Nihal de Silva
<wtrmrt@sltnet.lk>

The Road From Elephant Pass

An army officer's routine assignment to pick up a woman informant near Jaffna turns into a nightmare when the Tigers launch a massive attack on the peninsula and the camp at Elephant Pass. The two adversaries are forced to escape together through the rebel held Wanni and later, cross the abandoned Wilpattu National Park on foot.

Bitter enemies at the start of their journey, Captain Wasantha and the activist Kamala face innumerable threats from wild animals and a gang of deserters who make determined and violent efforts to capture the woman. The constant external danger, and their enforced dependence on each other, gradually erodes their enmity and distrust.

But a shocking revelation confronts Wasantha when he finally reaches Colombo. He is now compelled to choose between his friend and his country.

Winner Gratiaen Prize 2003

Winner State Literary Award 2004

The Far Spent Day

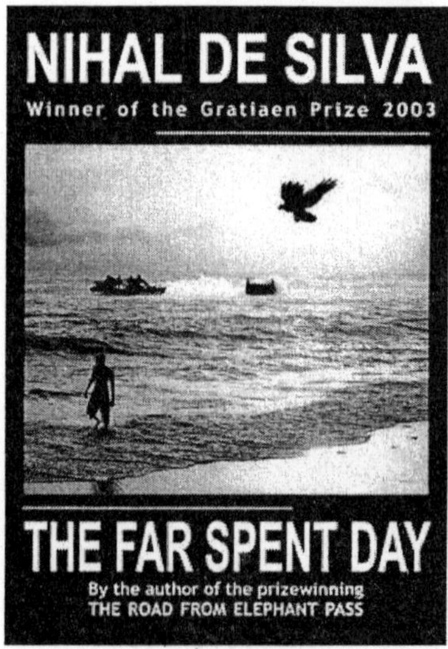

When Ravi returned after graduating overseas he wanted to help his father run their small family business. His well-meaning effort to stop a brawl escalates into a firestorm of violence as one party turns out to be the son of a Government Minister.

When Ravi is assaulted and hospitalized, his parents demand justice, but even this is considered an intolerable affront by the assailant's family. A series of ruthless attacks result in the death of Ravi's parents, ruin of the family business and loss of his home.

Driven to the edge of insanity by grief, Ravi fights back with the help of a young reporter, Tanya. But each strike only results in more violent and ferocious responses. When Tanya is also lost, Ravi prepares to carry out a final, devastating act of revenge.

But, looking within, he finds that the spiral of violence has also corroded his own soul....